Under the Influence

Under the Influence

A Novel

WANDA B. CAMPBELL

MICAH 6:8
BOOKS

Acknowledgments

As always, I thank my Heavenly Father for equipping me to pen stories that change lives, in addition to being entertaining. *Under the Influence* is novel eleven, and the voices in my head are still talking. *Under the Influence* is the most challenging novel I have written. I sincerely hope you enjoy Alexander's journey.

To my immediate family – **Craig, Sr., Chantel, Jonathan, Craig, Jr., Dinari,** and **Zaria**: I appreciate your support and allowing me to pursue my passion. Keep aspiring to be all that God has called you to be.

My Angel: Mimi still misses you.

Israel Houghton: Once again your music has been the fuel in my engine. Thank you for *Breathe Your Name*.

Wanda B. Campbell Readers & Supporters Facebook Group: Words cannot express how much I appreciate your support and encouragement. May our Heavenly Father continue to bless you with health, success, and long life.

Davina, Cassandra and Rhonda: Thanks for taking the time and keeping it REAL.

Fellow scribe, Officer Trenia Wearing of the SFPD: Thanks for sharing your knowledge and insight. Looking forward to seeing your work on stage.

While writing *Under the Influence* I was blessed to witness two of my children graduate college. Chantel and Craig, Jr., much success in your endeavors.

During the process of publishing *Under the Influence,* two of my biological brothers transitioned from earth to eternity within two weeks of each other. Fletcher and Roosevelt Townsend, thank you for the flavor you brought to my life.

To everyone who reads this book: May this novel bless and encourage you in every area of your life and strength your walk in the kingdom.

Happy Reading!

I love hearing form readers at:
wbcampbell@prodigy.net
Or, join me on Facebook at Wanda B. Campbell Readers & Supporters

Contents

Prologue. 1

1   Mama and Me 7

2   Bathroom Break. 15

3   The Girl with the Long Braids 23

4   Transitions 37

5   Little Man on Campus. 47

6   Miss Jackson 57

7   Challenges 69

8   Courting 81

9   Love. 97

10 The Investment. 115

11 Love and More Deception 133

12 The Proposition 143

13 Let Brotherly Love Continue 161

14 Happy Anniversary 171

15 The Whole Truth, And Nothing but the Truth 183

16 No Honor Amongst Thieves. 203

17 Freedom is Never Free 215

18 A Reason to Live 229

19 Self, Meet Me. 245

20 The Final Confrontation 253

21 Right to Remain Silent, but Why? 263

22 Freedom's Cry 271

Under the Influence

Prologue

I RELEASED MY HOLD and squeezed my orbicularis oculi muscles with such force dizziness threatened to overtake me. I learned in my eleventh grade Anatomy and Physiology class the name of the muscle that opens and closes the eyelid. Strange I would think of that now. I squeezed and squeezed, hoping God would grant me a miracle and change my circumstances. The adrenaline was wearing off and a tingling sensation tickled my hands, making me aware of the throbbing and the possibility something might be broken. In slow motion, I opened my eyes. Nothing had changed.

The room was still in disarray. The oak table at which I'd sat numerous times before presenting ideas and often persuading clients, remained turned over on its side. So were the leather chairs. Shattered glass from the cracked picture frames that lined the walls peppered the navy carpet. The off-white walls served as a canvas for the splatters of blood dripping down the wall and pooling on the carpet. The smashed multi-line speakerphone lay crumbled on the floor with its cords twisted around a chair leg. Useless now.

My attempt to relieve the throbbing in my hand by rubbing it against my shirt proved futile once the blood smeared my shirt. I'm not sure if the red sticky life-saving substance belonged to me, or my victim who lay motionless on the floor. I'm not sure if it was the blow to the head with my right fist, or the head slammed against the oak table that caused the permanent lifeless expression on the ashen face staring back at me. I'd snapped, zoned-out and couldn't remember the fine details. The piercing pain in my left jaw and the blood trickling from my nose were indication the victim had fought back.

How my actions would affect my wife and daughter, I didn't know. Would my business survive? Probably not. Would I spend the rest of my life tucked away in a six-dimensional space, contained by steel bars? Maybe. Would I blame my lack of control on a sudden loss of mental stability? I didn't think so. Did I regret finally standing up for myself? Absolutely not. Would God forgive me? I certainly hoped so. The only thing I knew for certain was my life would never be the same after I made two phone calls.

I stepped away from the body and paced the room several times before removing my cell phone from my back pocket. The thought occurred to run away, or to stage the scene to implicate someone else. I violently shook those thoughts away. I'd given too much control of my life to the person slumped on the floor. I refused to allow him to control me in death. I paced some more, then stopped abruptly and pressed 9-1-1 on the keypad.

"I'd like to report a murder," I said, when the operator asked the nature of my emergency. As if standing outside of my body and looking on, I gave my name and location then disconnected the call.

I walked over and hunched beside the person I once idolized, yet who'd caused me nothing but pain. With my throbbing hand, I dialed the second number and waited. With my free hand, I closed the victim's eyes.

"Alexander Bennett Jr., what's going on?" my mother answered. She was the only person who called me by my full name, usually when I was in trouble. I knew I'd interrupted her favorite game show, *Family Feud*, but this couldn't wait. My mother's infatuation with Steve Harvey would have to wait. My mother needed to know what had happened, and she needed to hear it from me.

With my sore hand, I grabbed the back of my neck. It didn't freak me out in the least that I'd touched a dead body with the same hand only seconds before. I was too worried about how to tell my mother I'd just murdered her son.

Back in the Day

CHAPTER 1

Mama and Me

EVEN AS A child, I was a morning person. I figured if the sun was up then I should've been up doing something. My mother, who also served as my alarm clock, never had to call me twice. In fact, every night I made a bet with myself to wake up before her feet touched the floor. I always lost the bet, because Mama was also a morning person. I learned years later Mama would shower, pray and read the Bible for at least an hour, before entering my room.

Instead of yelling my name from the doorway, Mama would sit on my bed and rest a palm against my forehead. "Protect my baby and bring him back to me safe," she'd say. Her palm would then be replaced by her warm lips. She would gather me in her arms and hold me for a few minutes while I inhaled what I thought was perfume. I learned later the soft scent wasn't some fancy perfume, but plain cocoa butter. At any rate, my mother always smelled good. She looked good too.

My mother's rich dark smooth skin gave new meaning to the phrase "Black is beautiful". She could have been a model or movie star. I'd seen the popular TV moms—Claire Huxtable and Vivian Banks. Through my seven-year-old eyes, Glenda Bennett left them in the dust. My mother wasn't a lawyer or a professor, but she was tall, smart, and always graceful. My mother never yelled at me and always listened to me.

I'd break up our quiet time by inquiring about my favorite meal of the day—breakfast. Then I'd bolt from the bed and skip to the bathroom. Mama would say, "Be sure to brush those back teeth," before heading to the kitchen to make breakfast.

That was our daily routine. Back then, I assumed Mama shared similar moments with my older brothers, Randall and Carlton. I didn't learn until years later how wrong I had been and how something so minor could sow deep seeds of discord and cause hatred to spread like ivy.

I used to sit at the kitchen table playing Tic-Tac-Toe when I was supposed to be eating waffles and sausage. I imagine I was like most seven-year-old boys and invented a more entertaining purpose for my food before devouring it. I would crumble the sausage and then flip the pieces from my fork into the syrup-drenched squares. On this particular day, I was two for three.

"Baby, stop playing and eat before you mess up your white shirt," my mother said, just as I was about to fling a piece of meat.

"Okay, Mom," I said, but flipped the meat anyway. The thought of staining the white shirt was a great idea I hadn't thought of when I began the game. I hated wearing white shirts every day to school, with khaki pants and a green cardigan sweater, but I didn't have a choice. That was the standard uniform at the private school I attended. My brothers, who were in junior high and high school, got to wear regular clothes. They also attended public school, but Mama said I had to attend private school, because that's what my father wanted and that's what he provided for. Mama was determined to fulfill his wishes.

I don't remember my father, Alexander Bennett, Sr. He died before my second birthday. I knew what he looked like because Mama kept their wedding photo hanging above the fireplace. Whereas my mother was black and beautiful, my father was the exact opposite. He was the palest white man I'd ever seen, but Mama loved him. She wouldn't date or even speak to a man unless it was related to business. "The love of my life is waiting for me in heaven," she'd say whenever I asked her about getting married again. Then she'd add, "I've had two husbands. One bad one, and one good one. I don't need another one."

Apparently, my father loved Mama just as deeply, because he took on the responsibility of raising my brothers as his own. I was told, my father wanted to adopt my brothers, but their biological father wouldn't allow it, although he refused to play an active role in their lives. Mama didn't mind his absence since he use to physically abuse her and my brothers.

I looked up at my mother, sitting across from me sipping tea, and I could see sadness. I knew she missed my father, because she always talked about him. She's always told me how they met and how good he was to her and my brothers. My father took Mama to stage plays and on boat rides. He bought her fancy clothes and a nice car. What Mama said she loved most about my dad was how gentle and attentive he was with her. He also sacrificed a lot for her. My father was from a town in southeast

Texas with conservative views. When my parents married, my father's family disowned him. My great-grandfather removed him from his will, effectively leaving him nothing of the family's oil business.

Mama said his death didn't make sense. According to Mama, my father was easygoing and considerate of others; always willing to help those in need. He was the top performer at the law firm and volunteered in local soup kitchens on the weekends. His clients loved him. He didn't participate in risky behavior. My father was just in the right place at the wrong time. He simply went to work on a Wednesday morning. Unfortunately for my father, a distraught client of a brokerage firm entered the crowded lobby of the twenty-five story office building in downtown San Francisco and fired an automatic weapon. My father was one of four victims. In the wake of the tragedy, the law firm established a trust fund for my education through college and living expenses. My father's life insurance paid off the house and all of the bills and left Mama with a sizeable bank account.

"Your daddy was good to us, even in death," Mama would often say. I agreed with Mama. Thinking back to age seven, I don't ever remember not having nice things. Mama didn't like expensive name brand tennis shoes, but made sure I had an ample supply of leather loafers or tie-ups. My shoes were never scuffed, and always shined thanks to Mama and the strict dress code at school. Instead of laundering my uniforms, Mama had an open ticket at the neighborhood cleaners. My dirty uniforms were dropped off, and a fresh starched and ironed supply was picked up every Saturday afternoon. Mama spent every other Saturday morning at the barbershop with me, while my brothers performed chores.

Unlike my brothers, who shared a room, I had my own bedroom with a full-sized bed and matching oak furniture and a toy chest. My toy chest seemed to always overflow. Every so often, Mama would change the décor to whatever cartoon character I was into at the time. I only remember a few times my mother denied me anything. I pretty much got everything I wanted thanks to my trust fund.

On one particular day, I wanted the new Super Soaker water gun I'd seen on TV. Mama didn't like guns because of how my father died. I didn't see anything wrong with the plastic toy with the extra reservoir. The kids on TV weren't hurting anyone. They were just having fun getting wet in the sun. I wanted to have some fun too, away from recess at school. My brothers were eight and seven years older, and too cool to play with me. I figured if I had the water gun, they'd find the time to play with me, since I'd heard them say how cool the toy looked during a commercial.

I cleaned my plate and finished off the apple juice before starting my campaign. I decided to go an extra step and place my dirty dishes in the sink. Surely, Mama would like that. She always fussed at my brothers for leaving their dishes on the table. I barely had my Teenage Mutant Ninja Turtle plate and cup in my hand when Randall stomped into the kitchen.

"Mama, you got lunch money?" Randall asked that question every morning. I guess that was one of the cool things about high school—you got to buy your own food.

I abandoned my scheme to impress Mama and focused on Randall. My oldest brother was way too cool. I wanted to be just like him when I grew up. He was fifteen and tall with long arms and big hands. He was the fastest runner in the world and the best basketball player at school. I heard him tell his friends that and I believed him. He was also the best-dressed freshman—whatever that meant—on campus. He had lots of friends and all of the girls wanted him. To do what with I didn't know, because Mama always called him lazy. Unlike me, Randall had big hair that leaned to the side. Mama allowed him to wear tennis shoes every day, but the shoes must've made his feet hurt, because Randall walked funny in them and he didn't tie them all the way up. Still, I would've traded in my loafers for a pair like his.

Randall didn't wear khakis or sweaters. He had what he called the "tightest fits", although the pants were baggy. I didn't like tight pants, but I wanted blue, black, red and gray jeans with designs on them like he had. I liked his white shirts. They were different from mine. Randall's white shirts looked like T-shirts with the arms cut out. He had big muscles that one day, I hoped to have. Mama wouldn't let him leave the house without what she called "a decent shirt" and jacket. A decent shirt was usually a loose jersey from his favorite sport teams.

"Boy, can't you say 'Hello' or 'Good morning' before you start asking for money?" She reached into her pocket and placed some rolled bills on the table. "You are just like your daddy." Mama frowned. "You smell like him too with that cheap cologne you insist on over-using every morning."

Every morning Mama complained about Randall's behavior and every morning Randall would grunt, "Good morning, Mama," through clenched teeth. Then he'd nod his head at me and say, "Hey, little man."

This morning I agreed with Mama, Randall smelled funny, but I still wanted to be like him. I hurried and placed my dishes into the sink. I wanted to ask Mama for the Super Soaker while

Randall was there. Since he liked the toy, he might help me talk Mama into saying yes. And he might play with me.

"Good morning, y'all. What's for breakfast?"

I whirled around from the sink. Carlton was finally up and ready for food. He was always the last one to get up and the first one to go to bed. I liked Carlton, but I didn't want to be like him. Mainly because Mama said he had the worms. "Boy, all you do is eat, sleep, and poop," she'd fuss whenever he ate the last of something. "You must have tapeworms living inside you."

Carlton was tall like Randall, but he wasn't cool. He didn't have as many friends as Randall, and as far as I knew at the time, girls didn't want him for anything. He was thinner and wore black-rimmed glasses. Unlike Randall, Carlton's voice wasn't deep, but squeaky like Alvin and the Chipmunks. He wore jeans, but only black and blue ones, and unlike me, he liked sweaters. Randall called him a genetic mistake, because he wasn't good at basketball, football, or track. Carlton wasn't good at any sport, but made good grades and like Michael Jordon had done a three-peat at the school's science fair. Still, he wasn't cool enough for me.

Mama pointed toward the cabinet, but didn't move. "There's a box of cereal in there, or you can make some instant oatmeal."

I noticed Carlton roll his eyes at Mama, but I didn't tell on him. Snitches were suckas, at least that's what Randall called me after I told Mama he had his friends over while she was at work. Besides, Carlton always rolled his eyes behind Mama's back.

Carlton reached over me and into the cabinet. "I bet the golden child didn't eat cold cereal," he said while dumping cereal into his favorite big bowl. It was the same bowl Mama mixed cakes in.

Mama stood, and like always pointed at me. "Don't worry about him. His daddy, rest his soul, provides food for him. Maybe if y'all," her finger bounced between my brothers, "dead-beat daddy paid some child support once in a while, you'd eat better. I spend most of my check trying to feed and clothe you and Randall. If this house wasn't paid off, I don't know how we'd survive."

Randall picked up the money and stomped out of the kitchen. Carlton slammed the refrigerator. My brothers always got mad whenever Mama talked about their daddy, money and food. Mama didn't seem to care about them being mad. I did care because that meant another day of playing alone in my room.

CHAPTER 2

Bathroom Break

UNLIKE AT HOME, at school I had plenty of playmates, but not the right kind. For some reason girls liked to hang around me. My thick curly brown hair was good, at least that's what the girls in my class told me when they insisted on touching it. My greenish-light-brown eyes made me cute, so the girls said, but I wanted to be cool like Randall with brown eyes, not cute. I liked the company, but I didn't like girls. They didn't like my superhero games or wrestling, but they liked me. Since I was outnumbered, I usually abandoned my impression of Batman for an imaginary tea cup and cookies. Then be forced to chase the girls until the bell sounded.

I was stuck, since most of the other boys in my class "mean-mugged" me. That's what Randall called it when a guy stared you down without a smile.

I noticed I was the only boy invited to the tea parties, and the hide-and-seek games with the girls. The boys in my class noticed also and began teasing me and picking fights. At first, I thought the shoves were part of a game, like the one my brothers played with each other. Randall and Carlton would push and jump on each other, wrestle and punch one another. Every time Mama would ask what they were doing, they'd say, "We're just playing." So, I laughed at the first few shoves, thinking I was finally making friends. Then one day I was so thirsty from the heat and chasing the girls, I couldn't stay away from the water fountain.

I didn't want to spend my playtime in line waiting for the boys' room, so I waited until the warning bell sounded before going to the bathroom. When I stepped from the stall, my new friends were crowded in front of the sink.

"Hey, guys, what's up?" I asked squeezing between them to the sink with the naiveté of a seven-year-old.

Oliver, the self-proclaimed leader of the pack answered, "Pretty girl, we're going to kick your butt!"

I giggled, thinking about the play fighting I'd seen my brothers do. I wet my hands with water, but didn't use the sandy soap from the dispenser then shook my hands. "Well, go ahead and try," I said, turning back around. I'd never had a fight before, but I'd watched Randall and Carlton enough to know how it was done.

"You think you better than us just because you bright. You look like a cat with those eyes. And you look like a girl with that curly hair. That's why the girls play with you. They think you a girl like them. You little fag."

I stopped laughing. I didn't know what a fag was, but Oliver sounded mad and his black face twisted, like his mother had made him eat spinach.

16

The three other boys laughed, and called me more names. One of the names Mama had grounded Randall for using, and the other name—homo—I thought meant that I liked to stay at home.

Confused isn't adequate to describe how I felt right then. I didn't know what it meant to think you're better than someone. I thought the girls played with me because I was cute, at least that's what they told me, not because they thought I was a girl. Why did Oliver call me a pretty girl, and why were his fists balled up?

I recalled something I'd heard Randall say many times when talking smack with his friends and used it. "Dude, you just jealous. Get a life," I said with my chin up, thinking I'd scored a point. Usually when Randall said it, his friends would wave a hand at him and walk away. My friends waved all eight of their fists at my face.

I fell back against the sink from the first blow. The second and third blows knocked me to the floor. A kick in the stomach followed the fourth kick. I lost count of the punches and kicks after a foot stomped my head. I didn't remember anything after that. I didn't know who broke up the fight or how long it lasted. The next thing I remembered were my mother's tears soaking my face.

I woke up in the hospital. Mama told me a campus supervisor conducting a bathroom check after recess found me on the floor, unconscious. My friends had done exactly what they'd set out to do and some. They beat and kicked my butt. My head hurt. I had several knots on my head and my lips felt big like when I'd gotten my cavity fixed at the dentist. It was days before I realized I was also missing a tooth. My chest and stomach ached, but Mama said nothing was broken.

The doctor let Mama take me home the next day and assured her I'd be okay, but Mama must not have believed him, because she took off work and stayed home with me. During those first three days, I don't remember a time when Mama wasn't by my side. She held me and fed me soup. She bathed me and massaged my little achy muscles.

My brothers were around also, but they didn't take care of me. If they were upset about me getting my butt kicked without getting one punch in, they didn't show it. Randall often bragged about how he and Carlton were the toughest dudes in the neighborhood. From what I could tell it was true, because no one messed with my brothers. Randall and Carlton Williams were revered, because everyone knew you couldn't fight one without fighting the other. And from what I'd heard their friends say, they'd never lost a fight. Maybe they were mad at me for losing the fight.

Randall would walk into Mama's room and stare at me laying in her bed. "You a'right, little man," he'd asked after awhile, then leave once I nodded my head. Carlton would stay longer and watch TV with me, but didn't talk much either. So, I was surprised the day I went back to school and they offered to take me to school for Mama. They'd only done that a few times when Mama had a special project due at work, and she had to force them then. Mama agreed, but told them she didn't want any problems.

I didn't know what Mama meant by problems, because I'd told her and the police officer at the hospital that I didn't know the boys who'd beaten me up. Snitches weren't cool, and I wasn't going to be one.

A block away from the house, Randall started drilling me. "Little man, tell us everything that happened, right now. I want details and names. And you better not leave nothing out."

"Yeah, and you better not lie," Carlton added.

I stretched my neck and looked up at Randall, who was holding my hand. "You want me to be a snitch now? You said that wasn't cool." I turned to Carlton. "So did you."

Randall and Carlton exchanged that twisted facial expression they often shared. Before the fight, I'd been practicing that same look.

Randall grunted. "We've got to teach him the full code," he said to Carlton, then looked back down at me. He waited until we passed two ladies walking their dogs before starting the lesson. "Little man, that's only true when you're telling on us to Mama. If snitching is going to get us, meaning the three of us in trouble with Mama, or other grownups, then it ain't cool. But you're supposed to tell us when mess is going down."

Carlton patted my shoulder. "We're your big brothers and we're supposed to keep an eye out for you."

"Really? I thought you didn't like me because you don't play or hang out with me."

"We don't like you," Randall confirmed, "because you're spoiled and Mama is always babying you. But you're our little half-breed brother and we have to look out for you."

"And we're gonna teach you how to fight, but you better not tell Mama," Carlton warned. "We can't have you getting your butt whipped like a little girl."

I imagine my smile showed the new gap in my mouth and my back teeth. I couldn't believe it; my brothers were going to spend time with me.

"Take that stupid grin off your face and tell us what happened," Randall ordered again.

Since snitching was now cool, and I wanted to be cool, I told them everything that happened, including names and descriptions. I even told them about the "friendly" shoves I'd received the weeks leading up to the fight.

"So you let these dudes punk you all this time?"

Carlton asked the question like I'd done something wrong. I didn't like Carlton questioning me, because he wasn't cool like Randall, so I shot back, "Randall pushes you around all the time."

The grip on my hand tightened as Randall explained, "We're brothers—blood. We're supposed to hit each other. It's called rough-housing and it makes us tough. That's why can't nobody in the neighborhood beat us." We stopped at a red light and Randall squatted to my level. "Look, little man, you don't let nobody, but us put their hands on you and get away with it. You always fight back. If you can't beat them all, you grab hold of one and beat the mess out of him. You never lay there like a sucka and take it. Mama babies you too much; you should know this," he added, standing to is feet. "If you were in public school, you would. We'll take care of it this time, but we're going to teach you how to fight, and you better not let this happen again."

"And if you tell Mama, we're gonna kick your butt," Carlton added.

As we crossed the intersection and continued on to school, I didn't think too much about what Randall meant by taking care of it. I was just happy to have my brothers around. I didn't need that Super Soaker after all to get their attention. I just needed to get my butt beat.

The Monday after I returned to school my teacher had the class make big get well cards for my friends—much like the ones I'd received from the class. Oliver along with the other boys who ganged up on me had gotten jumped by a group of older boys on the way home from school the previous Friday. They all were beaten pretty badly, my teacher explained, but Oliver got it the worst with a broken arm and a cracked jaw.

Perhaps it was denial, or maybe my seven-year-old innocence, but at the time, I refused to believe Randall and Carlton had anything to do with Oliver and company's beat down. What I do know is from that day until the day I graduated from middle school, Oliver and his gang never bothered me again. Neither did any other boys at my school.

CHAPTER 3

The Girl with the Long Braids

A LOT CHANGED DURING the two years after my first fight, at both school and home. I'd grown a little taller, but not much. My skin was a little darker, but girls still called me light-skinned. I ate more and grew out of my clothes sooner. Mama still coddled me, but at age nine I didn't like it. At least not in public; it wasn't cool. We still had our early morning ritual and I still got pretty much everything I wanted. The difference now was I included things for my brothers in my requests by pretending I wanted them. From what I could tell, Randall and Carlton didn't lack anything, Mama just had to work to have money for them. Their father still wasn't paying child support. Randall and Carlton still didn't like how Mama spoiled me, but since they were reaping the benefits, they didn't seem to mind so much. Thanks to me, they were the first kids in the neighborhood to have a PlayStation. The only time they let me play the new video craze was when Mama was around, since it was supposed to be mine.

At school, I didn't have to attend pretend tea parties anymore. I was known as the big man on campus, and not just by the girls. Mama and my teacher had convinced me to compete in the district's spelling bee. I didn't want to, but Mama said it would make my father proud. Apparently, he was a spelling bee champion at my age. I started to argue with Mama and ask how could a dead man be proud, but she had that dreamy look on her face—that look of love she had whenever she spoke of my father. Instead of disappointing her, I entered the competition and won first place. Then went on to finish second in the state trials. Mama was so happy I'd won the district, she invited the partners from my father's law firm to the state competition. Several of them showed up, and Mama made me take pictures with them.

Those trophies and ribbons shot my popularity to the next level at school. Girls now considered me smart and cute, and clung to me even more. After a story about my winnings appeared in the local paper and on a local news station, boys began speaking to me beyond the usual, "What's up?" Dudes started sitting at the same lunch table with me. I got invites to birthday parties, and for once, I wasn't the last one to get picked for kickball. I went from being one of the girls, to that smart dude on TV. I was no longer a square. I was cool, and I liked it.

At home, I was cool too—at least when Mama wasn't home. Randall and Carlton, now seventeen and fifteen, included me in on their chill time while Mama worked. Randall deputized me head of Security and Maintenance. I took my job seriously and worked hard to make my brothers proud. My responsibilities included making sure the house was clean and alerting my brothers and their friends when it was time for Mama to return home. Carlton taught me how to tell time and helped me to set a schedule.

Although I was nine, Mama still wouldn't let me walk home from school, so I took a bus, which let me off at the corner. Randall was supposed to meet me at the bus stop, but he never did, and I never told Mama. Randall and Carlton were always home when I walked in, playing video games, watching TV, or eating the food Mama told them not to. They weren't supposed to have company, but they did. Mama didn't know it, but half of the neighborhood kids enjoyed afterschool snacks from her refrigerator.

I arrived home every day, at the same time, except when the bus was late. My first order of business was to check with by brothers for any special instructions. I knew the routine, but sometimes they had special projects for me, like running to the store to pick up more potato chips. After the special projects, I'd start the maintenance part of the job. I'd have one hour to wash dishes and clean both bathrooms, straighten up the family room and start my homework before Mama got home while my brothers camped out in their room. At five thirty-five I'd knock on their bedroom door and announce, "Time to rise up." Within minutes, Randall and Carlton along with their friends would drift from the bedroom. Randall would open the windows and spray air freshener around the house after his friends filed out the door. Then he and Carlton would remove their clothing and discard them into the washing machine. Their clothes didn't look dirty to me, but they washed clothes every day. When Mama entered the house shortly before six the house was spotless and smelled like fresh rain, or apple spice depending on which air freshener Randall sprayed.

It was routine. After hanging her coat, Mama always hugged me and then thanked my brothers for keeping the house clean while she worked. Mama said it was the least they could do since Randall and Carlton ate up everything. My brothers would then hug Mama and tell her they appreciated her hard work in providing for them. On their way back to their room, they'd pat me on the head and say, "Good lookin' out, little man," for making them look good. To this day, I don't think Mama ever found out I was not only a spelling bee champion, but also the housekeeper.

In addition to being head of Security and Maintenance, I was also a dedicated student. I studied my brothers, especially Randall, with keen observation. Randall had grown even taller and had developed what he called his cool walk—walking with a slight forward lean and dip while dragging one leg. He now had facial hair and knotted hair on his chest. His muscles were bigger and his voice was deeper. Girls must have liked his voice, because they were always calling him on the phone. Another thing Mama complained about.

Carlton was different too. He no longer sounded like a chipmunk; his voice had dropped a few levels. The glasses he now wore were cool—brown with a shaded tint. The worms inside his body must have stopped eating his food because now Carlton was thick around the waist. He still didn't play sports, but could run fast. Like Randall, Carlton also had developed his cool walk, but his dip was deeper than Randall's. Girls called the house for him also, but Randall said all of Carlton's girls were ugly, calling them his leftovers.

In addition to the physical changes, my brothers seemed to change personalities, especially when Mama wasn't home. Most days they'd camp out in their room for long periods of time. After a while a stinky smell would hover around their bedroom door. I wasn't allowed inside their room, unless I was bringing them food. Even then, I could only stand in the doorway. When their friends came to visit, they'd all cram into the smelly room and close the door. I guessed that was the fun part about being a teenager—you didn't care about stinky rooms.

During the visits, I heard giggles and a lot of bad words coming from the room. Sometimes I stood at the door and listened and practiced saying the bad words. I'd gotten so good at using dirty words—that's what Mama called them—I used them on the playground at school. With my lean walk and vocabulary, I imitated Randall perfectly.

One day I cursed at a neighborhood kid for touching my football and Carlton gave me a high-five and said, "Way to go, little man." I had considered the boy a friend and the ball landed in his yard from a missed throw, but Randall said, "A man protects what's his at all costs," so I let the boy have it. I called him every name I'd heard my brothers say. I felt bad when the kid slumped his shoulders and walked away. He was hurt, but I had my brothers' approval. I figured the boy would get over it. I always did when Randall and Carlton cursed at me. Although I continued to see him on a regular basis, that kid never played with me again.

At some point, my brothers' visitors changed. The fellas were replaced with girls. Giggles and bad words transformed into moans and a rhythmic thumping noise. I still stood outside the door and listened, but the moaning didn't hold my attention like the cursing had. One girl, and sometimes two girls, would cram into that smelly room. I couldn't tell what game they were playing. Whatever it was it must have made them hot, because my brothers would come from the room without a shirt, sweating and go straight to the kitchen for some juice.

One day, in a rush to start the game I guess, they left the bedroom door cracked open. Curiosity got the best of me and I peeked inside. I just had to know what game my brothers and the girl with the long braids were playing. As I positioned my head in the opening, I had hopes of joining them and being more than the housekeeper and head of security.

From what I could see, the room was clean, but still stunk. One look at the group inside and I changed my mind about wanting to play their game. The girl with the long braids was sitting on the side of Randall's bed. My brothers stood in front of her with their pants down, passing what looked like a skinny cigarette between each other. I assumed the girl with the long braids didn't like to smoke, because they didn't offer her a puff. She did appear to enjoy putting my brothers' "private parts", as Mama called them, into her mouth. From the moans, Randall and Carlton seemed to like it too.

I didn't like it, and wanted to shout, "Yuck!" but I was afraid of being caught. Randall had warned me he'd beat me up if I opened his door without knocking. So I kept watching.

The girl must have gotten tired, because she lay back on the bed, pulled her skirt up and opened her legs. Randall, with his pants still down, got on the bed too. From my angle, I couldn't see what they were doing on the bed, but the familiar thumping and moaning began. After a while, Randall stood back up. Then Carlton got on the bed and the noise started again.

I had a bad feeling Randall and Carlton weren't playing a game at all. They were doing something they shouldn't, that's why they only did it when Mama wasn't home. But I couldn't stop watching, that day or any other day. From that day on, I became obsessed with what I'd seen. Whenever my brothers brought a girl, or girls home, I'd rush through my housekeeping chores and risk a beat down by cracking their door open and peeking inside. Mama didn't allow locks on the bedroom doors. Watching my brothers do those things made me aware of my private part, and excited me. This went on for weeks without me getting caught. I compared my size to theirs. I was much smaller, but figured when I turned seventeen, I'd be as big as Randall. I wondered what it felt like to have someone do those things to me. Under the covers at night, I'd stroke my body the way I'd seen Carlton do while he waited for Randall to finish his turn with the girl of the day. What I was doing felt wrong, but I continued the self-exploration because it felt good. Shortly after my ninth birthday, my luck ran out.

The Thursday started off like every other day. Mama and I shared our morning prayer time, and then I got dressed for school. I ate pancakes, eggs and bacon for breakfast. Except for my class winning the fifth-grade kickball tournament, school was uneventful that day. I ran all the way home from the bus stop. It had been six days since my brothers had a girl over and I was getting antsy. I wanted to see more. I didn't understand at the time, but the experiences aroused me.

I'm sure I smiled when I entered the house and saw the girl with the long braids sitting at the table, drinking a coke.

"Good, you're here. Now we can get busy," Randall said, and at the same time started for his room.

Like always, Carlton followed after the girl. "Don't forget to watch the clock. If Mama catches us, you're going to get beat down," he yelled his customary warning right before slamming the door.

I pretended I was Superman and zoomed around the house doing my chores. The dishes were washed and both bathrooms were cleaned in eleven minutes. Since I didn't have any homework, I left the family room for later—after the girl with the long braids left. I didn't want to miss too much of the action.

I did my usual tip-toeing to the door, then listened. I had to make sure the activity started before I opened the door. Otherwise, they might see me. The moaning hadn't started yet, but the stinky odor from the skinny cigarettes seeped beneath the door. I waited, patting my foot in anticipation. I also felt a tingling sensation below my waist. I went to the kitchen for a glass of water. When I returned, Randall's moaning and curse words had started. After spying on my brothers, I was able to differentiate between their sounds. Randall cursed and Carlton grunted. What I couldn't figure out was why they were making noises at the same time. Once I cracked the door open and peeked inside, I understood. Unlike the times before, both of my brothers were "getting busy" at the same time. Randall was on top of the girl with long braids, and Carlton was standing by her head.

I was so captivated by the scene, I didn't realize I'd taken steps into the room. I saw every move and heard every sound, but I don't remember lifting my feet or touching myself. But I must have done those things, because I was at the foot of Randall's bed, with my hand inside my pants, when Carlton yelled at me.

"Didn't we tell you not to come in here?" Carlton pulled away from the girl and pulled his pants up, while calling me bad words.

Randall looked over his shoulder, but didn't get up. He didn't have to; the names he called me hurt as much as his fist would have.

The girl with the long braids didn't say anything.

I didn't know what to say. I was caught. I started crying.

Randall finally stood up, but didn't pull up his pants. "Shut up, you little whimp! I told you about coming in my room without knocking. The house better be clean and you better not tell Mama!"

"I won't," I stuttered.

Randall walked over to the nightstand and picked up the skinny cigarette. "How long have you been buttin' into my business?" he asked, after taking a drag.

"You better not lie," Carlton warned.

"No a lot," I lied anyway. "I promise; I don't watch all the time."

Randall passed the skinny cigarette to Carlton, and then folded his arms. He had the same cool look on his face he used when he lied to Mama about doing his share of the housework. A smile appeared while looking me up and down. That's when I realized I still had my hand inside my pants. I snatched my hand out and tucked it behind my back.

"So you like to watch, do you?"

"No, not really?" I lied again, trying not to look at Randall's body.

The girl sat up on the bed and started laughing.

Randall smirked. "You little liar. You've been gettin' off watching us when you suppose to be cleaning the house."

I didn't know what the term "getting off" meant, but I defended myself anyway. I stuttered, cried and lied my way through an explanation. "No I haven't. I only saw a few times. I mean, I only peeked two, three times. All I saw was y'all sitting on the bed." I pointed at the laughing girl. "I didn't see you put your private part into her mouth. I promise I didn't see you get on top of her."

I covered my face and waited for Randall's fist. Instead of the usual blow to my stomach, roaring laughter filled the room. Randall, Carlton and the girl were laughing at me.

Randall patted my shoulder. "Sit down, little man. Since you like watching so much, I'm gonna teach you what's it's like to be a man."

I lowered my hands, but didn't make eye contact. "But I'm only nine. Mama said I'm too young to be a man."

Randall smirked. "Mama don't know everything. I bet she doesn't know you've been playing with yourself."

He was right. I would never tell Mama that.

"As your older brother and man of the house, it's my job to teach you how to handle your business. Now sit down," he ordered, more forceful. "We don't have all day."

I was crying, but I obeyed.

Randall pointed at the girl with long braids. "Get up and serve my little brother."

"Whoa man," Carlton butted in. "Are you sure about that?"

Randall's answer came out in giggles. "This way, I know the little perfect half-breed won't snitch."

The girl with the long braids giggled too, as she dropped to her knees in front of me. I slammed my eyes closed. She wasn't wearing any underwear. I felt her hands tugging my pants down.

"Stop crying, you little whimp! This will teach you to stay out of grown folks' business."

I wanted to tell Randall Mama said as long as he lived in her house, he wasn't grown, but I didn't. I stopped crying, but I didn't say anything. When my brothers pointed at me and made fun of how small I was, I tried to cover myself, but Carlton pulled my arms behind my back.

"Dude, you really are a *little man*," Carlton teased.

"That's 'cause he's half-white. I bet he stays that little the rest of his life," Randall added.

"Yeah, little man, this may be all you get. Ain't nobody gon' want that little thing."

The girl laughed, but didn't offer any insults.

I kept my eyes closed the entire time I got served. I didn't moan, curse or grunt like my brothers. I was too busy trying to decipher why I felt bad and good at the same time. I felt excited and afraid. I wanted to run far away from that room, but I also wanted to stay.

The girl with the long braids finished her task, then sat on the bed and lit a skinny cigarette. Carlton released my arms.

"I better not catch you in my business again," Randall barked. His pants were still down. "And if you tell Mama, we're gonna tell her you was doing it to. We cool, just as long as you don't open your big mouth."

I wanted to ask what "it" was, but I didn't. Like always, I didn't say anything. I was still confused about what had just happened.

"Now get out of here, and make sure the house is clean before Mama gets home," Carlton added.

The girl with the long braids never said one word to me.

I stood and ran from the room with my pants still down amidst laughter and that stinky cigarette smoke. Once inside my room, I tore off my school uniform. I didn't want to see or touch that uniform ever again. So unlike my brothers, I threw my clothes outside in the garbage can. I'd come up with a lie later if Mama noticed I was one uniform short.

After changing clothes, I finished my chores and alerted my brothers at the normal time, like nothing had happened. The girl left, and one by one, my brothers emptied out of the room. Randall opened the windows and sprayed air freshener. Carlton started the washing machine, then inspected my work. They brushed their teeth and gargled with mouthwash. To make the scene look convincing, they placed an open textbook on the couch. My brothers got all cleaned up for Mama, but didn't bother to show me how to get rid of the shame I felt. They didn't say anything to me.

When Mama came in and hugged me that night, I didn't want to let her go. I wouldn't have if Randall hadn't made a fist at me behind Mama's back. I wanted to be a baby again and have Mama rock me in her arms. I wished it were morning so I could cuddle next to her. But it wasn't morning and I was no longer a baby. Something happened to me in that room. I'd lost something, but at nine years old I couldn't identify what it was.

That night in bed, I didn't explore my body, like I'd become accustomed to doing. That night I cried myself to sleep. My days of spying on my brothers ended that afternoon.

The girl with the long braids continued to come by and serve my brothers, but she never spoke to me. It was like outside of what she'd done to me, I didn't exist. She was known by my brothers and their friends as the fat neighborhood freak. I learned years later her name was Trina.

CHAPTER 4

Transitions

M Y LIFE CHANGED rapidly and drastically after the girl with the long braids incident. Some of the details are still a blur to me. It seems I went from a scrawny fifth-grader to a high school senior overnight. I went from not caring about my appearance to being totally obsessed with how I looked. My body went through a metamorphosis too. I was now almost six-feet tall. My once- skinny arms and legs expanded with defined muscles. Curly brown hair not only covered my head, but my arms, armpits, legs and chest. I didn't like the hair in my armpits, because it was sweaty and stinky. Instead of traditional zits, my face became home to permanent blemishes— freckles. I hated my freckles, still do. At school, girls didn't seem to mind the invasion taking place on my face, but at home, I became known as "spotted half-breed little man" by my brothers.

Although I begged to attend public school like my brothers had, Mama made me continue in private school throughout high school. Glenda Bennett was determined I receive the best education my trust fund could pay for, so at seventeen I was still wearing khaki slacks and white shirts to school. The sweater had been replaced by a black blazer with the school's emblem on the pocket.

With minimal effort, I maintained a 4.0 grade point average through my senior year. For some reason school came easy for me. Mama attributed my ability to my father's good genes. Apparently, my father graduated at the top of his class too, and like him, I had several college scholarships offered to me from top schools around the country. During my junior year, Mama joined me on a trip back east for a college tour. She wanted me to attend Harvard, like my father had, but I had other plans.

I'm sure my father was a wonderful person—Mama still talked about him every day. I'd seen his degrees and special recognition awards. I'd heard from colleagues and clients how devoted and generous he was, but I didn't know him. My memories of Alexander Bennett, Sr. were implanted by second-hand accounts. He was more like a legend, whose story had been passed down through generations, than a father figure. I needed someone live and present to talk to and to seek advice from.

Due to no fault of his own, my father wasn't there when I fully reached puberty. He couldn't explain why I sometimes woke up with damp underwear. My father wasn't available to show me how to use a condom when I fully lost my virginity at fifteen to a neighborhood girl—a gift from Randall. My father didn't teach me the rules of the game and how to handle myself in the streets. Randall did. Carlton helped, but Randall was my biggest influence. And I still wanted to be just like him.

Due to lack of funds, Mama refused to use my trust fund to pay for my siblings' education. Randall and Carlton attended the local community college before transferring to state college. Both earned degrees—Randall in Accounting and Carlton in Nuclear Science. That child support never did kick in. In my opinion, my brothers had done well, and I didn't see any reason to travel a different path. Of course, I hadn't shared my plans with Mama.

At age twenty-five Randall lived in his own condo and owned a new Ford Mustang. Like his old bedroom door, the door to his condo was a revolving door for women. The only difference now was, he no longer shared his bounty with Carlton. I was still his housekeeper, only now I got paid to clean his pad once a week. At first Mama didn't want me working for Randall, but he convinced her I needed to learn how to earn money. Since Mama wouldn't allow me to work at a fast food restaurant, working for Randall was a safer option. Or, so she thought. On occasion Randall would offer me one of his chicks, but his endless supply of weed was off limits. "Mama's not going to blame me for destroying her golden child," he'd say whenever I expressed interest.

Randall still had a shadow, only now I occupied the space instead of Carlton. I'd always considered Carlton a nerd. He proved me right when he enrolled in graduate school. Pursuing an advance degree and with ambition of working for the government someday, didn't leave time for getting served by numerous girls and getting high. Not only did his priorities change, so did Carlton's personality. He was no longer satisfied following behind Randall. He was his own man.

I first noticed the change in Carlton at Randall's college graduation. That was the first time I'd seen Randall and Carlton's father. Mr. Williams showed up at the ceremony with what looked to be a teenager on his arm, and more than a little drunk. Throughout the entire ceremony, Mr. Williams boasted about how proud he was to have a son graduate college, and how much he'd sacrificed putting two sons through college.

The young woman, who upon further inspection I noticed was pregnant, encouraged him. "I know. That's why I'm working, to help you with the bills. All your money goes to your boys."

My mother was sitting directly in front of the loud pair, but not one time did she turn around or acknowledge their presence.

When his father greeted him, Carlton nodded his head, but didn't reciprocate the hug his father initiated. Throughout the declarations of selfless acts of love, Carlton removed his eyeglasses and glared at his father. He had to have felt like he was looking into the mirror, because Carlton was an exact replica of his father. As soon as Randall's name was called, Carlton left.

That summer Carlton didn't hang around the house with Randall. He stopped smoking weed and going to parties. Instead, he got a job tutoring kids. Randall called him a square, but Carlton didn't seem to care. A week after the fall semester started, Carlton announced he was moving out. He'd found a job close to campus and shared a four-bedroom house with some classmates. It wasn't until after he'd moved out that I realized he'd stopped referring to me as little man and half-breed.

I didn't mind filling the spot vacated by Carlton. It meant more one-on-one time with my idol, Randall. At seventeen, I should have been hanging out with friends my own age and making plans to join the "real world". I was making plans alright, but my definition of the "real world" was moving in with Randall and having fun while attending the local junior college. My brother and I weren't friends, at least I was his, but we had a good relationship. He told me what to do and I did it. I watched his actions and mimicked them. I didn't return the derogatory names he called me. I held him in the highest regard.

I decided to unveil my big plans to Mama one Sunday after church. We'd been attending the new neighborhood church regularly since the congregation started three years ago. The services were lively and engaging. Mama liked the minister's messages. I liked the youth activities. My brothers liked the fresh crop of ladies. It was a win for the entire family.

Mama was always in a good mood after Sunday service, humming as she prepared dinner. I walked into the kitchen and kissed her cheek. As always, Mama smiled at me with eyes full of love and adoration. It was the same smile that said, "Just ask, and I'll give you anything you want."

"Need some help?" I asked, reaching for an apron. Mama had taught me how to cook basic meals, so I wasn't a total dimwit in the kitchen.

"Sure. You can peel the rest of these potatoes." Mama held out the potato peeler and took two steps to the right. "You peel, and I'll cut while we talk about your future."

The oven wasn't on, but sudden heat swirled around me. Was Mama a mind reader now? "What future?" I played dumb, hoping to distract Mama. I wasn't ready to dive headfirst into an argument. I wanted to slip in my plans to move in with Randall and junior college after a spoonful of mashed potatoes and a gulp of lemonade.

Mama thrust the peeler in my hand, then picked up a knife and began cutting the potatoes that were already peeled. "Alexander Bennett, I had a good time at church today. Don't make me lose my joy like your brother did last week."

When Mama and I returned from church last week, a young woman was waiting on our steps. She was looking for Randall, said she hadn't seen him since telling him about her pregnancy three months ago. I don't know why Mama was upset. At least three other women had dropped by in the past five years with a similar story. Each time Randall swore the baby wasn't his. "I don't have sex," he'd say. "And when I do, I use a condom."

Mama would shake her head in disgust and grunt, "You are just like your daddy." None of the ladies ever returned with a baby.

I used a diversion tactic to regain control of the conversation—something I'd picked up from Randall. "The way you danced in service today, I doubt there's anything that could make you lose your joy. And don't think I didn't see Deacon what's his name talking to you after church."

The smirk on Mama's face was the closest thing I'd seen to a smile in regards to a man, aside from my father.

"The good deacon was just making me aware of his plumbing services, just in case I need some work done. Nothing special."

"Yeah right." I had her now. Mama wrung her hands, something she did when nervous or anxious. "I guess it was nothing special last week when he escorted you to the car."

Mama planted her fists against her waist. Her neck rolled in sync with the words of correction. "It was drizzling outside, and Deacon Hill escorted several people to their cars with his umbrella. If you weren't so busy chasing that girl in the short skirt, you would have noticed that."

I lifted my hands in surrender. I had been too occupied inspecting thighs to pay much attention to Mama. "You got me on that one. But from now on, I'm going to keep an eye on you."

"Don't worry about me," Mama said, while stirring cabbage. "You need to focus on selecting a college. In less than seven months, you'll graduate high school, and you haven't decided on where to go yet. We need to secure housing and transportation. I need to contact the administrator of your trust fund with details. If you're going out of state, arrangements have to be made."

I sat the potato peeler down and patted her back. "Mama, calm down. I have everything under control. I've even decided on a school and have made housing arrangements. Sort of." I hadn't asked Randall, but I was sure he wouldn't object to having a roommate.

A shocked expression rested on Mama's face, but only momentarily before a barrage of questions began.

Mama placed the utensil on the spoon rest and stood next to me. "Where have you decided to attend? Harvard? Princeton? Morehouse? I really don't want you to move far away. What about USC, or Berkeley?"

"I have decided to remain close to home. The east coast is too cold for me and the south isn't diverse enough."

I intentionally resumed peeling potatoes and left her hanging. Another tactic I'd learned from Randall. "Leave them hungry for more, so they'll do anything you want," he'd said. Of course, he was referring to girls, but I'd seen him manipulate Mama on several occasions so I knew the method worked on all females.

Mama's warm arm rested around my shoulder. "So, baby, where are you going? I want you to live on campus so you can have the full experience."

Her pride shown so brightly through her smile, I almost felt bad for manipulating her. "I'm going to experience everything. I promise. I'm moving in with Randall and attending Chabot."

Indignation replaced pride so fast I didn't see it coming.

"The devil is a lie!" my mother snarled, with fists planted at her waist. "Have you lost your mind?"

"W-what? H-huh?" In mere seconds my mother reduced me to stuttering.

"There is no way you're moving in with Randall! I don't care if he became the national spokesperson for the National Negro College Fund. You will not waste the opportunity your father has made available for you." Mama pointed her finger at me and rolled her neck. "You have the grades and the money to attend any school in this country. You will not waste your life at a junior college smoking weed and screwing everything walking with your brother. And that's final!"

I immediately shifted to step two on Randall's foolproof manipulation plan: Play stupid. "What? Randall smokes weed?" I may have overplayed it by gasping and falling back against the table.

For the first time ever, my mother raised a wooden spoon at me, as if to strike me.

"Alexander Bennett, Jr., do I look stupid to you? Boy, I will beat you down before I allow my oldest child to corrupt you. Letting you clean his apartment to learn the value of money is one thing, but sending you to live with that devil, ain't gonna happen."

The wooden spoon stayed in constant motion as Mama ranted and raved. I didn't say a word; I was too busy trying to stay out of striking distance.

"We will not have this conversation again!" Mama finally yelled and stormed out of the kitchen.

And just like that Mama won the battle. The following fall I enrolled in UC Berkeley.

CHAPTER 5

Little Man on Campus

LTHOUGH I'D GROWN up in the Bay Area and had passed by UC Berkeley on numerous occasions, I'd rarely visited the campus outside of annual field trips to the Lawrence Hall of Science. Even as a Bay Area native, the twelve-hundred-plus acres seemed like another world to me. Attending a prestigious private high school prepared me for the diversity, but nothing prepared me for my newfound freedom. I could come and go as I pleased, eat what I wanted and do what I wanted.

My academic scholarships covered the bulk of my tuition and books, allowing Mama to splurge some on my room and board. Most freshmen shared double rooms with twin beds. Thanks to my trust fund, I enjoyed a single high-rise suite with a private bathroom and kitchenette. Everything I needed was within walking distance, or assessable by public transportation, but Mama insisted I have a car for emergencies. I was less than thirty minutes from home. I could ride the BART train to every major hospital in the Bay Area by the time it would take me to get through the Berkeley traffic, not to mention the shortage of available parking spaces. Mama didn't care; she purchased a white five-year-old Toyota anyway. I left the car parked in her garage, and used it sparingly on weekends.

Randall thought the car was a waste of money too, but his rationale was rooted in the fact that Mama had refused to buy him a car, or act as cosigner. "If your father had paid one dime of child support, I'd have money to buy you a car," Mama had said when Randall asked years prior. Mama did buy him a nice watch for his college graduation.

I had hoped for one more growth spurt before high school graduation. I wanted to be over six-feet tall like my brothers. Thanks to my father's genes that didn't happen. My body stopped growing at five feet, eleven inches. I was officially the little man in the family. On a regular basis I lifted weights. What I didn't have in height I made up for with physique. My chest was broad and I had a six-pack. Now that I had the freedom to wear regular clothing to school, I selected fashions that highlighted my strong points. My freckles remained, but now I kept my thick haircut short. I didn't consider myself attractive, but I wasn't an ugly duckling either.

Unlike in high school, I wasn't the smartest kid on campus at Cal. Everyone on campus was smart with a bright future ahead of them. No one made a fuss over me, or complimented me when I did well on a test. Good grades were expected. I didn't earn extra credit for working after class on an assignment. No one reminded me of assignments either. In fact, in most of my freshman classes I was known by a number. For the first time in my life my mixed heritage didn't define me on campus. Cal's student body was a melting pot of cultures and ethnicities. I was only one of hundreds of bi-racial students. I didn't have to worry about being called "light bright" or "high yellow". I was just another student.

I made several new friends freshman year and was recruited by several fraternities. I hadn't planned on pledging because Randall hadn't. However, Mama had my father's former law partner explain to me the benefits of joining the brotherhood, and I decided to pledge the same fraternity my father had at the first opportunity. This made Mama happy and Randall furious. Carlton, who was nearing the end of a Master's degree, called and congratulated me on my selection. I'd been so obsessed with Randall, I didn't know Carlton had pledged a few years prior.

I was determined to stand out in the sea of students attending the Haas School of Business, but not at the expense of a social life. During the week, I studied hard and stayed a week ahead of the syllabus, but on the weekends, I hung out with Randall. I duplicated his dress, his walk and his lingo. Now that I was a college student, my oldest brother didn't seem to mind me club-hopping with him now that I received a monthly allowance from my trust fund. He even helped me get a fake ID. At the clubs, he'd introduce me as his younger brother, Alex, but when a chick expressed more interest in me than him, Randall reverted back to the term: little man.

It took me a few months to notice that although we both partied, I was the only one paying. I paid the cover charge, for the drinks and the gas. The only time Randall pulled out his money was to impress the ladies. He'd buy drinks and stuff money into the thongs of the dancers on stage, but never offered me a dime. I was the starving college student, well maybe not starving, but I was unemployed. Randall had passed his CPA exam and was working as a full-time accountant. The one time I mentioned the inequality his response was, "You're the little golden child. You can afford it." He skipped hanging out with me the following weekend. I hated being called the little golden child, but hated being left behind more. So I never mentioned the disparity again.

Near the end of the first semester Carlton called and asked if he could come and hang out for the day. The request surprised me. I rarely communicated with Carlton since he moved out and we'd never been close. I agreed, but didn't change my clubbing plans with Randall that night. I figured the bland encounter would only last a couple of hours. Beyond, "What's up?" and "How's school?" we didn't have enough conversation to fill an entire day.

He arrived at my dorm precisely at 10:00 a.m. Carlton, at age twenty-five and almost two degrees under his belt, still looked like a nerd to me. It was Saturday—the weekend—yet he wore khaki pants with a dress shirt instead of jeans and a polo shirt. His feet were stuffed in loafers and not the latest Nikes. He refused to trade in those rimmed glasses for contacts. One thing was new: his smile. I'd noticed it at Thanksgiving dinner. Carlton smiled more and appeared more relaxed. Uninterested, I attributed his change in demeanor to him being close to making some scientific discovery that would earn him that job he wanted with the government.

"What's up, man?" I hoped my facial expression didn't convey how dorky I thought he looked.

"Hey, little brother. How are you?"

I didn't expect a handshake, let along the hug my brother gave me. Sharing affection and expressing emotion wasn't something we did amongst each other. We rarely exchanged high-fives. I returned the awkward embrace, but only for a second.

"I'm good," I answered, contemplating what angle he was coming from. "Come in."

The smile never left Carlton's face as he looked around my private dorm. He walked over to my desk to where my laptop was, and picked up some books. "I've read all of these. That's some exciting stuff about the human mind. Don't you just love how the book challenges you to think outside the box?" His smile grew wider when he made the statement. It occurred to me that Carlton really loved academics.

I didn't share the same love for Psychology and Humanities, but I didn't want to embarrass my brother, so I played along. "Yeah, it's good stuff."

Carlton continued browsing, then did something I was familiar with. He went straight to the refrigerator and helped himself to a leftover half of my pastrami sandwich. Figuring out scientific formulas had done nothing to diminish his appetite.

"You don't mind, do you?" he asked after starting the micro-wave to reheat it.

Even if I wanted the sandwich, Carlton's grin wouldn't allow me to deny him the day-old snack. I'd never seen him look so content. "Help yourself."

He retraced his steps to the refrigerator. "Since you're offering, I'll take this leftover pizza too."

I laughed. "You're the human garbage can; eat it at your own risk."

My brother didn't miss a beat devouring the leftovers, but I noticed he prayed over the food. That was new. So was the fact that he'd been in my presence longer than five minutes and hadn't used profanity.

After discarding the trash, Carlton leaned against the mini counter. "So what's going on with you? Looks like you're adjusting well to college life. The last time I spoke with Mama, she raved about how well you're doing."

I chuckled. "Let's see if she feels the same after grades come out."

"Alexander Bennett, Jr., you can do no wrong in Mama's eyes. You could bring home straight "D"s and Mama would put a positive spin on it."

His smile remained, but I heard the pain Mama's favoritism had caused him. Although I'd acknowledged the difference Mama made between me and my brothers, I wasn't ready to address it.

"The last time I talked with Mama, she was cheering about your externship at the chemical plant." Randall always said avoidance was the best tactic when faced with difficult subjects. It worked; Carlton's eyes lit up.

"Really? Mom talks about me?"

In an instant, Carlton reverted to a little kid, eagerly awaiting his parent's approval. In his eyes were hope and fear. I didn't disappoint him and I didn't lie. I'd heard Mama bragging about her sons on several occasions; she just never bothered to express her pride to them directly.

"Man, Mama thinks you're either going to invent a way for humans to live on the moon, or create a bomb that will destroy the Earth. Either way, she brags, 'My son's name is going down in history for doing something big!'"

Carlton looked contemplative, like he was deciding if my words were true, then walked into my living area and plopped down on my futon.

I followed, still unsure why my brother was there in the first place. We weren't close. Despite being closer to Carlton in age, I gravitated toward Randall. Frankly, I had no interest in Carlton. He was boring, dorky and took life way too seriously. His sudden detachment from Randall also fueled my dislike toward him. Carlton never voiced anything negative about Randall to me, but I didn't like the fact that he dropped Randall for geeks in bowties. Randall wasn't perfect, but he was the closet example of a father figure I had, and I took offense to anyone who dissed him.

"So, man, what's up?" I asked to get the game started. I hoped he didn't want to borrow money; I'd already loaned my reserves to Randall. It was more like gave because Randall never paid back.

Carlton's expression changed from contemplative to worry. This had to be about money. I cut to the chase. "I already loaned Randall what money I had left from my monthly allowance."

His face twisted. "What? Man, I don't want your money. Just because I ate your leftovers doesn't mean I need a handout. I'm a grown man, and I take care of myself."

If it wasn't about money, then why was he here? And was he implying that Randall wasn't grown and responsible?

"I came here," Carlton continued when I didn't comment, "because I wanted to talk to you. Actually, I owe you an apology."

Now I was totally confused. "For what?"

Carlton stood and walked over to the window. I assumed he was admiring the Berkeley hills in the dead space that followed.

He removed his eyeglasses and cleaned them with a cloth from his pocket. Finally, he turned to face me. I hadn't seen that grim expression since my beat down in the bathroom. Maybe he'd gotten a girl pregnant?

"What's up?" I asked again.

His lips moved, like he was mumbling to himself, before he spoke out loud. "I'm sure you've noticed how I've changed over the past few years."

I nodded.

"In addition to engulfing myself into school, I've also experienced a rebirth. Meaning I've received Jesus as my savior."

"Huh?" That didn't make sense to me. Jesus had been the savior in Glenda Bennett's house for years. We may not have went to church every Sunday, but we'd known about Jesus all of our lives.

"I know we went to church as kids, but I didn't pay attention to what the preacher or anyone else said. I was too focused on chasing girls to care about my soul. Then in my third year of undergrad things changed. I changed. My focus is no longer on how many ladies I can screw and getting high. Now I care about serving and helping others."

"That's great." I still didn't see how I fit into the equation. "But you didn't have to travel two counties over to tell me that."

He nodded. "You're right. There's more." Several deep breaths later, he continued. "When we were younger, I did a lot of things I'm not proud of. I idolized Randall, because he reminded me of our father. I followed his lead no matter how crazy the idea."

My agitation with him dissing Randall must have showed, because Carlton raised his hands and retreated.

"I don't blame Randall for anything—the stealing, the weed, the alcohol or the sex. I love our brother and always will. I had a mind of my own. I obeyed Randall because I wanted to, but I'm still not proud of my actions." His head lowered. "What I'm most shameful of is what we did to you."

I chuckled at his concern. "Man, I know y'all didn't mean nothing by making me be the maid and making fun of my ethnicity. Y'all were just cracking jokes." At least that's the story I'd feed my psyche every time I heard the degrading words.

Carlton's head raised, and from the dread in his eyes I knew he was about to go somewhere I did not want to go.

"I regret those things too, but I'm not talking about that. I'm talking about the day Randall and I made you have oral sex with Trina."

The second the name slipped from his lips a knot formed in the pit of my stomach and I tasted bile in the back of my throat. I stood frozen as the sounds and smells of that Thursday came rushing back. *"Yeah, little man, this may be all you get. Ain't nobody gon' want that little thing."*

"You were too young. Randall and I were out of control. I shouldn't have stood back and watched. I should have stopped Randall instead of holding your arms. I wasn't so high that I didn't know what was happening was wrong. I saw the tears and fear in your eyes and didn't do anything about it. For that, I am so sorry. Please forgive me for not looking out for you. You were a kid and I was your big brother. I should have said something."

Tears dripped from Carlton's eyes, but I refused to show any emotion. That was in the past. I had moved on.

"No problem."

"I hope the trauma didn't mess you up too badly? I wish there was some way I could make it up to you." Carlton hugged me and whispered, "I love you, man."

"Me too." I returned his hug. Not because I wanted to, but because I wanted him to leave.

He shared more about his conversion and plans for the future. I think he mentioned a girlfriend. I couldn't be sure; I'd zoned out. I remember vividly closing the door behind him as he left the apartment.

Later that night after clubbing and getting high with Randall, my older brother and I shared two strange women. To this day, I can't recall their names.

CHAPTER 6

Miss Jackson

B Y JUNIOR YEAR, I'd adjusted to campus life well enough to balance an active social life, join several campus groups and maintain a high GPA. Mama was already probing me about grad school. I had been thinking about continuing on to a Master's in Finance, but wasn't sure I wanted to go straight through. I also hadn't pledged a fraternity yet. Mainly because Randall said it was a waste of time. He didn't belong to one.

Although I didn't stand out on campus like in high school, a variety of ladies were always within reach. Having my own pad made me a hot commodity and afforded me many friends with benefits. Even guys befriended me in hopes of using my spot to hold parties or to hide one girlfriend from the other.

I didn't mind the intrusion, but for some reason Randall did. Every time I cancelled on him and spent time with my classmates, he called me a fool for allowing them to take advantage of me.

At the end of each tangent, he'd ask to borrow money for the weekend. Turns out, I continued financing Randall's partying habit although I wasn't there.

I didn't see anything wrong with allowing my school friends to use my pad. At least they didn't ask to borrow money and never pay back. I did wonder why Randall always needed to borrow money from me. He worked a full-time job. He wore tailored suits to work and recently traded in his Mustang for a new BMW. One day I asked him why he always borrowed from me, his reply was, "You can afford it. And besides, I'm making up for lost time." I didn't dare ask him what he meant by that. As long as Randall spent time with me I didn't care.

I purposely limited my face-to-face communication with Carlton to the holidays. Even then, I kept the conversation to a minimum. During phone calls, I always had homework or a class that needed my attention. I didn't need him taking any more trips down memory lane. It took weeks and several sexcapades to get the events of my first sexual experience out of my head, and I wasn't going back there.

I consider myself warm-blooded. I love warm temperatures. Spring and summer are my favorite seasons. While my skin enjoyed the warm climate, my eyes feasted on a smorgasbord of female specimens parading around in shorts and mini-skirts. Following Randall's advice, I was always on the lookout for the next best thing. Although, I didn't fully buy into Randall's philosophy that women were only good for satisfying a man's sexual appetite, my actions said otherwise. I wasn't committed to anyone and didn't want a commitment or any emotional attachment. I wanted gratification, plain and simple.

Then I met Miss Jackson.

It was a Friday afternoon. The April temperature hovered between sixty and seventy degrees and the sky was clear. I'd just completed my statistics class and was headed back to my apartment for a snack. Instead of taking my usual route, at the last minute I heard music and decided to cut through Sproul Plaza. As I took the stairs leading from Upper Sproul to Lower Sproul, powerful beats of a steelpan drum and a bass guitar charged the atmosphere. Maracas shook in choreographed movements, and the trumpet squealed. Lower Sproul was packed with people dancing, all the way from the Student Union building on the east to Zellerbach Hall on the west. I had forgotten today was the start of the spring music series in Lower Sproul. Today a Calypso band provided the means of escape for us students.

I didn't dare join in with my schoolmates and gyrate to the beats. I considered myself a good dancer in the dark clubs while slightly under the influence of alcohol or weed. Dancing sober in broad daylight may've proven me wrong. Randall said I danced like an offbeat white boy and although the comment was made in the confines of a club, I heard his voice above the music and laughter in Lower Sproul. I didn't want to look like an idiot, so I stopped at the last step and watched the careless brave souls around me. I bopped my head and patted my feet, but that was all.

After the third song, I started toward my destination, only to be delayed again. This time the distraction came in the form of an African beauty queen. At least that is what she resembled to me. In the midst of the chaotic, yet peaceful scene, adjacent to the Packard mural, stood the finest woman I'd ever seen. She was wearing a yellow sundress that stopped just below the knee. She stood around five-feet seven-inches in the low-heeled gold sandals, and I figured weighed no more than one-hundred-twenty pounds. Even with my untrained eyes, I could tell she'd naturally grown the thick black hair flowing past her shoulders. A perfect set of hips rested between her small waistline and shapely legs. Both her fingers and toenails were painted yellow to match her dress. Dark skin as smooth as Ghirardelli's dark chocolate covered her toned body. She was simply beautiful.

Under normal circumstances I would approach any female and drop some lame lines and a few lies and walk away with a phone number and promise of a future date. However, there wasn't anything normal about this dark beauty. Just looking at her from twenty-feet away zapped my confidence. I looked down at my attire. Suddenly jeans and a striped button-down shirt wasn't stylish enough to step to Miss Sunshine. So in the midst of crowded Lower Sproul, I stood frozen, admiring her from afar. Her head moved to the rhythmic beats, but her feet remained planted as her lips moved. I thought she was singing until her angle changed slightly and revealed a hand-held tape recorder. Her head constantly turned, like she was scanning the crowd, perhaps looking for someone.

Anxiety overwhelmed me and my rational thinking faculties turned into mush. I told myself I couldn't let her see me looking so casual. The woman didn't know me and probably had no idea I existed on the planet, but I fed myself the notion that she'd be disappointed with my appearance. I dashed behind a pillar the second she turned and began walking in my direction. The veins in my neck thumped inside my sweaty skin until the yellow sundress passed by me, leaving a fruity scent in its wake. Swaying hips always aroused me, but I didn't dare peek at the Nubian queen's backside. When I finally stepped out of hiding, the yellow dress was nowhere to be found. After using the back of my hand to wipe the sweat from my forehead, I dashed to my apartment without looking back.

Later that evening as I prepared for an outing with Randall, I tuned into the campus news station on my laptop. The cyber station was a good resource for keeping up with campus events and documentaries on hot social topics. I'd just sprayed starch onto my slacks, and had only intended to steal a glance at the screen, but the Nubian queen in the yellow sundress on the screen captured my full attention. I nearly burned a hole in my slacks watching her lips move as she reported on the music festival. Her voice wasn't soft and sexy like I'd imagined, but strong and authoritative. She enunciated each word perfectly, relaying important facts about the performers and the festive crowd. My knees buckled when she looked into the camera and ended the report in a much softer voice, "For CalTv, this is Tamara Jackson." Logically, I knew she wasn't smiling at me, but in the fantasy I'd created in my mind, she was speaking and smiling at an audience of one—me.

I stood frozen until the iron's sensor alerted me seconds before I burned a hole in my pants. I had to meet this Tamara Jackson, but how? I could try and contact her through the CalTv e-mail system, but there wasn't a guarantee she'd receive my message. Besides, what would I say? From the few things I knew about her, name and major—she had to be a journalism major to work on CalTv—Tamara Jackson was out of my league. Even in cyberspace, her natural beauty radiated. Her mannerisms were that of a classy woman. A woman that wouldn't be found in the clubs I frequented.

I slipped into my pants and regulated Miss Jackson to a shelf of wishful thinking in my mind. My cell phone sounded just as I stuffed several condoms into my front pocket. Figuring it was Randall calling to see why I hadn't left home yet, I waited until the fourth ring to answer.

"Hello."

"Man, what took you so long to answer the phone?" I was right. It was Randall. "Why haven't you left yet?"

I tried my hand at bluffing him. "You called my cell, what makes you think I'm still at home?"

"Negro please, CP time is about the only black characteristic you have. You get dressed slower than any woman does. Maybe because secretly you'd like to be one, *little man*."

At twenty, Randall's insults about my mixed ethnicity and manhood still hurt, but as always, I didn't stand up to him. I was banging just as much tail as Randall was—sometimes the same tail. The only difference was I didn't take money from women. Randall took money from me and nearly every woman he screwed more than once.

"Whatever, man. I'm leaving now," I said in resignation, suddenly wanting to pounce on the first woman I saw to prove my brother wrong.

"Don't forget to bring an extra two-hundred for the strip club. Since it's my birthday, I want a private show. If you're here in twenty minutes, I might let you watch."

His laughter filled the line, but I didn't find anything funny, since I was financing his freak show. Every time we went out Randall conjured up an excuse as to why I should foot the bill. Randall felt since I was the rich half-white boy, I could afford it. I didn't tell him about the increase in my allowance, for fear he'd find a way to spend that too.

"See you in a few." I disconnected, and grabbed a few more condoms. Tonight I planned to prove to Randall that I was just as much of a man as he was. My brother's approval meant everything to me.

I couldn't tell if I proved my point or not. I woke up the next morning on Randall's couch with a girl I'd last seen in his room. Randall's bedroom door was closed. Although the Cisco I drank aided in my memory lapse, I'm sure I had sex, but with whom, I didn't know. My clothes were strewn all over the living room. The woman cuddled beneath my arm was naked, and I was still wearing a condom.

The usual dose of pride and satisfaction my ego got after a night of wild sex, evaded me. Probably because I couldn't remember the events. The longer I lay there with the woman whose name I couldn't recall, the more thoughts of my first sexual experience resurfaced. Time had passed, but nothing had changed. Girls had to be high or under the influence of alcohol in order to be with me. And I had to have a buzz to do it. There were a few sober times, but I can't say I enjoyed them. I was too focused on performing. I never received complaints, but I didn't get rave reviews either. I had yet to experience making love, but had mastered acting out lust. Unlike in times past, today lust left me empty.

For once, I wished my father was around. Perhaps he could explain why multiple sex partners hadn't been enough to erase the emptiness in my spirit. In the gospel according to Randall, sex and money were the answer to everything. I'd had both, but still found myself lacking. Something was missing from my life, but I didn't know what. I couldn't share my thoughts with Mama; she still believed I was a virgin—a lie I didn't bother correcting. Since receiving salvation, Carlton was now too geeky and too deep for me to relate to. So I kept everything bottled up inside and prayed I lived up to Randall's expectations.

The sweaty body next to me mumbled something, and stale alcohol breath fanned my nose, nauseating me. Without consideration or care, I pushed the woman away, causing her to fall on the floor. I hadn't meant to push so hard, but there were three things I couldn't stand on a woman: morning breath, alcohol breath and cigarette breath. The nameless naked woman didn't seem to mind the floor. She simply curled into a fetal position and went back to sleep. I used that as my opportunity to escape. I dressed without showering and left the apartment without waking Randall. I needed to be alone to figure out why sex no longer satisfied my emotional needs. Maybe it never had, but that's the lie I fed myself. Today, I no longer believed the lie, but I wasn't ready for reality either.

———◆◆◆◆———

En route to statistics class Monday morning, I stopped at the local Starbucks for an energy boost to get me through the morning. After celebrating Randall's birthday all night, and then studying all day on Sunday, I needed a lift. Normally, I preferred to patronize one of the many local coffee houses near campus over franchises, but today my fatigue outweighed my social-economic conscience. I'd just claimed my venti coffee and turned toward the condiments' station when my world shifted off its axis. Within arm's reach was the lovely Miss Tamara Jackson.

Today she wore black jeans. Underneath the matching jacket, a cream-colored blouse. Her clothes weren't skin-tight, but still flattered her figure. She'd traded in the low-heeled sandals for high-heeled boots which made her look taller. With her hair pulled back into a ponytail, her high cheekbones were more defined and so were her eyes. Just as I thought from a distance, her beautiful dark skin was flawless. Instead of carrying a backpack on her back, Miss Jackson wheeled her school supplies around in a black leather bag.

Without warning, she started toward me, and I nearly panicked. Was she going to speak to me, and if so, what would I say? She solved the dilemma for me when she walked past me and collected her drink from the barista, leaving the scent of fresh apple wafting around my nose.

I continued on to the condiments' table with my drink. To say I was disappointed she didn't notice me was an understatement. I wasn't any more prepared to meet her than I was two days ago, but it would have been nice to have been greeted by someone of her caliber. Without engaging in conversation, I could tell Tamara was a woman of class and self-worth. Unlike the women at the clubs Randall and I frequented, Tamara displayed dignity and confidence. She walked with her head held high, like she had a bright future ahead of her that didn't involve spreading her legs open to strangers.

She was definitely out of my league, I resolved, and proceeded to absentmindedly add cream to my espresso.

"You'd better wake up before you make a real mess."

The light tap on my shoulder in no way prepared me for my first interaction with the beautiful Miss Jackson. Dumbstruck, that she had not only spoken to me, but had also touched me, I stood zombie-like with my mouth open. "Huh?"

Her head nodded, like she was trying to bring my attention to something on the condiments' counter. "Your cup; your drink is overflowing."

I was so zoned into her beauty and the fruity scent permeating from her, I couldn't understand her words until I felt warm liquid against my pants leg. In my trance, I'd poured too much cream in my coffee, causing the cup to overflow. What was supposed to be an energy boost was dripping in a steady flow over the counter's edge and onto my pants.

"Oh crap," I said, suppressing the normal expletive that would have flowed from my mouth in this situation, and set the creamer carafe down on the counter and grabbed a wad of napkins. Figuring it was useless trying to clean the coffee stain from my pants, I focused on cleaning the counter before the brown liquid trickled to the space occupied by Miss Jackson.

"Let me help you with that," she offered, before lifting my cup and walking away. By the time she returned the condiments' counter was clean again.

I expected her to toss the cup. What I didn't expect was for her to return with a fresh cup of coffee, but that's exactly what she did.

"I assume you drink regular? Don't worry about it, it's on the house." She set the sleeved cup down with such care I envied the morning staple. "I wouldn't worry about those pants. A little Shout® or an egg yolk will get that out," she added, before retrieving her cup.

The woman's beauty and consideration left me speechless. I attempted to thank her, but my tongue got tied. I stuttered over the words "thank you" until I gave up and just nodded.

"Have a good day, Alexander Bennett."

"You know my name?" I'd found my voice, but it projected a few octaves higher than normal, making me sound like a bad Prince impersonation. I didn't care. I liked the way my name sounded off her lips.

Her pensive facial expression made me wonder if she considered me developmentally challenged. "Yes, unless you're wearing someone else's ID and perpetrating as a student? I doubt that, since it's obvious you're not a morning person."

Her tone was more jovial than accusing, and I couldn't help but laugh as she pointed out the obvious. I'd totally forgotten about the lanyard around my neck. I'd spilled coffee and developed a speech impediment in a matter of seconds. It was official; this woman's presence rendered me a complete idiot.

I didn't need to look at the badge resting between the lapels of her jacket to know her name, but I did anyway and was treated to the outline of two perfect-sized breasts. "Miss Jackson," I managed after clearing my throat. "Thank you for your help this morning. I hate to think of what would have happened if you weren't here to rescue me." I couldn't tell her she was the reason I'd made the mess in the first place.

She grabbed the bar on her wheeled bag. "Glad I could help, but get some rest. I can't promise I'll be here to save the day tomorrow." With every word, she stepped toward the door.

"What about the day after?" Out of desperation, I asked the question to keep her from leaving. Randall said the longer you engage a women in conversation the chances of getting what you want increases. I didn't want to take advantage of Tamara, but I did want her company. For the first time my motives were pure, and for the first time, the tactic didn't work.

"Good-bye, Mr. Bennett," she said, and continued out the door.

Rejection never felt better. Tamara Jackson may have been out of my league, but I'd scored a small victory. The short, half-breed, freckled-faced kid with coffee-stained pants had been touched by an angel.

CHAPTER 7

Challenges

OWARD THE END of my junior year, I faced challenges, but keeping up in school wasn't one of them. Finals were strenuous, but not overwhelming. My grades were good and I was on track to graduate on time. I still straddled the fence about grad school, which frustrated my mother. I didn't care. Mom's happiness would have to wait. I had a bigger challenge to conquer.

Since the impromptu sighting of Tamara Jackson a month prior, Starbuck's had become a daily stop for me. Even if I patronized the local coffee house first, I would stop by Starbuck's in hopes of bumping into Tamara. After several fruitless attempts, I changed my routine. I not only went in the mornings, but midday as well. Sometimes, after checking inside, I'd sit outside at one of the tables—like I was doing now—and watch the door before going home to watch a recorded news story on my laptop.

I honestly don't know when I became obsessed with Tamara Jackson. In addition to stalking her at Starbuck's, I couldn't fall asleep at night without watching her on CalTv. Her smile was the image I drifted off to sleep with. While brushing my teeth in the mornings, I wondered how she brushed her teeth—up and down, or in a circular motion. Yes, I was definitely obsessed.

I had no desire for a relationship—not that she'd be interested in me, but I wanted to get to know her. In our brief interaction, her kindness and giving spirit had shone through. Granted, it was only a cup of coffee, but the gesture made an impression on me. Normally, women gave me what I wanted as long as I gave them what they wanted. It was an even trade: money and drinks in exchange for sex. I had a feeling Tamara would never barter her goodies, and I liked that.

I was just about to give up and settle for another cyber fantasy when Tamara strolled toward the front door with the wheeled bag in tow. She disappeared inside the coffee house before I could get my bearings.

Now that I'd accomplished my mission of seeing her, I didn't know what to do next. I'd been too focused on seeing her to concentrate on having a conversation. I paced in front of my little table trying to plan my next move, or should there even be a move. I'd lived in the Bay Area all of my life, and had never experienced the sudden spike in temperature that had sweat gathering at the base of my neck. My palms were sweaty, and my throat dry although I'd just finished a tall beverage. Fluid accumulated in my armpits. It wouldn't be long before the sweat absorbed my deodorant and give way to a foul smell even I didn't like. I grabbed my backpack and threw my empty cup away. I was going home, back to my fantasy.

"Hello, Mr. Bennett." Her voice arrested me before I could take two steps. "Haven't seen you around here lately."

I turned and faced her, and was glad I hadn't seen her coming. The up-close view heightened the pleasure. Her hair was pulled back in a ponytail, and she was wearing walking shorts and a Cal sweatshirt with matching blue and gold Nikes. The simple attire yielded stunning results. I doubted there was ever a moment when this woman wasn't beautiful.

I'm sure I blushed. "You remembered my name?" I couldn't believe she actually remembered my name.

Her smile appeared natural, like it was her normal facial expression. "Of course. How could I ever forget the clumsy, stuttering man with the cute freckles?" She set her beverage on the table. "Mind if I join you, since this is the only free table? Or, are you waiting for someone?"

Not only did I blush again, but I'm sure I also turned a shade of red. No one since high school had shown any delight in my freckles. No way was I going to refuse her anything.

"Please have a seat. I promise not to spill anything on you. That should be easy since I've already finished my drink." I attempted to pull out the chair for her, but she beat me to it. I reclaimed my seat, hoping my slowness didn't leave a bad impression. Randall had taught me impeccable manners with the ladies. Granted, they were to be used as a way to get between their legs, but I did have good manners.

She claimed the seat with the gracefulness of a swan. "I'll be sure to leave before you decide to get another drink." Her smile conveyed she was only joking. "So have you made any messes lately?" she asked, after taking a sip of what I recognized as a caramel Frappuccino by the brown drizzles on top.

"No. That only happens when you're around. Or, when I'm looking at your image."

"What? You've only seen me once. Don't blame me for your coordination problem."

I wanted to retract the truth with a lie the second her face twisted, but I couldn't. Now I had to explain at the risk of sounding like an idiot. I swallowed my pride and broke a rule from Randall's Player's Handbook: Never explain yourself to a woman.

"Well, Tamara, if I may call you by your first name?"

"We'll see after I hear your explanation."

Most people would have read her neck-rolling as attitude, but I found the gesture adorable.

"Ms. Jackson, you're a beautiful woman. In fact, you're the most astounding woman I've ever seen. I can't help it if your presence renders me an imbecile." I hoped my words didn't sound lame. I'd used those lines too many times to count, but today was the first time I meant them. "I spilled my coffee that morning because I was thinking about you."

She stood and looked around our immediate area, like she'd lost something. "When did this patio turn into an outdoor club? That's the only place you could've recycled that line from." Her girlish laughter softened the blow to my ego. "Mr. Bennett, you didn't even know I was standing next to you; didn't know I existed until I caught your attention. But that was a good try." She reclaimed her seat and began sipping her beverage.

"Actually, I saw you in Lower Sproul at the concert a few weeks back. I didn't speak then, but I've been watching you on CalTv ever since. I've been hanging around here, in hopes of running into you again, since the morning I spilled coffee all over my pants." I hadn't meant to tell the whole truth, but for some unexplained reason I felt the need to be honest with Tamara. I didn't think I had a chance with her, but her impression of me was important.

"For real?"

I nodded. "For real."

She set her cup down, almost in slow motion. "In that case, yes, you may call me Tamara." She blushed ever so slightly, easing my fear of rejection. "Now that you've found me, Mr. Bennett, what is it you'd like to say to me?"

I didn't have an answer, and from her smile, she knew I was stuck. I stalled anyway. "Please, call me Alex. My mother is the only person who addresses me by my birth name."

"Alright, Alex, I'm listening. What burning words had you hunting me down for weeks?"

"No words. Honestly, I just wanted to look at you."

The truth, although foreign to me, seemed to please Tamara. An appreciative smile rested on her face.

"Somehow, Alex, I think you sincerely mean those corny words. That's the nicest compliment I've received in a while. Thank you." She resumed nursing her drink, before retrieving her laptop from the wheeled bag.

"Come on. I'm sure you get that all the time from your boy-friend or significant other." Being a glutton for punishment, I had to know if she was attached to a man or to a woman. The campus was loaded with beautiful women who preferred a wom-an's touch over a man's. I hoped Tamara wasn't one of them.

She opened the laptop, but didn't turn it on. "To answer your not-so-subtle question, I don't have a boyfriend. I haven't dated a guy since freshman year." She let the statement hang, like dangling a fresh bone just out of a dog's reach. She sipped more

Frappuccino and turned on the laptop before finally looking up. She must have read the anticipation on my face, because she giggled and added, "And I've never dated a woman and never will. I'm one-hundred percent heterosexual."

I hadn't meant for my sigh to resound across the table, but the relief was short-lived.

"What about you? You can't have a serious girlfriend if you stalked me for weeks, but do you have any boyfriends stashed away? Are you straight or bi?"

The question was valid and to be expected in the cultural climate we lived in, but that fact didn't stop me from being offended. Maybe Randall's constant jeering about my sexuality had finally begun to taunt me. Whatever the reason, I didn't like being asked about my sexual preference, especially since I couldn't brag about how many women I'd conquered.

"I'm one-hundred percent heterosexual also, and no, I don't have a girlfriend," I answered honestly, "unless you count school."

She tapped the keyboard. "Tell me about it. School takes up all of my time. I don't know what I was thinking when I double-majored in Journalism and Psychology. With my work-load, I won't have time to date until after graduation. Which suits Judge Jackson just fine," she added, after taking a sip.

Just as I thought, Tamara had brains to match her beauty. Intellectually, we were on the same level. "Judge Jackson?"

"My father is criminal Superior Court Judge Earl Jackson. If he has his way no one would ever date his baby girl. 'Fifty percent of the male population in your generation are dogs, and the other fifty percent are recovering dogs,' he says." Her eyes pierced me, like she was trying to determine which percentage group I fell into.

"And you take your father's words as law, I assume?" I remained poker-faced. Something Randall taught me.

"Not always. I usually rely on the Holy Spirit to direct me."

The fantasy was officially over. Not only was Tamara the daughter of a criminal judge, but also a Christian. I'd end up in jail and in hell if I touched her.

"I don't want to keep you from your work. I have a paper that's due tomorrow, that I need to work on," I announced, and at the same time stood to leave. It was only a partial lie. The paper wasn't due until the following week. "It was nice seeing you again. Perhaps we'll meet again when we're not so busy."

For a split second, disappointment veiled her face, but she quickly recovered. "Perhaps. Good luck on your paper." Her smile and nod were a clear indication I'd been dismissed.

Before I could completely turn to leave, she began typing as if I were never there. Although I'd just brushed her off, I didn't like the ease in which she returned the favor. I walked away totally confused, and knowing I would see her again.

<hr />

Studying for finals consumed me, but didn't stop me from thinking of Tamara. It just wasn't as intense. My determination to ace my finals outweighed my attraction, especially now that I knew for certain we were traveling on two different paths. I'd never had the privilege of meeting a girl's parents and doubted I'd measure up to the judge's standards. Based on what Tamara shared, her father was a pretty good judge of character when it came to young men. If I did manage to fool her earthly father, I still had God to contend with. I was already on the man upstairs punishment list for the girls my brothers and I corrupted at the neighborhood church. There was no way I would show up on the radar again. The preacher used to talk about one reaping what one sowed. I'd sown enough bad seeds to reap a crop of damnation already.

I gave up the quest and hoped the infatuation would end soon. I stopped watching CalTv and no longer frequented Starbucks. With finals, summer school and weekend escapades with Randall, I had more than enough to occupy my time.

During summer break, I stayed with Mama and commuted to campus for summer classes. Mama was so happy to have me home, she cooked me breakfast every morning like old times. She also nagged me about my social life, making me promise not to turn out like Randall.

Turns out at least two of the pregnant girls who'd shown up on my mother's doorstep weren't lying. Court ordered paternity tests proved that Randall fathered two children, both daughters. Randi and Kendall. The same court also leveed hefty child support orders, which included arrearages. Randall was so angry with his baby mamas for taking him to court, he vowed never to have anything to do with his daughters, who were now five and three years old. And he didn't. He wouldn't even visit Mama if he knew his kids were around. If the child support wasn't automatically deducted from his paycheck, I doubt if he would have paid it, although he'd moved up in the company and was making nearly six figures.

Mama tried to make up for lost time and Randall's lack of concern, but it was nearly impossible with the girls asking where their daddy was, and the mamas complaining about how trifling Randall was. Mama and I put up a good front as much as possible and tried to bond with the girls. Carlton joined the effort by taking the girls to the movies and trips to the neighborhood ice cream shop.

My nieces enjoyed the time Carlton and I spent with them, but I knew from experience their hearts longed for their father's love and acceptance. I felt bad for them. My father was absent because someone callously took his life, and even in his death he loved me enough to provide for me. Randall was alive and well, yet he showed more regard for the chicks at the club than he did his own flesh and blood. I didn't like Randall's actions, or lack thereof, but he was my brother and I loved him. And like everything else, I overlooked this character flaw.

Mama had arranged to keep the girls so they could attend Vacation Bible School at the neighborhood church for the week. Mama said with Randall as a father, Randi and Kendall needed all the Jesus they could get. Randi insisted I come with them the first night, and being the softy I was, I rushed home after class to grant her wish. I had every intention of tipping out while they played and learned about Jesus.

The registration process took longer than expected. I estimate there were at least one hundred kids roaming around. After Mama completed registering the girls, I affixed name tags on the girls and with their little hands tucked into mine, started for the fellowship hall.

Dark-chocolate skin in a knee-length flaring red dress and gold sandals blocked my path. It was Tamara. She was the last person I expected to see in my neighborhood at Vacation Bible School, and to my dismay, I was happy. Looking at her was like drinking a glass of ice water on the hottest day of the year— refreshing and soothing.

She bent to the girls' level, and addressed them first. "Welcome, Randi and Kendall. I'm so happy you could join us tonight. My name is Tamara," she said, pointing to her name tag.

"Hi." The girls answered in sync, then released my hands and shook Tamara's extended one. My nieces must have liked Tamara, because neither of them looked scared anymore.

Tamara returned to the upright position and finally made eye contact. "Hello, Alex. I didn't expect to see you here. Are these your children?"

The fruity fragrance emanating from her clogged more than my senses. I also couldn't speak until Mama jarred me in the side. "Answer the young, single woman. She's asking you, not me. She can look at me and tell I'm too old to have children that young," Mama stated with a smile that communicated her approval of Tamara. I bet Mama scanned Tamara's left hand for a wedding ring the second she walked over.

"Hello, Tamara. These are my nieces." I thought I saw relief wash over her face.

"Do you know each other from school? I don't recall seeing you in service before," Mama pressed.

"We've run into each other on campus. I attend a different church, but I always volunteer here for Vacation Bible School. My uncle is the pastor here and I really enjoy the children."

Mama's eyes expanded twice the normal size. "That's great. You love kids and the Lord. You are such a pretty girl. Are you dating anyone?" So Mama was going to match-make right in front of my face.

Tamara blushed. "Thank you. And no, I don't have a boyfriend."

"Good. Alex is single too."

"Mama! Not here!" My cry fell on deaf ears. In a matter of seconds my mother gave a mini sales pitch on what she considered my best qualities, much to my embarrassment.

"Alex is a little shy, but he has a great personality. He's caring and respectful. He doesn't smoke, drink or do drugs. He loves children and can clean a house better than most women. He can cook too. He's been baptized and believes in Jesus. He's an 'A' student, and plans to own his own business someday." Mama turned to me like she expected me to add something. I didn't. Mama had done a fine job of creating a false image of who I really was.

Tamara laughed while looking down at her watch. "That's good to know, Mrs. Bennett, but it's time me and the girls joined the rest of the group. Come on, ladies." My nieces cheerfully accepted her extended hands. "It was nice meeting you, Mrs. Bennett."

Mama beamed as Tamara and the girls walked away. I stood frozen in place until Tamara called over her shoulder, "Have a good summer, Alex."

I didn't return the salutation, and at that moment, I had no idea how good my summer would eventually turn out. I wasn't spiritually connected to Jesus like Mama believed, but I was discerning enough to know running into Tamara at a place I normally wouldn't have been had divine intervention written all over it. And at Mama's urging, not that I needed it, I took advantage of the situation.

I returned to pick the girls up a few minutes late, in hopes of having a few minutes alone with Tamara. I lingered outside until the parking lot was nearly empty before I got out of the car. Just as I was about to stroll toward the entrance, Tamara and the girls exited the building, heading straight toward me.

79

The smile Tamara wore lacked her normal radiance. She stopped within inches of me and released the girls' hands. "See you tomorrow. Don't forget to practice the memory verse for tomorrow. I want you to win the prize."

I opened the back passenger door and waited for the girls to climb inside, all the while wondering what I could say to Tamara to make her interested in me. Tamara made the choice for me.

She leaned slightly back with one hand on her hip and a finger pointed in my face. "Alex, I get you don't want to see or talk to me, and I'm fine with that. Since I make you uncomfortable, I'll assign the girls to another group leader tomorrow. That way you won't have to hide out here to avoid seeing me."

She stomped away with what I considered too much attitude for a church girl, but cute nonetheless. Watching her ponytail sway to the rhythm of her hips, I became the hunter Randall trained me to be and went after my prey.

CHAPTER 8

Courting

C OURTING A WOMAN was something I'd never done before, never really desired to do, but that's exactly what I did the summer between my junior and senior year. From the moment Tamara stomped away from me in the parking lot, I pursued her. The knowledge that I'd made her angry, compelled me to set things right with her. Driven by my emotions and not by my hormones, I followed after her, calling out her name. When she wouldn't stop, I ran in front of her and blocked the church entrance. She stopped, huffed and folded her arms, and for the first time in my life, I begged a woman to listen to me.

After I explained I wasn't trying to avoid her, but was actually hiding out in hopes of speaking with her alone, the attitude relented. She unfolded her arms, and without a word, snatched my cell phone from my waist clip, then thrust the phone in my face after punching the keypad several times.

"If you want to speak to me, try using the phone since your direct communication skills suck."

"I told you that only happens with you." As I accepted the phone, I treated myself to the soft feel of her hands. The thrill was short-lived, but at least she didn't scowl when she snatched her hand back.

"Whatever, Alex. Now get back to the girls. You shouldn't leave them in the car alone."

I glanced back at the car. "You're right. What's a good time to call you?"

"As soon as you pass a public speaking class. Now go."

Her sassiness drew laughter from me and for once, I wasn't concerned about the honking-like noise coming from me. I called her that night and every night after that. On the second day of Vacation Bible School, I totally relieved Mama of her chauffer duties. For the rest of the week, I dropped the girls off early and then lingered afterward to spend time with Tamara. I'd help her set up before and clean up afterward, figuring the sooner she got out of there, the sooner I'd get my nightly dose of therapy. That's what Tamara was to me: therapy.

I was the hunter, yet Tamara controlled our conversations. No matter the topic, she always steered the subject back to me. She seemed to be on a fact-finding mission about me. She wanted to know my thoughts on everything from the weather to controversial topics like the probability of the first woman president. Maybe it was the journalist in her, but she listened and responded like she was really interested in my bland life. Naturally, I omitted my extra-curricular activity with Randall. She called my parents' relationship a romantic tragedy and guessed I was a spoiled brat being the youngest—a fact I didn't dispute. She wanted to know about my childhood and how growing up bi-racial in a single-parent home affected me emotionally. Her soothing phone voice coupled with the mental image I stored of her, made it easy for me to open up about my life. Family dynamics I could handle, and from my perspective, I did not bear any emotional scars.

She gave as much transparency as she desired, and for the first time I listened to a woman's thoughts and aspirations. Tamara had goals of writing and producing documentaries, and planned to use the Psychology degree to help counsel people with emotional disorders and adjustment problems. She was the oldest of Judge Earl Jackson's three daughters. Her mother was a bio-chemist, working on cancer research at Stanford Hospital. Her maternal grandparents were both physicians, and her paternal grandfather, a lawyer. Her heritage was saturated with class and wealth, yet she wasn't snobbish or snooty. She wasn't superficial or boastful. Tamara Jackson was simply the sweetest woman I'd ever met. She planned to marry and have children. After observing her interact with the kids for a week, there wasn't any doubt in my mind she'd make the perfect wife and mother. She was patient, nurturing and affectionate. Quite frankly, I was jealous of the attention and care she lavished on the kids. I wanted to feel her hand in mine and be wrapped in her welcoming embrace.

More than my nieces, I dreaded the last day of Vacation Bible School. It meant my time with Tamara had come to an end. We'd still have an occasional phone call, but my daily dose of her beauty would cease. I didn't have class on Friday, which allowed me to hibernate in my room most of the day.

Mama entered my room without knocking and asked if I was feeling up to taking the girls to the church—a question she didn't want to know the answer to because she didn't let me answer. Like old times, Mama sat on my bed and fingered my thick curls while grinning.

"Your dad courted me with roses. I bet Tamara likes roses, most women do."

Subtlety was never one of my mother's strong points.

She walked over to my closet and pulled out a hanger. "This tan linen outfit really looks nice on you and compliments your skin tone." She laid the outfit on the bed and looked at her watch. "If you hurry, you can get a haircut before the after-work crowd comes."

"I don't need a haircut."

"Yes, you do. Women like clean-shaven men with fresh haircuts. There's no way Tamara will turn you down with the roses, this outfit and a fresh haircut. Make sure you present the roses in front of a group—women like that, too. "

Mama had taken her matchmaking skills to a new level. Making suggestions was one thing, but selecting my clothes and telling me how to look was out of line. Fortunately, for Mama, I agreed with her selection and ideas, so I didn't voice my displeasure of her telling me what to do and wear. Neither did I voice my perceived inferiority to Tamara. What I did do was follow my mother's advice and went to the barbershop.

That night I arrived early to pick up the girls. I watched the group presentation from the back of the fellowship hall. Parents and grandparents watched and celebrated the kids, but I only had eyes for Tamara. It was a good thing my nieces were in her group, otherwise, I would have missed their presentation. After the dismissal, I refused the cake and punch offered and made a beeline to Tamara. She was sitting with my nieces, making my chances of being humiliated minimal. If her attitude was tart or distant, I could present the roses to my nieces instead to save face.

"Hello, ladies." I swear my knees were knocking as I stood next to her.

She looked up at me, and for a brief moment I thought I saw admiration resting on her ebony face, but she voiced her usual greeting, "Hey, Alex," without mentioning the dozen red roses in my hand.

"Uncle Alex, did you see me sing? I knew all the words and didn't mess up."

The expectancy in Randi's eyes tugged at my heartstrings, and for once, I wondered if Randall was making a mistake by avoiding his daughters. Even children need validation. I hunkered down to my niece's level. "Of course I did. You were wonderful. And so were you," I added turning to Kendall, who at age three appeared just as anxious for my approval. I removed two of the roses from the bunch and gave one to each of my nieces, who blushed.

I hugged and kissed my nieces, but my senses were keenly aware of Tamara's intense stare. I adjusted to my full height, and was greeted with warmth and adoration I'd never received from anyone other than my mother. I extended my arm, knowing my gesture had met Tamara's seal of approval. "These are for you. Thank you for teaching my nieces all week."

"I love roses." She first sniffed, then cradled the bundle in her arm. Her eyes blinked rapidly. "Thank you. It was nice getting to know you. Enjoy the rest of your summer. See you around campus."

She turned to walk away, leaving the next move on me. Within seconds, I made the move that would change my life forever—a move I would never regret.

"Are you hungry?" I actually stuttered. She faced me again and after clearing my throat, I repeated the question. "There's a great sushi buffet I'd loved to take you to after I drop the girls off. That is if you don't mind sharing a meal with a spoiled bright freckle-faced dude."

Her lips parted into a huge smile, and I swear I saw heaven in her eyes. "Sure. I'd love to share a meal with you." She leaned in and added, "Just so you know, I like freckles. I'd go out with you even if I wasn't getting a free meal."

For the first time ever, I allowed myself to freely enjoy the moment. Even I didn't recognize the hearty laughter pouring from me. "Wait here. I'll be back in ten minutes." I turned to the girls, who were sniffing the flowers, like Tamara had, and grabbed their free arms. "Let's go before she changes her mind."

With me jogging through the parking lot and driving forty in the twenty-five-mile speed zone, I made it back to the church in eight minutes and thirty-five seconds. The tires on my Camry screeched when I stopped alongside the curb nearest the entrance. Much to my delight Tamara was waiting right there, smiling. In addition to the roses, she now had a purse and sweater draped over her arm. She was just as anxious to spend time with me as I was with her.

I took her to dinner that night, and every free night we had after that during the summer. Tamara's schedule was more compact than mine, with all of her volunteer work and church activities. That left us with three evenings to hang out together. Our routine worked fine until I wanted more. I couldn't get enough of her sensuality. Her voice soothed me and her smile relaxed me. Her conversation stimulated me and her scent intoxicated me. Before counting up the cost, I committed to joining her on Saturday morning deliveries for the Meals on Wheels community program. I'd do anything to spend more time with her, even if it meant getting up at six in the morning on a Saturday. Sleepiness could be cured with coffee, but I hadn't planned on Randall's opposition.

I had to cancel our standing Friday night strip-club-hopping appointment. I couldn't take a chance on oversleeping and missing my time with Tamara. Even more so, I didn't need to fantasize about a stranger who was using me for money, when I had the real thing. Tamara and I weren't officially a couple, but if and when that happened, I intended to be faithful.

The first week I cancelled on Randall, he didn't ask too many questions; just cursed and hung up on me. By the third week, he demanded to know why I was messing up his weekend groove. I told him I was seeing someone from school, thinking he'd be pleased, but that wasn't the case.

"So you're kicking your brother to the side for some skank?" he stated more than asked. "Those come by the dozen at the club."

It's a good thing those words were spoken over the phone, otherwise, I may have punched my idol in the face. Instead, I defended Tamara's honor as if we were actually in a relationship. "She's not some stank, and not the type of woman who'd be seen in a club. She's smart, has class, and knows her value as a woman."

"So what is she doing with you?"

I didn't have a comeback for Randall. I'd been wondering the same thing. "We're just friends, but I still don't want you talking about her."

"Whatever, man. When you finally hit it and quit it—'cause I know your small, half-breed, slow self haven't tapped it yet—hit me up."

His words stung, but I refused to acknowledge how deep the hurt ran. I remained silent.

"And another thing, ain't no piece of tail good enough to desert your family for. And don't be blowing our money on her," he added before hanging up.

I stood frozen long after, pondering his words about deserting family. Hadn't he done just that by rejecting his daughters? My nieces were the sweetest, lovable kids. They weren't high- maintenance. All they required was a little attention and time, but Randall didn't care about them. And just what did he mean by "our" money? Did Randall actually believe he was entitled to my trust fund? He certainly didn't have a problem partying on my dime, but he had to have known it was my money, and I could spend it how I saw fit.

That weekend after the Meals on Wheels program, I treated Tamara to an early lunch mainly to spend more time with her, but also because I was starved. After a night of fitful sleep, I'd overslept by ten minutes and missed breakfast. That day I discovered that in addition to being beautiful and compassionate, Tamara had a love affair with pancakes. The national chain had a promotion on summer fruit and pancakes, and Tamara tried all four varieties. I watched in awe as she devoured eight pancakes then leaned back and rubbed her stomach. A smile of complete satisfaction rested on her face. Her eyes closed, and I thought she'd slip into a deep sleep, but then she bolted upright and asked a question I honestly didn't know the answer to.

"Do you have a personal relationship with Jesus?" The words rolled off her lips again after I didn't answer the first time.

I didn't know how to answer the question. I believed in God, Jesus and the Holy Spirit, although I didn't practice the teachings I'd heard in Sunday sermons. Did I have a relationship with Jesus? I wasn't so sure after my last visit from Carlton. I prayed on occasion, but didn't read the Bible or attend church on a regular basis. I drank and smoked weed on weekends with Randall. I'm sure screwing strange women didn't classify as Christian behavior.

I stalled. "Why do you ask that?"

"It's like this," she said, still rubbing her stomach. "I'm a Christ-follower, and my faith is very important to me—to my entire family actually. I plan to teach my future children the teachings of Christ and raise them to love others, like Jesus does. That being said, I can't get into a deep relationship with a guy who doesn't share my views on faith." She paused and looked away, like she was unsure of her next statement. "And, well, since you insist on dating me, I have to know."

Dating? I didn't realize we were dating. Sure I spent all my free time with her and constantly thought of her. I'd upgraded my wardrobe in hopes of impressing her and may have slipped and addressed her as "sweetheart" once, maybe twice. I hadn't had sex or desired another woman since hooking up with her at Vacation Bible School. Okay, I was dating her, but I didn't think she'd seriously consider me relationship-material.

"So we're dating?" I stuttered, and she laughed in my face. I remained stone-faced, trying to logically figure out how to answer her question and process that I may have a girlfriend. I'd never had a girlfriend. Booty calls didn't qualify.

Her laughter ceased. "I'm sorry. I must have misread your actions." She looked down at her empty plate, embarrassed.

"You didn't misread anything," I said, gaining confidence from the fact that I was acceptable to the sophisticated Tamara Jackson.

"Then why has your face turned two shades of red since I said the 'D' word? Don't worry about sparing my feelings. Be honest. If you're not courting me, then say so. We can still be friends."

Her glossy eyes belied her words. My heart soared, because now I knew she really liked me and didn't just consider my freckles a novelty. All she desired from me was honesty, which I freely gave.

"I like you a lot, but honestly, I didn't think you'd be interested in a relationship with me."

Her eyebrows furrowed. "So you think I've been spending all my free time with you just for company? I can get a puppy for that."

"True, but I doubt his freckles would be as cute as mine." We both laughed, releasing the tension.

"I should have never told you I like them on you."

For the first time since the spots appeared, I began to feel comfortable with what I characterized as a deficiency. "I'm glad you did." A comfortable silence rested between us. "Now to answer your original question. I do believe in God, I wouldn't say I have a personal relationship. I grew up attending church, and on occasion still do. My mother and older brother have a direct line to God. I pretty much leave the praying to them." Her smile disappeared, and just that quick my world took another turn.

From that moment on our relationship changed. Tamara and I still spent time together, but instead of spending meaningless hours at movies and restaurants, Tamara took me to church.

I spent the rest of the summer and most of the fall courting Tamara and learning about Jesus. Sunday morning services weren't a problem, but the midweek Bible study and Singles' Ministry sessions were new. Tamara allowed me to hold her hand and hug her, but that was as far as the affection went. She never voiced it, but I got the message her body was off limits during the first Singles' Ministry class she invited me to. The leaders presented Biblical principles for dating, and grinding between the sheets wasn't one of them. I appreciated Tamara's stance on purity, because that meant if she wouldn't open her legs for me, she wouldn't spread them for anyone else either.

I found most of the sermons motivational, and applied some Biblical principles to my daily life. I even bought a Bible and took notes during Bible study. I added a morning prayer to my daily routine, and I must admit I began to experience a sense of peace and joy. I was totally confident in my decision the Sunday I walked to the altar and accepted Jesus as my Lord and Savior. I felt free and ready for my new life as a Christ-follower. Carlton reached out to me after learning of my conversion from my mother, but I was too busy and I didn't see the need to fit the nerd into my schedule. I read the Bible every day and listened to worship music while studying. I stopped drinking and stopped watching porn. The one thing I didn't do was stop hanging around my old friends who weren't believers. I couldn't give up Randall—he was my brother, father figure and only true friend.

Randall accused me of being a traitor and complained I was allowing a skank to come between blood. He didn't buy into the salvation message, and accused me of only going to church to please Tamara. In hopes of proving him wrong, I introduced him to Tamara. I just knew once Randall met her, he'd see she wasn't a hoochie, but a refined woman with a good heart. My hopes were shattered the second Randall laid eyes on her. After scrutinizing her from head to toe, Randall scowled and walked away. His actions confused Tamara, and I apologized by making up an excuse about him being tired from working. Later, Randall made it clear that I wasn't good enough for Tamara, and one day she'd dump me. I believed him and became a closet Christian—clubbing and freaking on Saturday, and praising the Lord on Sunday.

I wasn't happy with my double life, and at first I tried to resist by setting boundaries. After having dinner with Tamara on Saturdays, I'd follow Randall to the club and foot the bill, but I wouldn't drink, smoke or pick up girls. Randall in turn started sending girls to entice me. When I didn't take the bait, he berated me in front of the ladies and I became known as the "little man who couldn't rise to the occasion" around the club. To cope with the embarrassment and to prove Randall wrong, I started drinking again. Under the influence of alcohol was the only way I could bring myself to screw a strange woman while in a relationship with Tamara. During Sunday service I'd vow never to fornicate again. I prayed Tamara couldn't discern my previous night's activities. I really cared about her and wanted our relationship to grow, but I couldn't handle Randall's mocking. And truth be told, I didn't like disappointing Randall.

Finally, the fall semester of my senior year began and ended my charade. I was so busy with school projects, that I didn't have time for clubbing. Randall said he understood, but still occasionally borrowed money from me for his weekend exploits. Oddly enough, my intense schedule increased my prayer life. My senior year was the most challenging as far as academics went. For the first time ever, I fought hard to maintain a 4.0 GPA. Tamara worked twice as hard, being a double major. We literally only spent time together on Sunday mornings at worship service and Sunday dinner. Of course, I got my daily dose of her on CalTv recorded programing. Occasionally, we'd meet for a study session at Starbucks since Tamara refused to be alone with me in my apartment. We didn't talk much during the sessions, with both of us studying, but just being in one another's presence strengthened our bond.

Tamara was becoming my friend and a person besides my mother I could look to for support and encouragement. It was her confidence in me that persuaded me to attend grad school. "Babe, you have the brains to go all the way and build the foundation for a multi-million dollar company. Why settle for working for someone when you can be your own boss?" she had said in reference to opportunities an advanced degree would afford me during one of our late- night phone sessions. I was so glad she couldn't see my face. I'm sure my flesh blazed red—it does just before tears fall. I coughed to conceal how much her words affected me. No one but my mother had expressed that much confidence in me.

Tamara prayed for me daily during our early-morning brief phone conversations. She shared scriptures with me via text and laughed at my corny jokes. She always greeted me with "Hello, handsome." The woman worked wonders on my ego. When we were together people stopped and stared at us—mainly her. Students I passed on a regular basis without so much as a head nod, would pause momentarily and greet us when Tamara was on my arm. Thanks to frequent appearances on CalTV, Tamara was a "big woman" on campus, and I was just honored to be in her presence.

One Sunday dinner in early November, Tamara dropped a bomb on me. "It's time you meet my parents. How about Thanksgiving dinner?"

I gulped down a forkful of macaroni and cheese without chewing, and nearly choked. *Meet the parents?* Why on earth would she want me to meet her parents? Were we that serious? Actually we were. I had been faithful the whole semester. I would venture to say the infatuation had past and I was falling in love with Tamara, but fear prevented me from telling her. Standing before the judge and biochemist could cause me heartbreak. What if Judge Jackson disapproved of me? What if Mrs. Jackson detected an abnormal gene in my DNA that rendered me unworthy of her daughter's affection?

"Well?" The expression of hope and anticipation on her face made it impossible for me to refuse her. "Are you ready to meet my dad? Don't let the title scare you. He comes off as a tough guy, but he's really a big teddy bear."

Bears kill, ran through my mind.

"And mother's personality is similar to mine. We're both quiet, yet strong-willed and focused. My sisters are more laid back than I am, but very intelligent."

"Sisters," I stuttered. "So the *whole* family will be there?"

"Not the whole family, but my sisters and grandparents and several aunts and cousins. It is Thanksgiving," she added with a smirk.

The sudden queasiness and rise in temperature had nothing to do with food or the weather. Whereas I was fearful of taking our relationship to the next level, Tamara embraced the idea.

Tamara's perfectly manicured hands reached across the table and dabbed my forehead with a napkin. I loved how attentive she was, but the act emphasized my failure to conceal my fear. I would rather have her pretend not to notice me sweating like a pig.

"Maybe you could have dinner with your family, and then stop by for dessert with us," she suggested as a way to calm my anxiety.

I liked that, but pride prevented me from accepting the alternative. "Dinner with the Jacksons is a wonderful idea. Then we'll spend Christmas with my family."

Tamara relaxed against the booth. Sheer joy veiled her ebony face. "I'm looking forward to spending the holidays with you. I know you'll love my family. Just be yourself, and they'll love you too."

Just be yourself. That would be easy if I wasn't in the presence of social royalty. I needed to brush up on my manners, politics, the stock market and sports just so I'd be able have an intelligent conversation with the Jacksons. Even if Tamara and I didn't get the happily ever after, I wanted to make a good impression. I took a gulp of water and mentally viewed the next three weeks. I needed to squeeze some quality time in with my mentor.

CHAPTER 9

Love

THANKSGIVING DAY ARRIVED, and although I'd managed to squeeze in several occasions to hang with Randall, I was still ill-prepared to meet the Jackson family. My time with Randall proved to be a waste of time. Ironically, he wasn't interested in teaching me how to impress the Jacksons, but he thrived on schooling me on how to manipulate the panties off unsuspecting women.

He finally voiced his true opinion after I'd postponed a study session for the third time. "Man, I'm not helping you impress that broad. I'm still not cool with the fact that you let that chick come between us. She's cute and all, but why are you going through all this for a piece of tail? Her stuff can't be that good."

My jaws tightened, but I remained silent. I was used to Randall disrespecting women, but Tamara was different. She deserved better.

"You are hittin' that?" he pressed when I didn't respond. "You better get all you can now, because you know this ain't going nowhere. This is a college fling. Once daddy hooks her up with one of his frat brother's kids she's going to drop your little johnson."

"Tamara's not like that. She's special." I was trying to convince myself. I feared getting too close to Tamara for fear she'd discover I wasn't good enough.

"Ain't no broad that special."

Randall went on a tangent about how trifling women are. I guess he forgot our mother was a woman and worked hard to raise him after his father abused and abandoned them. The fact he neglected his own daughters eluded him. So did his sexual and mental abuse of women.

I left his apartment feeling like a fool and deflated. Why had I bothered to ask Randall about something in which he knew nothing about? And why had his words resurrected insecurities about my sexual ability? I stayed at Mama's house the night before since it was a long holiday weekend, and to get some much-needed validation only a mother could give.

I showered and dressed in the brown single-breasted suit I'd purchased for the occasion for two reasons—Tamara liked me in brown and I wanted to impress Judge Jackson. I even splurged on a new pair of dress shoes and 14-karat gold cufflinks. I'd gotten a haircut the day before and trimmed my mustache. Outwardly, I was prepared for the Jackson clan, but internally, I felt inadequate.

"Come in," I said, assuming the knock on the door was Mama coming to offer me a pep talk.

"Hey, little bro, what's this I hear about you going to meet your girl's family today? Sounds like this is getting serious." To my surprise and disappointment, it was Carlton. I didn't know he'd arrived, and I would have preferred an ego boost from my mother. During my limited conversations with Carlton, he'd been supportive of my budding relationship. He could relate since he was in love, or "sprung" as Randall would say, with his college sweetheart. Love hadn't elevated Carlton's wardrobe. The slacks and bow tie he had on moved him up to captain of the geek squad in my book. The square-rimmed glasses and loafers only made matters worse. He leaned against my dresser with that goofy grin, like he was expecting me to share my business with him. I decided not to disappoint him since it was Thanksgiving—a day for family.

"We're not headed down the aisle, but we're steady." I turned to the mirror and attempted to tie my tie.

"Moms said she's beautiful. A chocolate doll is what she called her."

The smile parted my face before I could put up a macho façade. "She's a dime piece." I undid the knot I'd made in the tie and started over.

"And her dad is a criminal judge?"

I heard Carlton move behind me, but was too focused on making a Windsor Knot to care what he was doing. "Yeah. And her mother is a bio-chemist. She comes from a long line of lawyers and doctors."

Carlton's whistle pierced the air. "And she's saved. Little brother, you hit the jackpot. I can't wait to meet her."

At the moment I wasn't feeling too lucky. I was too nervous to fully appreciate how blessed I was to have Tamara in my life.

"Let me help you with that." Carlton turned me to face him, and proceeded to undo the crooked knot I'd made and replaced it with a perfect Windsor Knot.

Leave it to the geek to get it right the first time, I thought, but voiced, "Thanks, man." I turned back to the mirror and brushed my low-cut hair and attempted to splash on cologne. I missed and anointed Carlton, who was standing behind me, instead.

Back in the old days Carlton would have laughed in my face and belittled me, but not today. He simply patted my shoulder and thanked me for helping him smell good, and we both enjoyed a lighthearted laugh.

"Calm down, man. Just be yourself, and you'll be fine. Tamara wouldn't have invited you if she didn't think you'd fit in. And you definitely wouldn't be meeting the family if she didn't care about you."

The simplicity of his advice was brilliant, but I was too nervous to accept it. Years of being labeled inferior had taken its toll. Besides, what did Carlton know? He'd been dating the same woman, who was just as geeky as he was, for two years.

"Thanks. You're probably right." I didn't desire to bond with Carlton, but since he'd helped me with my tie and seemed genuinely interested in my life, I asked him what was going on in his world.

I'd been so caught up in my own world, I didn't realized Carlton would graduate in a few weeks with his Master's degree. I also didn't realize he was ready to settle down. He'd planned to propose to his college sweetheart for Christmas.

"Congratulations. I'm sure she'll say yes." Now that Tamara was in my life, I could appreciate his happiness. "Did you tell Ma and Randall yet?"

His smile spread, taking the focal point on his face away from his glasses. "Mom is ecstatic, and well, you know Randall. He thought I was crazy and whipped for wanting to commit to one woman. Then when I told him Monica and I hadn't had sex, and wouldn't until marriage, he called me stupid."

"That sounds like Randall," I interjected, although I no longer agreed with Randall's assessment.

"I told him, club-hopping every weekend and throwing money away on strange women for an erection, while neglecting his daughters was stupid. At least I don't have to worry about catching something, and I always have my own money."

Carlton was a geek, yet he had the courage to stand up to Randall. I both admired and despised him for that. "What did he say to that?"

"After he punched me, he asked to *borrow* twenty dollars."

I laughed then, but later on the drive to the Jackson home I pondered the path my idol had chosen and wondered if the situation presented itself would I have the courage to travel my own path without Randall's blessing. I cared deeply for Tamara, but Randall had been with me my whole life. His tutelage molded me into the man I was. I needed him in my life.

I pressed the doorbell on the Jacksons' Blackhawk estate at exactly one o'clock. That left me with only an hour of forced conversations before dinner was scheduled to be served. I'd expected an older woman in a maid's uniform to answer the door. Instead, I was greeted by a vintage version of Tamara. The woman was tall and regal with salted edges along the temples with smooth dark skin that glowed just like Tamara's. Even dressed in black slacks and a sweater with a big gold turkey across the front, I could tell she was physically fit. Although not as appealing to me as Tamara's scent, a soft fragrance permeated from her.

"You must be Alexander. Welcome to our home," she said, while leaning in for a light embrace. "Tamara has told us all about you."

"Thank you. It's my pleasure, Dr. Jackson," I practically stuttered, wondering how she could be so sure of my identity. Did my appearance scream *lower class?*

Her dismissive wave accompanied the same smirk I'd seen on Tamara's face when she was irritated about something. Then her facial muscles relaxed. "At the lab, I'm Dr. Cynthia Jackson. Here, at home, I'm Cindy, Mama, or Honeydew."

"Honeydew?" The first two names I got, but the last one boggled me.

"My husband will have you arrested for calling me that. That's his pet name for me, reserved only for him. Since your mother is alive and well, and might take offense to you addressing a woman you've just met as 'Mama', Cindy will be fine."

Her sincere smile set my anxiety at ease. I decided I liked Mrs. Jackson and let my guard down. "Okay, but I will put a 'Miss' on that. My mother taught me to respect my elders."

She stepped sideways to allow me entrance, but I stood there, awestruck at how down to earth she was.

"Why are you standing outside?" Tamara appeared next to her mother, practically glowing and wearing a sweater similar to her mother's, except Tamara's turkey had lights. "Come on. We won't bite."

"Speak for yourself," a bass tenor voice bellowed from behind the ladies. "I'll attack any stranger, especially one who has my daughter's head in the clouds and my wife smiling."

The ladies laughed and stepped sideways, leaving an unobstructed view of the man of the house.

From the sudden burning in my cheeks, I must have turned two shades of red. I'd assumed Judge Jackson was tall, dark and majestic. By his commanding tone, I expected a stern face with a pointed nose and piercing eyes, a cufflink shirt and tie with pointed shoes. His voice was deceiving. What stood before me was a fair-skinned, dark-wavy-haired, freckled-faced, gold-rimmed-glasses-wearing man, only about an inch taller than myself dressed in black jeans, a black sweater with gold and silver turkeys, and tan loafers. His physical appearance didn't match his tough no-nonsense reputation at all. In that instant, I identified two truths. One, there was validity to the theory that women look for men like their father, and two, the Jackson family had a serious turkey fetish.

I recovered and smiled at the ladies, fully understanding how Mrs. Jackson knew who I was and why Tamara loved my freckles so much, but I didn't linger. With my head held high, I entered the home and walked straight to the man of the house and extended my hand. "Hello, Judge Jackson. I'm Alexander Bennett." I expected the firm grip, but the pulling caught me off guard.

"I know who you are," the judge answered and practically steered me into the foyer and down a hall. "Tammy has been singing your praises more than mine. It's time you and I had a talk."

I followed along, shaking, and not knowing what to expect. I imagined Judge Jackson would interrogate me and then throw me out, and command Tamara never to see me again. With his connections he'd probably had a background check done, and knew my exploits all the way back to kindergarten.

"Daddy, go easy on him." Tamara's plea fell on deaf ears. Her father continued through a maze of turns and down some stairs and didn't stop until he closed the door to his private chamber.

I expected wall-to-wall bookshelves, a huge desk, and a gavel to strike once he passed judgement. Once again I was wrong. Judge Jackson's private chamber was the ultimate man cave. Pool table, mounted flat screens, miniature golf green, mini-refrigerator, wet bar and a massage chair. He even had an old vinyl record player and an extensive record collection. I looked around in awe. I'd never considered a tough criminal judge would have a playroom.

"Wow!"

"Where did you think I was taking you," Judge Jackson asked, "to the basement for an execution?" I started to laugh in kind with him, but that's when I noticed the shotgun mounted on the wall. "Have a seat." He motioned to a bar stool, then opened the refrigerator. "What kind of juice would you like—cranberry, apple, orange or prune?"

If I wasn't afraid of that shotgun, I would have laughed in the man's face. What normal person offers his guests prune juice? Had he mistakenly read my worry for constipation? "Apple juice fine," I answered after mounting the stool.

After setting the round apple-shaped glass in front of me, Judge Jackson joined me at the bar, but he wasn't drinking anything. I'd just broken the seal when the interrogation began. "Talk to me," he ordered, more than asked.

I set the bottle down. "What would you like to know?"

With the same intense piercing stare Tamara had, Judge Jackson laid his cards on the table. "Alexander Bennett, Jr., I want to know all about you. I have a good idea of who you are from my daughter and the background investigation report, but

I want to hear who you are in your own words. I want to hear what your goals are and how you plan to accomplish them. I want to know your likes and hobbies. How solid is your walk with the Lord? And most importantly, what are your intentions toward my daughter?"

I gulped down almost half of the bottle to lubricate my suddenly parched throat. The judge had done a background check. He knew all about me. My responses would be a test of my honesty and character. What were my intentions with Tamara? Even I wasn't sure of that.

I heard Carlton's words, *Just be yourself.* "Well, sir," I started after clearing my throat. "There really isn't much to me. I'm from the Bay Area, reared by my mother and two older siblings. I'm a Finance major, and plan to start graduate school next fall. If things work out, I'm considering starting an investment firm someday."

Judge Jackson remained silent. He was either weighing my words or waiting for more disclosure. His elbows rested on the bar and his fingers formed a teepee. He wanted more.

"My mother believes in God, and took me to church when I was a kid. Since meeting Tamara, I've established a personal relationship with Christ and have surrendered my life to him," I said truthfully. I'd been clean for weeks—no alcohol or strange women.

He nodded for me to continue.

"Your daughter is a wonderful person. She's intelligent, beautiful and has a heart of gold. I care about Tamara deeply and have no intentions of hurting her. I only want what's best for her."

He smiled, as if he liked my answer. "Then that makes two of us." He stood and walked back to the refrigerator for a bottle of juice. Upon his return to the bar stool, the Judge fired direct questions at me. Some questions he asked twice, I believe to see if I'd come up with a different answer. So much for being superficial. When Judge Jackson finished, I felt like I'd been stripped naked.

"Well, Alexander Bennett, Jr., I think you're a good man," he said, patting my shoulder. "If you're half the man your father was, you'll do fine in life."

My head jerked upward.

"That's right. I knew your father. A group of Bay Area lawyers used to meet on Saturday mornings at the golf course—to argue the law more so than to play golf. That was before I took the bench. Some of my best legal sparing matches were against Alex. After you were born, he spent more time bragging about you, more than he did arguing the law. He was a proud father, and would be pleased with who you've become. Saturday mornings were never quite the same after his death."

The judge's voice drifted into silence. I sat there, struggling with my emotions. The thought that Judge Jackson may have known my father had never occurred to me. To be honest, I'd become so detached from my father's memory, I rarely thought of him. Yet, Judge Jackson's words made me proud. They also made me a little angry. Why did I have to experience my father's greatness second-handed? Wasn't there some criminal who could have died in his place?

I swallowed hard. "I had no idea you knew my father."

"I know you come from good genes. You're focused, educated, with a bright future. You don't have a criminal record and you serve God. For those reasons I'm going to give Tammy my blessing to keep dating you. Although I don't think my blessing will make much of a difference. That girl thinks you're the best thing since sliced bread."

"Really?" My attempt to suppress my grin failed.

"Your father wasn't good at naiveté and neither are you."

We laughed, and he shared more memories of my father, then he showed me his record and gun collections. A subliminal message, I suppose. When we finally emerged from the man cave, Tamara's siblings and extended family had arrived—all wearing turkey designs of some sort. Not the thing I would expect from a prestigious family.

Tamara rushed to my side as soon as I stepped into the great room and gripped my arm. "Are you all right? He wasn't too hard on you, was he?"

I wasn't expecting my chest muscles to constrict when I looked at her, but her concern overwhelmed me. Worry had replaced the joy in her eyes. At that moment I came out of denial and accepted the truth—Tamara's feelings for me weren't superficial, but fear kept me from relishing the revelation.

"I didn't beat him up too bad. The bruises will heal in a couple of days." Judge Jackson slapped my back, and I winced like I was in pain.

"Daddy! What did you do?" Tamara's melodious voice dropped at least three octaves. Her arms fell to her side with bawled fists, like she was ready to pounce on her father. Daddy, you—"

Her dad and I, along with everyone else present, laughed in her face, preventing her from finishing the rebuke.

"What's so funny?"

"You are," her mother said, from behind. "Why don't you introduce Alex to everyone? That shouldn't take long since you find a way to mention him in any conversation about any subject. It's like we already know him." The room erupted in laughter again.

"I know that's right," a younger, lighter version of Tamara said. "The other day I asked her to proofread my final paper and instead of reading, all she talked about was Alex's plans for grad school and how hard he studies. After an hour, I gave up and e-mailed the file as is. I might fail because of her obsession with Alex."

For the first time ever, I witnessed eye-rolling from Tamara, and knew the girl had to be her sister. "Next time don't wait until the last minute," Tamara snapped.

I wanted to laugh with everyone else, but couldn't. Tamara's irritation bothered me, especially since I was indirectly the cause of that discomfort. Protectively, I placed my arm around her shoulder. "Sweetheart, relax. It's Thanksgiving."

Tamara's scowl transformed into the smile I loved and my rock-solid abdomen began to quiver. Something I couldn't explain was happening to me, yet I welcomed it.

Throughout the day, Tamara and I endured more jesting about our relationship and our interaction, but she didn't seem to mind as much with me by her side. Her relatives thought we were a cute couple with good chemistry. Before Judge Jackson said grace, her grandmother attacked by asking me where my turkey was after staring me up and down. "We get into the holiday spirit around here. If you're going to be part of this family, you'd better learn to assimilate," she said, without smiling.

I stuttered, while trying to digest that she'd accepted me beyond being Tamara's boyfriend. "I apologize. I didn't know."

"I'll excuse you this time," she said, before Tamara could come to my defense. "But come Christmas, I'd better see an ornament, a tree, or snowflake of some kind on your body. You can spray paint the nativity scene across your forehead, doesn't matter as long as you participate in the tradition."

Tamara squeezed my hand and whispered, "I'll explain it to you later."

After an extensive prayer and everyone giving words of thanks, we feasted on a traditional meal much to my dismay. Television portrayed wealthy African-American families as bourgeoisie and out of touch with the average African-American family. I was expecting roasted duck and caviar. I admit the cornbread dressing and yams were some of the best I'd ever tasted.

I sat around the fireplace with the Jacksons and listened to Tamara's grandparents share stories of growing up in the south and watched videos of holidays past. I learned the Jacksons came from meager beginnings. Tamara's great-grandparents were working poor sharecroppers living in a three-room house, yet they managed to send all four of their children away to college. Without the resources to buy gifts, the Jacksons celebrated the holidays by making costumes from old clothing and gunny sacks. Instead of opening presents, the Jacksons spent the day eating and playing games dressed in holiday attire. Although money was no longer an issue, the Jacksons continued the tradition to the third generation. Which explained why Tamara's aunts' heads were covered in feathers.

I got a glimpse of Tamara's competitive side in a game of dominoes with her sisters and cousins. Most importantly, I witnessed normal male and female interaction. Tamara's parents, along with her uncles and aunts, addressed one another by endearing terms and affectionately touched each other. The men pulled out chairs and helped feed the children. It was a partnership of mutual respect. I liked the Jacksons' portrayal over Randall's sexist ideology, and allowed my mind to fantasize about sharing genuine affection with Tamara and raising a family together. We would equally share in the rearing of our brown babies—a boy and a girl. I'd read them stories and tuck them in at night. If I arrived home first, I'd start dinner and we'd do the dishes together.

Tamara tugged me to follow her, but I couldn't move. The profundity of my thoughts paralyzed me. I wanted to build a life and make babies with Tamara! It was one of those exceedingly and above all I could ask or think kind of blessings the pastor preached about.

She nudged me again. "Come on, let's sit outside for a while. There's something I want to tell you."

I followed her lead to a backyard gazebo, and immediately anxiety took over. What was she going to tell me? I'd been on my best behavior all day. She couldn't break up with me less than five minutes after I'd accepted my true feelings for her. I sat down, leaving room between us. I didn't want her to hear the pounding in my chest.

"Get over here, Mr. Bennett." The order was accompanied by a gentle pull on my arm. "And stop shaking. I haven't bitten anyone in two days."

When had her smile become the antidote for whatever ails me? I inched over, only slightly sure I wasn't about to get served the benediction.

"This has been the best holiday ever," she stated, while inter-locking her arm with mine. "I'll never forget this Thanksgiving. Thank you for sharing the day with me and my family." Her eyes lowered, and an uncharacteristic shyness emerged. There was more, but she was going to take her time.

"You're welcome. You know I'd do anything for you. I would have had Mama sew some feathers on my shirt had I known about the tradition."

A nervous giggle escaped. "Feathers and lights would go good with those freckles. There's always next year, but I can't imagine next year being better than this one." Her head rested on my shoulder, but I knew there was more, so I waited, basking in her scent and warmth. The woman always smelled good. I didn't have to wait long.

She raised her head, leaving a sudden coldness where her head had been. "Today is the best holiday ever, because this is the first holiday I've been in love and spent the day with that person. My family likes you, and I know once they get to know you, they'll love you as much as I do."

"You have a wonderful family. They're funny too." *What did she just say?* I considered myself a good listener, especially when it came to Tamara, but she couldn't have said what I thought she said. "What did you say?"

With eyes locked on mine, she repeated the words I'd heard countless times in my dreams. "I love you."

"What does that mean? You love me with the love of the Lord? Like a big brother?"

"I'm in love with you Alexander Bennett, Jr., freckles and all. The love I have for you is from the Lord, but there's nothing brotherly about it." She looked perplexed. "You can't tell from my actions? You don't think I'd bring just anyone home to meet the folks, do you?"

"I believe you care about me, and we've grown closer, but love? Do you really think you love me? Don't say that if you don't mean it. I'll understand if you just want to be friends—"

"Alexander Bennett, Jr., sit down and be quiet!"

Tamara's uncharacteristic yell zapped me from my rant. I didn't realize I was pacing up and down the gazebo steps. I stopped dead in my tracks, but didn't face Tamara. I was too embarrassed and didn't know what to do. My fantasies always ended once she said the words without any response or action on my part. This scene wasn't in *Randall's Relationship Rules*. I'm sure I turned beet-red, trying to chart my next move.

When I didn't move, Tamara stepped in front of me. "I'm sorry. I didn't mean to scare you. I thought you felt the same, but it won't kill me if you don't."

Tamara's glossy eyes and hollow voice tumbled my wall of self-preservation. She loved me, and I'd hurt her. My actions implied I didn't feel the same.

"Of course, I love you. I think I started falling for you the first time I laid eyes on you," I admitted. "I just can't believe you love me. The idea that you love me is overwhelming," I stuttered and started pacing again. "I don't know what to do. I'm so happy."

She grabbed my forearms, forcing me to stop and face her. Her eyes were still glossy, but she was smiling again.

"I don't have experience in this area, but I believe the occasion calls for a kiss. At least that's how I imagined I'd seal the moment I expressed my love for the first time."

I inched closer to her with the goofy grin my brothers used to make fun of, but I couldn't help it. From the moment I first saw her I've wanted to kiss her. "I agree." My arms went around her waist, and her fingers interlocked at the base of by neck, filling me with so much of her scent and warmth, I thought I'd pass out. It was too surreal. If I was fantasizing again I wasn't going to face reality until after the kiss. I felt my head inching toward hers and prayed my breath didn't stink.

The moment of impact sent me spiraling into a sea of euphoria. Her lips were softer than I'd imagined, and her arms cradled me like precious cargo. We massaged each other in perfect sync, as if our lips had choreographed the event, and we were just puppets on a string at their mercy.

Tamara blushed once the adventure ended. "I'm new at this, but I think that was pretty good."

Looking down into her angelic face, I couldn't tell her I was a novice at kissing as well. Screwing strange women didn't include kissing. I didn't think it sanitary, considering where those women readily put their mouths. At age twenty-two, I'd finally experienced my first meaningful kiss.

"That was better than good. So does this mean I can kiss you regularly now?" Randall would berate me for asking a woman for affection, but I didn't care. I was in love with a woman who loved me.

Her answer was to cup my face and kiss me again. "I'd like that. But nothing too heavy," she added after a pause, "I don't want to lead us into temptation."

"I promise not to cross any boundaries, if you promise to confess your undying love and devotion every day." I added my own spin to the declaration, believing love equaled devotion.

"You have a gorgeous smile when you're not stressed. You should try relaxing and being happy more often."

"I am happy now that I know you feel the same about me as I do about you. I can relax now, since I know you don't want me for my freckles alone."

I imagine we resembled love-struck adolescents, holding each other, grinning and giggling for no visible reason.

Judge Jackson's baritone voice boomed through the yard, confirming our child-like behavior. "Alright kids, that's enough cup-caking for one day. Come on back inside. It's time to dance."

"Yes, sir."

"Coming, Daddy."

We answered, but didn't move before expressing the sentiment again and enjoying one more kiss. We walked back to the house holding hands and still giggling.

While taking those steps for the first time in my life I experienced real happiness. I was in love with a woman who loved me for me. Tamara was committed to me, and I was the only person she'd completely opened her heart to.

My phone vibrated again. I didn't answer it, knowing the text was from Randall. He'd texted earlier and offered me the opportunity to finance the evening at an exclusive swingers' club. I wasn't going. God had overlooked my imperfections and blessed me with my heart's desire. I was not going to trade in Tamara's love for meaningless sex. I turned the phone off and spent the remainder of the evening dancing and sneaking pecks from my girlfriend.

CHAPTER 10

The Investment

"YOU'VE GOT TO be the dumbest fool in the world!" Randall may have been laughing, but he meant those words when he declined to be my best man. From the moment I expressed my intention of marrying Tamara over a year ago, until now—the day before the wedding, Randall had been rebuking me for allowing a woman to control me. If he'd taken the time to get to know Tamara, he would have known control had nothing to do with it. Tamara was simply love personified, but Randall didn't know anything about love. Whenever Tamara joined my family for Sunday dinner, Randall didn't have more than two words for her. He did, however, make a point of staring her up and down, with his eyes lingering longer than necessary on her breasts. Once I walked into the kitchen and found him staring at her rear end as she helped Mama prepare dinner. Instead of being angry with Randall for lusting after my fiancée, pride filled me because I finally had something Randall wanted other than money.

Randall had matured over the past year—at least where reckless spending was concerned. He still didn't spend time with his daughters, but he managed his money better and had bought a house. The swingers' club had become his preferred hangout over the strip club, but he'd stopped asking me to finance his escapades. He'd also graduated to a new stimulant—cocaine. He'd been promoted to senior accountant so I didn't think his occasional ride on the white horse—as he called it—was a problem.

I'd completely stopped going out with Randall right after Tamara and I became engaged. Sad to say, our Thanksgiving love confessions weren't enough motivation for me to give up the social scene altogether. During the first year of our committed relationship, I yielded to pressure from Randall and participated in random sex fests at the swingers' club. I did drink to help take the edge off cheating on Tamara, but never touched cocaine, and I always repented.

Ironically, the face I remember most from the swinging scene was not some voluptuous female's. It was Randall's. Hanging in the balance between reality and an alcohol-induced fantasy, I clearly recall the night I opened my eyes and found Randall staring at me—almost in a trance—as I received a blow job. I don't remember if the stranger did a good job or not. What I do remember is my brother so engrossed in my activity that he stood there openly pleasuring himself. After a while, he turned and disappeared into the red-lighted room. I thought Randall's behavior was odd, but never addressed it. The tables had finally been turned from the day he caught me watching him and

Carlton get served by the girl with the long braids. In a strange way I felt vindicated and proud.

He continued our one-sided phone conversation. "I don't know where I went wrong with you and Carlton. How many times do I have to say it? Ain't no broad's stuff worth no putting a ring on it. Although, for a piece of Miss Jackson, I might walk by the jewelry store. And I wouldn't have spent all that money from our trust fund on a ring, like you did. I wouldn't walk by the pound for Carlton's broad."

Randall laughed at his assessment of our sister-in-law, but I didn't. Monica may not have been a beauty queen, but she had a sweet and caring personality and held the utmost respect for Carlton. *Did he say 'our trust fund'?* Mama adored Monica, and Carlton worshipped the ground Monica walked on. The two geeks were perfect for each other. They'd been married for a year and both had landed dream jobs and were expecting their first child.

Honestly, I admired Carlton and Monica's relationship and secretly prayed Tamara and I would enjoy the same. I'd watch and listen to Carlton interact with Monica and then imitate the same with Tamara. Of course, I could never tell Carlton that. I didn't buy Randall's theory that love was for wimps. I was in love, although I didn't fully comprehend what it meant to love someone. From Tamara, I received unconditional love and acceptance, but I didn't have a clue how to love her in return. I wanted the love story I'd heard so much about from my mother. I was smart enough to know that Tamara was my soul mate and chances of me doing better than her were slim and none.

She'd supported me emotionally with a listening ear and encouraged me through my Master's, which proved more challenging than I'd thought. Tamara knew how to calm my anxieties and build my confidence just by being there, or with a gentle touch. Tamara was a good kisser and loved showing affection. On a few occasions we came close to breaking our purity vows. Surprisingly, it was me who cooled things off. I loved Tamara and didn't want lust to be the foundation of our sex life. She appreciated my commitment to her and to God, especially since I'd been sexually active a few times during my freshman year—that's the sanitized story I told her.

Now, the night before the wedding Randall wanted to treat me to a bachelor "party" at the swingers' club. One final rump before lockdown was what he called it. I tried to convince him I didn't want or need a bachelor party, at least not the kind Randall had in mind, but he wouldn't listen. He hadn't bothered coming to the gathering Carlton organized with the fellas from church the week before, saying he didn't want to be in the company of God and geeks. I enjoyed the wholesome fellowship and saw a cool side of Carlton I didn't know existed.

Randall was relentless in his quest to open my eyes to the limitations I was placing on myself by getting married. After a week of mocking, pestering and guilt trips—Randall still accused me of placing Tamara before him—I gave in, figuring I'd hang out long enough to satisfy Randall, then tip out when he disappeared into one of the back rooms. With my plan formulated, I disconnected the call while Randall was still ranting and got dressed.

I'd planned to drive, but Randall arrived in a chauffeured limo. Inside were three female faces I'd never seen before attached to scantily clad bodies. By the giggles and glossy eyes, I detected Randall and his posse were already under the influence of some substance. I said a quick prayer for strength to resist temptation and climbed into the vehicle. The second I sat down corks popped and so did two of the girls onto my lap. I knew I was in trouble then. Randall handed me a glass of champagne. I accepted the drink for show; I didn't have any intention of indulging in the warm liquid or the women. In sixteen hours, I would marry the woman I loved and respected. The only woman good enough to be the mother of my future children.

I leaned forward and around the chick perched on my right leg at Randall, "What's all this, man? You didn't have to get a limo, I could have driven my car." I'd recently traded in my used car for a new Audi. I used achieving my Master's as the excuse to splurge, but I really wanted a new car for Tamara to drive after we were married. Surprisingly, Mama agreed and pulled the funds from my trust fund without hesitation—until my twenty-fifth birthday next month, she was still the executor. Mama also withdrew enough money to lease a townhouse in an upscale neighborhood.

"Only the best for you, little brother," he answered, after taking a sip from the glass of the chick on his lap. "You've always had the best of everything. Why change now?"

I moved the hand of the girl on the left away from my inner thigh and back onto her lap. "You didn't have to put yourself out for me." I was hoping to distract his semi-high mind from jumping on his soapbox about my father's provisions.

He smirked. "Trust me, I didn't put myself out. If I couldn't handle it, I wouldn't be here. I'm making an investment in our future."

"What?" I started to ask for clarification, but Randall kept talking.

"I think you're stupid for getting married and planning to hit the same piece for the rest of your life." He snickered. "You always were a little slow. You have book smarts and money, but you must have been studying for a test the day common sense was handed out. I'm not going to mention your faulty equipment. Tamara is going to be very disappointed."

His roaring laughter and the girls' giggles chilled me, and before I realized what I was doing, I'd gulped down half of the champagne, barely tasting it.

"You can't really help your little deficiency or those spots breaking through your skin. It's your blackness trying to come out. Blame them on your rich white daddy. It's a good thing he left you all that money, or you'd be totally jacked up and worthless to me."

I refused to accept the drug-induced words as a reflection of what was in Randall's heart.

He was my brother and idol. Surely, he loved me. He was just saying those things to loosen the girls up. Nevertheless, his words hurt and embarrassed me.

Randall kept talking and the ladies kept giggling and rubbing. Randall kept refilling my glass and I kept drinking. An unfamiliar wooziness invaded my body. I felt my body slipping to the floor, but was defenseless to stop the downward spiral.

To this day, I don't have any recollection of what happened that night after I passed out. My next conscious thought was a loud pounding noise against the window of the limo. I reached up to where I thought the door should've been and got air. I rolled over on what should have been a leather seat and feather-like particles tickled my nose. The pounding against the window intensified in conjunction with the pounding in my head. I rolled until my body pressed against a big object and could go no further. Then I heard my name. I forced my eyes opened and lurched upward. The pounding invaded my head causing my eyes to slam shut, but not before I noticed something familiar. The object I was pressed against was my couch. I was on my living room floor. What happened to Randall and the limo? I wondered. I didn't have time to come up with an answer; the pounding continued.

"Alex, are you in there?"

It was Carlton. Even in my groggy state I recognized the worry in his voice. I tried to answer back. My mouth moved, but no sound came out. With my eyes shut, I crawled toward the banging and used the doorknob to pull myself in the upright position. I had to grab Carlton's fist before the noise drove me insane. It had better be an emergency that had the geek yelling and banging so early in the morning. He'd only been elevated to Best Man because of Randall's refusal.

"Alex!"

I swung the door open ready to put my brother in check when he gasped and his glasses fell from his face.

Carlton stepped back and scrutinized me. "Man, what happened to you?" He replaced his glasses and scoped me from head to toe. "Alex, what's going on? What have you done?"

"I haven't done—" I started to lie, but stopped because I couldn't remember what I thought was the past eight hours.

"Man, look at you! You're supposed to be at the church in an hour. You're a mess and you smell like the back room of a ho house!"

Carlton's look of disgust and disappointment bothered me, but I couldn't deal with that at the moment. His words were more important. "I have to be at the church in an hour? What time is it?" I slumbered toward the kitchen to view the wall clock. On the way I caught a glimpse of my image in the wall mirror above the couch. I swear I shrieked like a girl. Except for my socks and underwear, which were on inside out with a used condom hanging out, I was naked. I had dried lipstick all over my face and torso and a few hickeys. My hair I could fix with the fresh haircut I was planning to get that morning, but there was no way I could meet Tamara at the altar with fresh hickeys. I couldn't remember what happened so I wasn't sure if I'd even used the condom properly. Even if I could hide the blemishes, I couldn't take the chance of giving Tamara a sexually transmitted disease. What had I done, and why had Randall allowed it to happen knowing I was getting married in a few hours?

"What happened?" Carlton repeated the question, but with less anger, when I slumped over the couch. I knew the attempt I made to hide my tears failed when I felt his hand on my shoulder. My brothers, or at least Randall, had always considered me a wimp. I didn't want to solidify the label, but at that moment I didn't care. My whole world had fallen apart. I had to call off the wedding and break Tamara's heart by admitting I'd been unfaithful. The love she had for me would evaporate into hate, all because I listened to Randall. Why had I listened to him? I shouldn't have gotten into the limo. I should have kept my freckled-face behind at home.

"Randall," I moaned, because the ache in my chest nearly suffocated me.

"Randall! You went out with Randall last night!"

"He wanted to hang out with me. He felt neglected." No sooner had I got the words out Carlton pulled me upward and spun me around to face him.

"Why the…would you do something like that? Neglected my…He wanted to make you look like a fool as always. He doesn't care nothing about you getting married or being saved. Our brother is all about himself. Always have and always will be. After all this time and money you've blown on him, I don't know why you can't see that."

Carlton's words may have held some truth, but I was too stuck on the fact that he'd used profanity to care. I hadn't heard those words come from his mouth since his rebirth. I must have really let Carlton down, but his feelings didn't mean anything to me.

"Tamara's going to kill me," I whimpered. "I really screwed up this time. I don't even remember what happened last night."

"What do you mean, you don't remember? Were you smoking, drinking, snorting or all three?"

I took it as a rhetorical question until Carlton started shaking my shoulders, demanding an answer.

"All I remember is drinking champagne and feeling woozy."

"Let me guess, Randall offered the drink. Did you watch him pour it?"

I knew where Carlton was going with this. I hadn't seen Randall pour the drink, but then I had no reason to watch my brother. Sure, I'd seen him slip goodies into the drinks of unsuspecting females, but Randall wouldn't do that to me. He had nothing to gain. "No," I finally answered. "Randall wouldn't do that to me."

"You can't be that naïve." My head dropped, indicating my answer.

Carlton's hand touched my shoulder, but not forcefully. "Look, Alex, I accepted a long time ago that Randall is your favorite. Randall is your idol. I'm the nerdy brother you tolerate. I don't need my degrees to know I wasn't your first choice as Best Man. I only got the privilege because Randall declined. It's fine if you love Randall more than me, but make no mistake about it, Randall doesn't love anyone but himself. Trying to please him will always leave you holding the short end of the stick. This is not all Randall's fault." He pointed at my chest. "You have to care enough about yourself to stop allowing our brother to make a fool out of you. If Randall cared about you, you wouldn't be standing here with your drawers inside out." He looked around. "And where are the rest of your clothes?"

Carlton's words cut like a freshly sharpened blade slicing the fantasy world I'd created to pieces, but I wasn't ready to accept the truth. Randall's assumed betrayal would have to wait. I was about to lose the one person besides my mother who loved me unconditionally, who saw the good in me and brought out the best in me. Tamara was my sunshine, and yet for most of our relationship I'd deceived her. I'd also been unfaithful to God, but grace and mercy would take care of that. I doubted Tamara would be as forgiving for the public humiliation of being left at the altar would cause. And her family? I'd become so attached to them, her father called me the son he never had. Her mother cooked me special desserts and she and Mama had become friends. Mama. Would Mama lose respect for me? The weight of my decision to please Randall knocked me to my knees, sobbing.

"Man, get up and stop crying." With more strength than I thought my geeky brother had, Carlton pulled me to my feet. His voice was firm, but not angry. "We don't have much time. Jump in the shower while I make some phone calls."

In a daze, I staggered to my room where the garment bag containing my tuxedo hung on the closet door. I spotted my clothes from last night in a pile on the bed. My wallet lay on top. All the cash was gone, but at least Randall didn't take my bank card. My bags were already packed for our two-week honeymoon in Paris—a gift from Tamara's grandparents. I imagined Tamara would go to Paris without me and return with a new love. I didn't care what Carlton said or thought about me, I wailed like a colicky baby. The steaming hot pellets may have washed away the stench, but the water didn't touch my shame.

When I stepped back into my bedroom from the shower my wedding garments were laying on the bed, and Carlton stood leaning against the dresser with a thermos of steaming liquid.

"Sip this while you get dressed. You can finish it in the car. And hurry up, we have to be at Renell's in twenty minutes. Bring the shirt and jacket with you. You can finish getting dressed after Renell works her magic."

"What magic? Who's Renell?" I asked defensively, but accepted the drink. I'd had enough tricks and strange women to last me a lifetime. "I'm through with all that."

Carlton stood upright and stared me down. "Do you want to get married today, or not?"

"Of course," I heaved out. The muddy-like substance nearly made me gag. "Are you trying to kill me?"

Without blinking, Carlton said words so powerful, it would take me years to fully grasp their meaning, "I'm trying to be your brother, best man and friend by making sure you get to the altar. You may be a few minutes late, but if it's the last thing I do, I'm going to make sure you move forward with your life and become your own man."

I took another sip, then obeyed. I really didn't have a choice. Carlton wasn't going to leave without me. And honestly, I didn't want him to. I needed my big brother to fix my mess. I didn't see how he could do it. Maybe the scientist had a time machine that could give me a do- over for the past twenty-four hours. Carlton loaded my suitcases and garment bag into his car while I dressed, but I couldn't stop crying. I'm sure I looked ridiculous being led by the hand to the car with my head down with the thermos pressed against my chest, wearing tuxedo pants, dress shoes and a T-shirt, and crying. I expected Carlton to make fun of my emotional state like Randall would have, but he never said a word, at least not aloud. His mouth moved the entire drive. I hoped he was praying for me, because at that moment I couldn't pray for myself.

Renell turned out to be a college friend of Carlton who owned an upscale spa and beauty salon complete with an adjourning barbershop. No sooner had I stepped inside the establishment, Renell hugged Carlton and then ordered me to take a seat in her chair. My butt barely touched the chair before I was draped and surrounded by more unfamiliar faces. I sat at their mercy, while they filed, scrubbed and rubbed various areas of my face, hands and neck. In less than an hour, I had a total makeover, complete with a manicure and haircut. I don't how she did it, but Renell created a concoction and rubbed it into my skin. The cream smelled like mint, but it evened out the hickeys on my face and neck. It even worked on my chest. I looked like I'd been airbrushed for a photo shoot. Renell's staff assisted me in getting dressed so I wouldn't ruin their work. When I looked at the completed product in the full-length mirror, I thanked God for covering my sins. All evidence of whatever happened the previous night was totally gone.

"Renell, you're a miracle worker," Carlton exclaimed, while Renell sprayed cologne on me.

"Thank you. Really, thank you. How much do I owe you?" The words fumbled out as I dug for my wallet.

Carlton started for the door. "That's already been taken care of. Let's get out of here. You're already late."

This time my brother didn't have to hold my hand. I followed with my head held high. I had hope again, and for the first time *I* saw myself as handsome. Inside the car, Carlton handed me a bottle of water and small bottle of pills.

"Take two of these now, just in case, you caught something," he ordered. "Take two more tonight, and then two a day for the next five days."

I read the bottle, then readily took the antibiotics without hesitation then tucked the bottle in my travel bag. A simple "thanks" seemed inadequate for what I owed Carlton, but we didn't have a bond beyond that. So, I mumbled, "Thanks," and directed my attention to the song playing on the radio.

On the ride to the church I had Carlton stop at the bank; I needed to replenish the cash Randall took and to make sure no non-authorized transactions had occurred on my account. Once Randall had "borrowed" my VISA debit card from my wallet and made an on-line purchase without telling me. I didn't find out until I received an e-mail from the bank stating I was overdrawn. I couldn't let something like that happen on my honeymoon. With my chaotic morning, I still made it to the church just a minutes before the limo carrying Tamara arrived.

Our wedding was so beautiful, I still tear up at the remembrance of it. I can't recall the exact layout of the decorations and flowers, or every face of the two-hundred-plus guests. What

I'll never forget is Tamara, my angel dressed in white, making deliberate steps toward me on the arm of her father. Her flawless ebony skin glowed with a brilliance that nearly blinded me. Her smile was sure and the love and admiration shining in her eyes, humbling. As she recited her vows with surety, tears flowed down my cheeks. Not from joy, but from shame. The force of how much Tamara loved and respected me felt like a hammer pounding my chest. She loved me fully, the way her faith commanded. Her love was pure. My love was tainted and full of lies. I didn't deserve her. I wanted to drop to my knees and beg her forgiveness, but I couldn't without embarrassing her. So between choking back tears, I vowed to love, honor and cherish her from that day forward. I vowed to forsake all others for her. Inwardly, that included Randall and his playmates. When the reverend pronounced us man and wife, I thanked God for rescuing me again and vowed to live the rest of my life serving Him. Then I gathered my angel in my arms and kissed my wife.

I remember my wedding reception for two reasons. The first being that was the first time I felt confident and secure enough to dance in public. Offbeat as I may have been, I couldn't stop dancing. I was happy. When Tamara grew tired, I danced with my mother, mother-in-law, and new sister-in-laws. The second reason I will never forget my wedding reception is Randall.

I hadn't seen him at the church, so I thought he would boycott the celebration altogether. I was in the middle of enjoying a slow dance with Tamara when Randall's voice boomed from behind me. I turned around with excitement that my brother had shown up to share the most important day of my life with me. Then my heart nearly stopped. With her arm interlocked with Randall's was one of the girls glued to my lap less than twenty-four hours ago. Randall hadn't bothered to dress for the occasion, opting to wear jeans and a football jersey. At least the woman revealed less skin than the last time I saw her, which wasn't saying much. They both bore sheepish grins, as if they knew something I didn't, and reeked of alcohol. I could tell from the gloss in Randall's eyes, he'd also been snorting lines. I couldn't think fast enough to pray before Randall opened his mouth.

"Hey, little man. I guess congratulations are in order," he said slapping me on the shoulder. He looked Tamara up and down. "Welcome to the family. Can't say I'll treat you like a sister. I mean, what are the chances of this arrangement lasting? No sense in getting close."

The woman whose name I still didn't know, giggled.

I couldn't breathe.

"Excuse me," Tamara asked.

"I read somewhere that fifty percent of marriages end in divorce within seven years," Randall clarified, then added while staring me dead in the eyes, "usually for infidelity or money. I wonder how your story will end."

Beads of sweat saturated my forehead and my cheeks burned. I knew my brother was selfish, but to bring this woman to my wedding and threaten me was beyond comprehensible. What did he want? I looked around for my mother, anybody to put an end to this nightmare.

"Our story will end only in death," Tamara answered with assurance. I wanted to agree with her, but neither she nor I knew what happened last night.

"Oh, really?" Randall smirked and stepped into my personal space. I nearly gagged.

A snorting sound now accompanied the woman's giggling.

"Hey, Randall. What's up, brother?" Carlton stepped between us just as Randall opened his mouth to say what I knew would end my brief marriage. "Are you okay?" Carlton asked, forcing me backward, away from Tamara and Randall.

"That's the girl from last night," I managed to mumble before bending over. Randall's appearance and disposition had already embarrassed me. Now I was about to embarrass myself by barfing in the middle of the dance floor.

"I got this. Pull yourself together," Carlton ordered, forcing me upright and stuffing his handkerchief in my hand.

I heard Tamara request a glass of water, but I was too busy dredging sweat from my face and praying for divine intervention to notice my mother and Tamara's parents had joined us.

"Randall Williams!" my mother started in. "Have you lost what little sense you had? How dare you show up here high and embarrass your brother, not to mention me. You have the nerve to drag this half-dressed airhead on your arm, and you haven't spoken one word to your daughters sitting over there. You are worse than your trifling daddy." She pointed at Miss Giggles. "Take this trash and get out." Although my mother's voice remained low, I'd never heard such anger and disgust coming from my mother. How would she sound once Randall ratted me out?

"Mama, you always take up for your golden child!" Randall brushed against Mama, but didn't get another word out.

"Not here and not now," Carlton said, after grabbing Randall's arm. "If you say another word, I promise you'll come off this high a lot sooner than you'd like to. You and your guest are leaving. Now." Randall's mouth moved to speak, and Carlton's open palm went up. "I mean it. Shut your mouth and leave."

Finally, the woman stopped giggling.

To my surprise and relief, Randall complied without further resistance. To my knowledge, Randall always dominated Carlton in authority and strength, but today the younger ruled the elder. As I watched Randall's retreating back, with Carlton following close behind, I knew God had dispatched an angel that day to save me from Randall's drug-induced sabotage. Throughout the confrontation neither Tamara, nor her parents said a word.

Carlton never shared the details of what happened once he and Randall reached the parking lot. I did notice Carlton icing his fist once he returned inside the reception hall. That day I saw my brother in a different light. He may have been a geek, but he was also the perfect best man for me.

CHAPTER 11

Love and More Deception

I USED RANDALL'S SLIP of judgment to build the platform for my excuse for not having sex with my wife on our wedding night. After Randall left the reception, I began complaining of nausea and light-headedness from the alcohol stench that lingered. I didn't dance anymore and sat with my head in my lap. I added gagging and several trips to the bathroom to the act. I alternated the dramatics, with profusely apologizing to Tamara and her family for my brother's behavior. Once inside the hotel room, I continued the shenanigans by forcing myself to purge and then crawling to the bed. I'd changed into my pajamas while in the bathroom, just in case the hickeys reappeared. I'd also taken the second dose of antibiotics.

Tamara was the perfect caregiver, helping me sip on ginger ale she'd ordered from room service. Then without a word of complaint she climbed in bed beside me, cradling me in her arms, and prayed for me. Tears filled my eyes as guilt ate at me for depriving my wife of the loving she deserved and had waited for, but I couldn't take the chance of infecting her with a sexually transmitted disease. She'd started taking birth control pills a month before the wedding, so I couldn't use the risk of pregnancy to justify wearing a condom. I had to allow the antibiotics time to circulate through my system for at least two days.

"I'm sorry, sweetheart," I whispered, honestly.

"Don't worry, babe. We have the rest of our lives to express our love."

I rested my head against her bosom, repenting, until I feel asleep.

From the time, we boarded the plane at 6:00 a.m. the next morning, and all during the eleven-hour flight from San Francisco to Charles de Gaulle airport in Paris, I held my wife close to me. I kissed her, rubbed her arm, held her hand, anything to communicate how much she meant to me. I didn't want her to think I didn't desire her, or that she'd made a mistake. Although Tamara was sympathetic to my supposed illness, I saw disappointment on her face every time I looked at her. I didn't have to pretend during our first night in Paris. We were both dead tired by the time we settled into the hotel, and climbed under the covers fully dressed.

On our third day of marriage, I awakened Tamara with soft music and warm kisses. She received my affections until I went for her lips. She jumped off the bed, grabbed her travel bag and sprinted to the bathroom. "You can't kiss me until I brush my teeth," she called over her shoulder. Tamara always presented me with her best. I loved that about her.

I followed her into the bathroom and started the shower.

"Okay, you can kiss me now," she announced, but when she turned around she didn't move. I guess my appearance startled her. I'd undressed while she brushed her teeth. "Oh," she whispered then nervously wrung her hands, like she didn't know what to do next.

I'd never seen my angel unsure of herself, but I loved her this way. With all of my imperfections, my refined wife needed me. I was the only person on earth she trusted with her most precious gift. I prayed I would meet her expectations, and then held her in my arms and finally got my kiss. Tamara didn't offer any resistance as I undressed her and carried her inside the shower, but she did insist on wearing a shower cap to keep her hair dry. Time passed in slow motion as we cleaned each other's bodies with the aid of jasmine-scented suds and hot water pellets. The sensual experience shook me, almost scared me, when I realized this was the first time I experienced foreplay. My previous experiences—the ones I remember—were of the "hit it and quit it" nature.

I turned off the water and rested my chin against my wife's head. I didn't want her to see me cry, not yet anyway. My bravado deserted me as I dried her with a towel. Tamara's body was too beautiful to be real. She helped me turn the covers back, and then laid on the bed and with the sweetness of honeycomb, beckoned me to join her.

The consummation of my marriage destroyed every myth I had about making love. In that Paris hotel, I learned not only had I never made love, but I didn't know anything about physically expressing love. What I'd been vicariously doing was substituting selfish physical activity for satisfaction. With Tamara it was different. My wife unselfishly gave me all of her without reservation. She was a virgin, but not once did she complain, nor did she attempt to shield her desire and pleasure. She totally surrendered to my administrations and let herself completely go. Her love shattered every wall of my self-preservation, and for the first time the idea of love moved beyond the physical for me. When we reached the pinnacle of euphoria, I didn't know who I was anymore outside of her. I'm sure my face burned crimson as tears flowed down and lapped beneath my chin, but shame and embarrassment weren't present. My angel kissed every inch of my freckled face, mixing our tears. I nestled my head in her bosom and for the first time truly thanked God for blessing me with such a wonderful gift. From the depths of my soul, I vowed to cherish her forever.

Paris was beautiful, at least what we saw of it. We enjoyed strolls down Avenue des Champs-Elysees—window-shopping. On Bastille Day, we watched Europe's largest military parade cuddled in each other's arms from our second-story hotel balcony. We savored great food and music and kissed in front of the Eiffel Tower. The museums were magnificent and rich in culture, yet what I enjoyed most were the lazy days in bed.

Even now, I count my first two weeks of marriage as the happiest days of my life. I was freely able to be me without pretense or reservation and Tamara embraced all of me. She'd always been affectionate with me, but now that we were married, her expressions escalated. It was as if she couldn't get enough of me. She wasn't ashamed to kiss me in public and let everyone know I belonged to her. Not once did she complain about my pale body or look away when I undressed. We made love with the lights on, and she loved kissing my freckles. She seemed to crave me, and I took pleasure in satisfying her. I also prayed that once we returned to the states she wouldn't change. As happy as I was, I still wondered if I had what it took to keep her happy over time. She was my wife, my angel, but was I a novelty to her?

The first Sunday dinner at Mama's house after we returned from our honeymoon and settled in, my mother presented me with information that changed my life for the better and for the worse. I'd already started looking for work. With a Master's degree in Finance and work experience from two internships, I expected offers to start pouring in at any moment. I'd already started the process for the CFA credential—I'd decided to build a career as a Financial Analyst. My wife wasn't materialistic, but I wanted to provide Tamara with the life she'd been accustomed to. I didn't want to deny her anything and I didn't want her running to her father to meet her needs. I respected Judge Jackson, but Tamara was now my responsibility. With planning and budgeting, I would be able to keep my angel looking good and happy until I built tenure with a prestigious firm. Mama's announcement changed all that.

Carlton and Monica were out of town and according to Mama, Randall hadn't bothered to say if he was coming or not. I hadn't heard from or seen Randall since he almost ruined my wedding day six weeks ago. His actions hurt, but I was too engulfed in marital bliss to deal with the depth of the pain. Besides, I believed in my heart, had Randall been sober, he wouldn't have tried to destroy my happiness. I learned from Carlton, that Randall's recreational habit had increased to daily use. Poor attendance had earned him a week's suspension without pay from his job. At least that's the story Randall told Carlton. Randall would say anything to manipulate someone for money. In a sense, I hoped Randall wouldn't show. I wanted to enjoy my Sunday with Tamara and Mama, and the soul food feast in peace.

"Son, I'm so proud of you," she said, just as I stuffed a forkful of cornbread dressing in my mouth. After kissing my forehead, Mama sat down at the dinner table beside Tamara and patted her hand. "And, I'm so glad he chose you for a wife. I finally have a daughter."

"I love you, too, Mama Glenda." Tamara smiled briefly, then reached for a fried chicken wing.

I nearly choked, laughing with food in my mouth. I couldn't help it. I was finally happy and my two favorite girls were happy.

Mama pushed my glass of lemonade toward me. "That's why I'm so glad I can finally transfer your trust fund over to you without any worries."

I gulped down half the lemonade before I realized what my mother said. "Huh? I'm sure Graduate school and the car pretty much wiped that out. It should be just enough left to tide me over until I find work."

A mischievous grin rested on Mama's face as she spooned collard greens on her plate. "That's what I wanted you to think so you wouldn't be wasteful. I wanted you to learn how to manage money. I didn't want you to become lazy and feel entitled. I wanted you to work hard and not depend on your inheritance."

I reached for cornbread that looked and tasted like cake. "Entitled? What inheritance?"

Tamara slowed her attack on the macaroni and cheese and looked at Mama.

"Baby, your daddy wasn't just an employee at the law firm. He was one of the founding partners, which means he profited from every client he brought in, and new clients referred by his old clients. Since his death, his share has been deposited into a trust fund that you and I share. And, as a founding partner, his estate receives a percentage of the firm's annual profits. That's how we were able to pay for your education and that new car. That, and those oil fields in Texas."

"Texas?"

"Oil?"

Tamara and I shouted simultaneously.

Mama kept piling her plate, like she hadn't just dropped a bombshell.

"Not everybody in your father's family disowned him when he married me. His uncle, Joseph—his mother's brother—didn't have any children, but he loved your daddy like a son. When Uncle Joseph died, he left his fifty-thousand acres of oil-soaked land to your father. When my dearest Alexander died, he willed the land to you."

"What?" I stuttered. "Fifty-thousand acres? Oil? What am I going to do with all that land? Oil?"

"You don't have to do anything. Uncle Joseph signed a deal with an oil company granting them drilling rights to the land. The oil company pays his estate annual royalties for the privi-ledge." Mama smeared butter on her cornbread before continuing and answered my question before I could ask it. "Alexander Bennett, Jr., you're not only a college graduate, you're also a multi-millionaire. I'm not too bad off either. I already made an appointment with the lawyer to transfer everything over to you," she added as a side note.

Mama beamed with joy, but Tamara and I gaped at each other. The new revelation left me at a loss for words. I didn't know if I should be happy or not, because this was the first time I actually saw the partiality my mother expressed toward me against my brothers, and I didn't like it. If Mama had the means to contribute to their education, why didn't she? And, why did she work so hard, and spend so little money? Mother dressed plainly and drove used cars.

"Mama, I don't understand," I continued to stutter. "You've been sitting on money all this time?"

"Baby," she said, after savoring more cornbread, "I haven't been sitting on anything. I've been working with financial planners and investing my money wisely. Trust me, there were many days I wanted to splurge, but I had to make the money my dearest Alex left me last." Once again, she answered my questions before I could ask. "I wanted to help Carlton with school, since he was trying so hard, but the stock market took a nosedive. I couldn't take the chance on my future retirement. I don't want to be a burden on my kids, so I let him find his own way. I knew he had the drive to make it. I prayed for him all the time and helped when I could from my salary. I was so glad the market had turned around by the time he got married. It felt good to give him the down payment on his house. I'm so proud of him." Her eyes blinked rapidly—something my mother did to hold back tears.

I'd never seen my mother get emotional over Carlton. I wondered if Mama expressed her adoration to Carlton. I'd never seen it, but then again I didn't know my mother helped Carlton purchase his home.

Mama cleared her throat and forked some greens. "Now, that oldest child of mine," she continued after swallowing. "I won't give him a dime. I love him, but Randall is too much like his daddy. He is a selfish manipulative liar, always has been. In kindergarten, he used to talk the other kids into giving him their lunches." Her head shook from side to side. "Randall doesn't care about anyone but himself. I had hope for him until he kicked his own daughters to the curb. He refuses to spend time with them and barely talks to them. Whatever I had for Randall is in a trust account for Randi and Kendall that he can't touch."

I agreed with Mama for thinking about the girls, but I resented her for bad-mouthing Randall. My brother had his faults, but Mama made him sound evil. Of course, I didn't challenge her.

"And now that his drug use has escalated, he's really not getting any help from me."

My head snapped up. "Drug use?" I feigned innocence, and as usual, it didn't work on Mama.

"Alexander Bennett, I'm not nearly as slow as I look. It was more than alcohol that had him flying at your wedding. I know Randall's been smoking weed since high school. He's doing something else now. I smoked weed before, and I ain't never been so high that I forgot to go to work for three days. And, he's always broke. He makes good money even after child support, so why is he always broke? It's because he's spending money on drugs. He's smart. I don't know why he insists on ruining his life and the lives of everyone around him."

I confirmed Mama's assessment without saying so. "What are we going to do about it?"

"We ain't going to do nothing. I pray for him every day, but that's about all I can do until he wants help. You need to focus on your new wife and your career, and leave Randall to God. You've always idolized your brother. I'm so glad you didn't get caught up in his foolishness," she added, while shaking her head.

In my wife's presence, I appreciated my mother's narrow-sightedness when it came to me. My mother had no idea just how tangled I had been with Randall's mess. I was done. Now that his substance abuse had increased, I wouldn't be giving him any money. Since he'd so readily laid claim on my trust fund, I was not going to tell him about my inheritance. Randall would feel entitled now that I'd struck oil, and I had a wife to consider. Like my mother, I didn't understand Randall's behavior. Randall was intelligent and charismatic enough to accomplish anything; however, he chose to float through life on the wings of drugs and women. My heart ached for him.

"Baby, don't worry. He'll be alright," Tamara said, rubbing my shoulder. "We'll add him to the prayer list at church."

That was my angel, always there to comfort me. Without having to voice it, Tamara perceived my mood changes and nourished me with words of peace. I resumed eating, but at a much slower pace. I couldn't help but wonder how far my brother would let drugs take him before turning his life around.

CHAPTER 12

The Proposition

T HE THINGS I enjoyed most about being a newlywed
were the adventures and spontaneity. Tamara dispelled
every myth I had about church girls being rigid and conservative when it came to sex. My wife worked as a part-time
reporter for the local television station, but once she entered our
home, she traded in the career dresses and suits for outfits that
fully displayed her assets. Often I'd come home from a long
day of interviews and find my wife wearing skin-tight, short, or
see-through clothing, and sometimes practically nothing and
high heels, waiting to serve me dinner. She wasn't ashamed of her
body and wasn't bashful about letting me know she wanted my
hands on her body. It didn't take long for us to create a special
memory in every room.

A peaceful atmosphere was important to Tamara. She filled
our home with soft music and fragranced it with scented candles

and fresh flowers. We didn't argue and worked as a team in every area, even prayed together. Sundays after church service, we alternated Sunday dinners between the Jacksons and Mama's house. Sometimes we all ate together, like one big happy family. I cherished those moments most of all.

The transfer of my inheritance was competed three days after our sixth-month anniversary. It all seemed surreal—me married to Tamara and a millionaire. I offered Tamara the option of being a stay-at-home trophy wife, but as I expected, my angel wasn't having it. "I didn't spend six years earning two degrees to sit at home and look pretty," she said, when I made the suggestion.

Financial security didn't make us wasteful. We decided to finish out the lease before purchasing a home in a gated-community. I eventually secured a job as a Financial Analyst. I wanted to gain experience before Tamara and I started our non-profit organization to assist leading the financially insecure into financial freedom. I did splurge on my nieces by matching Mama's contribution to their college funds. Carlton and I had never spent much time together, but since my marriage and the birth of his son, we conversed regularly. True to his character, Carlton didn't ask for a dime when I shared the news of my newfound wealth. I respected him for that, and paid off his student loans. I felt I owed him that much after he saved my wedding day. After an uncharacteristic hug, he warned me of sharing the news of my fortune with our brother. I still hadn't seen him since my wedding, but I'd spoken to Randall sporadically on the phone about nothing in particular. By coincidence, Randall started calling a few days after my inheritance released. As much as I wanted to, I didn't have the courage to confront him, even over the phone, about how his recreational habit interrupted my wedding day.

I ignored my conscience and concentrated on making a home with my wife.

Since she loved them so much, I routinely brought Tamara a caramel Frappuccino home. Without fail, she'd shower my freckled-face with kisses, like I'd given her a diamond ring. She was so easy to please and built my ego in the process; I made it my mission to please her. I pulled into our reserved parking space with every intention of pleasing Tamara all night long. I hadn't taken three steps when my stomach knotted. Standing across the pavement, leaning against his car with his arms out, was Randall.

His suit fit looser, but he was dressed from head to toe in designer labels. On his face, which was obviously thinner, rested the trademark smile he used for manipulation. Funny thing was, I used to spend hours trying to imitate that very look. Today, I found it disturbing, but I was happy to see my brother. The fact the he was clean-shaven, and obviously coming from work, proved the accusations about his drug use were exaggerated.

"Hey, little man," he hollered, and latched his arms around me and patted my back. "What's up?"

Randall's uncharacteristic affectionate greeting threw me off balance. I almost dropped Tamara's drink. I returned the embrace half-heartedly and stepped back, not wanting to spill my baby's drink.

"I didn't expect to see you today. What's going on?"

He wiped his nose. "I got to have a reason to see my little brother? I thought we were closer than that."

I couldn't tell if he was sincerely offended or not, and honestly I didn't care. Bland phone calls were one thing, but I didn't realize how much I'd missed my big brother until now. I wanted to share my ideas with him and get his opinion. My father-in-law thought my idea of a non-profit community service organization was brilliant, but Randall's approval would mean so much more.

"Of course we are." I laughed after shoulder-butting him. "Come on inside. I can't wait to fill you in on the latest happenings in my world."

"That's what I'm talking about." Randall practically skipped his six-feet-plus frame behind me.

In the back of my mind, I heard Carlton's warning, but once I stepped inside my unit, I had a bigger problem. Just that quick I'd forgotten I no longer lived alone. I had a wife—a wife who liked to welcome me home in sexy outfits. Today, Tamara was wearing the short skin-tight black lace tank dress that I loved, but left nothing to the imagination. Her arms were around my neck with lips pressed against mine before I could warn her.

As Randall brushed past us, a curse slipped. "Girl, I didn't know you had it going on like that!"

Tamara gasped and ran to our bedroom. I stepped in front of Randall in an attempt to block his view of my wife's retreating backside, but it was too late. Randall's trained lustful eye had already seen more than enough to whet his appetite.

"Man, your broad is bad! No wonder you kicked me to the curb," he said, still looking in the direction she'd disappeared until a door slammed.

Now that I was married, I no longer glorified in Randall's lusting after Tamara. Neither did I care for the derogatory term, "broad". I walked into the kitchen and set the drink on the counter before correcting him. "Tamara is not a broad. She's my wife, and your sister-in-law. You should treat her as such.

Would you like something to drink?" I asked as if I hadn't just checked my idol for the first time.

"When are you going to let me hit that?"

I'd reached into the cabinet and pulled down a glass before I deciphered my brother's request. "What did you say?" Randall stepped back. I think my raised tone surprised both of us.

"Come on, man. Don't act like we haven't shared or tag-teamed before."

"But Tamara is my wife, not some trick!"

"My bad," he corrected, holding up his palms. "She's a piece you were dumb enough to marry in order to hit. What's the problem? Are you afraid I'll get whipped like you are, and won't be able to leave it alone?" He leaned in close and whispered, "Or, are you scared after she gets a dose of some real power, she won't want your little twig anymore?"

I stepped away from the counter and paced the length of the kitchen. His innocent expression boggled my mind. It was as if he truly believed his idiotic words, but that wasn't possible. Randall was not stupid, and at the moment, he wasn't high. I considered his question for a split second. Not because I thought the request made sense, but because of my nagging fear of Tamara losing interest in me. "I'm going to blame that nonsense on that stuff you've been snorting for destroying your brain cells," I said, giving him the benefit of the doubt.

As always, Randall dismissed my comment by swearing. "Man, Mama and Carlton don't know what they're talking about. Today is Wednesday. I only occasionally do coke on weekends. I didn't miss three days of work; they misplaced my vacation request."

Randall had an answer for everything. Curiosity and pain made me ask, "So that's why you almost outed me at the wedding? It was a Saturday, so you were high?"

"I was trying to keep you from making a mistake. You do know this marriage thing is not going to last. You'll be divorced within three years. I understand why you're so possessive. If I had limited time with my favorite toy, I wouldn't share either. But if the opportunity arises, I ain't turning nothing down."

My brother had questionable character, but I always thought he had morals. Now I wasn't so sure. "Tamara is not a toy," I said, through clenched teeth. "She's my wife, and you need to respect that."

He sat down on my couch and planted his crossed feet on my coffee table. "What you need to respect and always remember is, I'm your blood; she's not. Family always comes before a piece of tail."

"What about your daughters?" I wanted to ask, but didn't.

"Like I always say, women are only good for two things: sex and money, and not always in that order. The sooner you learn that the better."

I studied my brother through eyes of pity, because I realized then Randall had never experienced the love of a woman outside of our mother, whom at times he claimed didn't care for him because of his resemblance to his father. In Randall's mind, he'd never experienced love; therefore, he didn't understand love, or know how to give love. He felt mistreated by Mama, which in turn made it easy for him to disrespect women and avoid his daughters. Randall was a lost soul. At least that's the rationale I fed my psyche to justify why my brother, mentor and idol had just stated his desire to screw my wife.

As a Christian, I had to take the high road and be understanding and tolerant of Randall's behavior, and try to see things from his perspective. I never had reason to question my mother's love for me. Mama showered love on me, almost to the point of obsession. I couldn't even begin to put into words what Tamara gave me.

I decided to change the subject to something Randall was an expert on. Being a CPA, I was sure Randall would love my idea of educating people about money matters.

"I have something I want to run by you," I said, straddling the barstool across from him. I wanted an unobstructed view of his first reaction to my idea.

"We'll get to that later. I only came over here to discuss a business proposition," he said, sitting upright. "Now that you're finished with school, I can stop working for other folks and start my own business. I'm sick of people telling me when to work."

My chest began aching from the blow of rejection from my mentor and idol. I masked the pain with a smile. "That's great, but how do I fit into the equation?"

"How do you fit?" he shrieked. "Bro, you are the equation."

Randall's laughter filled the room as the ache in my chest migrated to my stomach. "What are you talking about?"

"Now that you finally have full access to the rest of your white daddy's money and the royalties from them oil fields, you can finance my business."

"How did you know about that?" I stammered. "Did Mama tell you?"

"Man, you know Mama doesn't tell me anything, at least not directly. I eavesdropped on a conversation Mama had with one of the partners from the firm at the house, years ago. While he was breaking everything down to her, she was too busy thanking Jesus to notice me peeping around the corner." He leaned back and returned his feet to my table. "Man, I've been waiting a long time for this. I signed the lease for the office building yesterday, and hired an interior decorator to spruce up the place. I shouldn't have a problem pulling some of the clients over to my company. I've already been courting some corporate accounts."

I'd never seen Randall so excited, and yet, I couldn't share in his selfish joy. "Sounds like you have it all figured out."

"Yep. All I need from you is a check for two hundred fifty thousand for now." He snapped his fingers. "On second thought, make it out for three hundred thousand. It's time for me to get a new ride. I'll collect the rest of my first million later."

For what seemed like several minutes, I just stared at him trying to decipher if he was serious, or playing a practical joke. There wasn't anything practical about his request, and the expectant smile on his face indicated he indeed expected me to underwrite his adventure. Sure, I'd given him money in the past and financed his fun, but now I was a married man and Randall's behavior had become suspect.

"What do you mean first million?" I had to be sure I fully understood the implication.

"I also want a new pad, but I'll wait until after the business is up and running for that."

My jaw dropped. All those insinuations Randall made over the years about my money being his money were real in his mind. For the life of me, I couldn't figure out why he felt entitled to my inheritance. I didn't mind helping him out, but he was asking for way too much.

"Well?" he pressed. "Are you going to write me a check, or do an electronic transfer?"

I looked down the hallway to make sure my bedroom door was still closed. I didn't want Tamara to hear in case Randall chose to disclose my many secrets once I refused him.

"Man, I can't commit to something like this without more information, and without talking to my wife."

He jumped up. "Your wife! She ain't got nothing to do with my money!"

"She has everything to do with it. We're married, so it's not just my money. It's *our* money," I tried to explain.

"You're right, it is ours." He pointed at my chest. "Yours and mine! This ain't got nothing to do with that skank."

I grabbed his wrist and moved his hand, taking note his wrist was thinner. Another reason I couldn't allow this craziness. "That's the last time you're going to stand in my house and disrespect my wife. You don't have to like her, but you will respect her if you ever expect to see a dime of our money." My chest began to pound, this time from adrenaline. I was defending my wife's honor against Randall! He must have been just as shocked as I was because his head jerked backward. Since I had dove into deep water, I kept swimming. "And another thing, before I even consider giving you a one-time gift to help you start your business, you need to get your drug use under control."

Randall's face bore the same bewildered expression he had when Carlton checked him at the wedding. Any other time and any other person, Randall would have cursed and fought. This time he slowly backed toward the front door, but he didn't exit quietly.

"Take all the time you need to get the little woman's permission. Just remember, I had you first and blood will always be thicker than water. I am the one who's always looked out for you. I taught you everything you know. Most importantly, I know your secrets. The way I see it, you owe me. You will never get to happily ever after until you take care of me. You got two days," he added, before slamming the door.

My cheeks burned as heat singed my body. This could not be real. My brother did not just threaten to blackmail me into giving him a small fortune. All my life, I've done nothing but try to please him. True, Randall looked out for me over the years, and I respected and defended him, even when he was dead wrong. I didn't deserve this. Did Randall actually care so little about me, or was the threat the coke talking? Randall couldn't rationally think trusting a substance abuser with large sums of money was wise.

I paced the living room, wondering what Randall had on me anyway. Would Randall trade in his player's card and tell my wife I was much more experienced than I'd led her to believe? Other than the night before the wedding, which I still don't remember, I hadn't done anything foul. I'd been completely devoted to God and to my wife. What could I possibly owe Randall? Before I came up with an answer, Tamara stomped into the living room wearing a sweatshirt and leggings.

"You should have told me you had Randall with you. I wouldn't have been walking around here half-naked had I known your lustful brother was here."

My breath caught. Had she heard Randall's ridiculous request to have sex with her? "What do you mean lustful?"

Her fists hit her waist, and for the first time I saw my wife express anger. "Alexander Bennett!" She hadn't addressed me by my name since marriage. I was her "honey" or "babe". "Save does not equate to stupid! Randall has done nothing but lust after me since the day we met. In fact, the day he met me, he stared at my boobs and behind without ever looking at my face. It took him almost a year to hold eye contact with me. Thanks to you, he no longer has to guess what lies beneath. Now I'll never be able to look him in the face."

"I'm so sorry, sweetheart," I apologized, embracing her. "Randall was outside waiting when I pulled up. I should have called you the second I saw him. I was so happy to see him, I got side-tracked." Tamara briefly received my embrace, but didn't voice acceptance of my apology.

"What did he want?" she snapped, pushing away from my grip.

Her actions and facial expression disturbed me for two reasons. Until now, I didn't know she disliked Randall, and this was the first time Tamara pushed me away. Disliking Randall I could handle; he wasn't on my list of favorite people at the moment either, but her rejection hurt.

"Well, what did he want?" she pressed when I didn't readily respond.

I gave it my best spin. "He wants to start his own accounting business. He's already found a building, and has clients lined up. He's—"

"Does he also have a trip to the altar and rehab lined up?" she interrupted. "The only business Randall Williams needs to start is one that involves spending time with his daughters. I hope you told him as much. Every girl needs her father. Even if he is trifling," she added under her breath and took a sip of her now-melted drink.

"I didn't know you disliked my brother so much." I had to turn this back around on her, if I had any chance of giving Randall a dime. "You always talked about expressing unconditional love. I never would have guessed you harbored hatred in your heart." I stomped down the hall toward our bedroom. I heard her gasp, but I didn't stop. Another thing Randall taught me: Maintain control by making the woman chase you. I'd never planned to play manipulation games with Tamara, but her earlier rejection was too fresh for me to care.

"Alex!" she called, after me. I'd barely plopped down on the bed with my arms folded behind my head when she came huffing through the door. "It's true, your brother has character traits I don't care for, but I don't hate him."

I remained quiet and continued staring at the ceiling. My wife knew exactly how to get my attention and shatter my resolve.

"What I hate is," she explained, while straddling me and cupping my cheeks, "the person you become when Randall's around. Whenever he's around, your confidence and thinking ability evaporates. It's like he controls you. You'll do and say anything to please him."

If my ego wasn't already bruised, first by Randall, and now by my wife, I would possibly have pondered those words for truth. Instead, I pouted like a spoiled brat and struck back. "If he controlled me, I would have given him the money he wants. But because I have a mind of my own, I told him I had to talk to you first. So I guess it's you who controls me."

Rapid blinking wasn't enough to camouflage the pain my words had caused. Tamara, always a lady, didn't yell or scream. She simply released my cheeks and maneuvered off the bed, this time withdrawing physically and emotionally.

"Alexander Bennett, the money is yours and you can do whatever you please with it. If you believe in giving a blank check to a drug user, then go right ahead. Do whatever you have to do to maintain your freedom, but don't ever accuse me of controlling you."

I pounded the bed and spat an expletive after Tamara left the room. Randall's visit lasted less than thirty minutes, and in that short period of time he'd managed to disrupt my fantasy of a happy home.

Tamara didn't speak to me again until she climbed into bed wearing a loose-fitting, floor-length, thick, checkered thing I had never seen before. I couldn't tell if it was a gown or a dress. Even her feet were covered with socks. After a bland, "Good night, Alex," she turned her back to me. I got the message loud and clear: Don't touch me. Tamara normally fell asleep cuddled against my body.

I obliged her, and did one better. I didn't acknowledge her presence. Tormented by her femininity, I tossed and turned all night, fighting the urge to touch her. That flannel blanket-looking garb did nothing to conceal her womanly scent.

Pride and fatigue bound me to the bed the next morning, and prevented me from praying and having breakfast with my wife. I laid still, faking sleep, listening to her hum and move around the house. I was so angry she'd slept all night and woke up happy, I didn't budge until I heard the garage door close. Tamara demonstrated to me that she could carry on without me, just as Randall had warned. Now, I had to convince myself I was complete without her.

I climbed out of bed and trudged into the kitchen. Tamara's perfume tickled my nose with every step I took. By the time my hand touched the cabinet for a cereal bowl, I stopped lying to myself. I was miserable. After reading the handwritten note attached to the refrigerator, contrite accompanied my misery. Tamara kept our daily morning prayer tradition by writing her prayer for me. She covered every area in my life, including our future business venture. She signed off with *I ♥ u*, then said she would make me enchiladas for dinner.

I slumped against the counter and surrendered to reality. Tamara wasn't plotting a way to rid herself of me the way I'd been imagining all night. She loved me unconditionally. I'd offended her, but my attitude didn't control her love. Why had I lashed out at her in the first place? My angel never rejected me. What made me interpret her body language as rejection? I would search for those answers later. What I needed to do now was follow my wife's lead and pray. I retrieved my phone from my nightstand and sent Tamara a text message apologizing and praying she'd have a good day. I signed off by telling her I'd take care of dinner and how much I loved her. She responded immediately with a smiley emoticon. My world was back on its axis, but I wouldn't be whole until Tamara was in my arms.

The second my angel entered the house that evening, I show-ered her with affection, which she readily received and hungrily returned after we made a commitment never to go to bed angry again. We paused just long enough for me to feed her the straw-berry/banana whipped cream-topped pancakes I'd prepared. Then I carried her to our bed and loved her from head to toe. I made a vow to myself never to let my fear come between us again. I prayed I would keep that promise.

"Lord, give me the strength to do this," I prayed, once I spotted Randall standing in front of the building, carrying a briefcase and grinning. He looked like a true businessman in his tailored suit and alligator shoes. When he called at the crack of dawn, he insisted we meet at his new office since it was in close proximity to my bank. I'll admit, I'd never seen Randall display this level of excitement about anything before. Under different circumstances, I might share his enthusiasm, but he was blackmailing me.

I reached for the latch, but Randall grabbed it first and opened the car door.

"Come on," he ordered, then wiped his nose. "We barely have time for a quick tour before the bank opens.

"Sure." I stepped from my vehicle, obliging him as always, and delaying the inevitable. I followed Randall inside, half-listening to his renovation plans. The space included a reception area, conference room, and of course, a big executive office. He retrieved fabric swatches and paint samples from his briefcase. He even had carpet samples from Home Depot. He produced an application for professional liability insurance. Randall had everything figured out, even the financing—me.

He glanced at his watch. "Let's head to the bank before the lines get long," he suggested, then slapped my shoulder. "What am I talking about? We don't have to stand in line. You probably have your own personal banker watching over that oil money." He started for the front door, and once again, I dragged behind, second-guessing myself. Given the chance, Randall could be a successful entrepreneur.

"Hold up," I said, before he opened his car door. "We need to talk about this first."

His face twisted. "What's there to talk about? Everything's in order. You just need to give me my money."

The cockiness and entitlement returned, only this time I was determined to stand my ground, figuratively anyway. *Randall may knock me out and leave my lifeless body in the street after my next statement.*

"That's exactly what we need to discuss. You have a good idea, and I'm sure one day you'll do well in business." I paused, summoning courage. "But I don't think it's wise to give you that kind of money while you're still using. Maybe after you attend a treatment program and stay clean for at least a year."

At first, I thought my reasoning made sense to him. Randall stepped away from the car and paced the length of it, both his jaws and fists flexed. When he stopped directly in front of me, I braced myself, anticipating a blow across the jaw.

"So you think I have a drug problem?" he asked rhetorically. "I don't have a drug problem, but you will have a divorce problem if you don't give me my money," he snarled. "One conversation with that hot wife of yours and the fairytale life you have will be over."

His threat nearly made me flinch, but I held my ground. "See, that's where you're wrong. It's not your money. It's mine, and I don't think it's a good idea to give you money when chances are you'll stick it up your nose. Tell Tamara anything you like, she trusts me, and we'll work through anything together." At least that's what I hoped. "Besides, Randall, we're brothers. You wouldn't do anything to purposefully hurt me."

"You don't know me very well, do you?"

The deadening tone chilled me. The death stare unnerved me. I held my ground. "What's that you preach about family loyalty?" I attempted to turn the tide of manipulation, but quickly lost the battle.

"Your half-breed behind don't mean nothing to me, unless you got my money." Randall proceeded to curse me with less regard than he'd give a wad of spit. I absorbed every word, inwardly praying fervently, rebuking the spirits of cocaine, alcohol and any other substance I could think of. Those words were coming from a demonic force, not the brother I loved. "I'll teach you to put that broad before me," he vowed before spitting in my face.

By the time I used my shirt end to clean the saliva, Randall's tires were screeching into traffic.

CHAPTER 13

Let Brotherly Love Continue

E XCEPT FOR CONSTANTLY looking over my shoulder and wondering, is this the day Randall would destroy my marriage, the next four months of my life were normal. My job and preparations for the CFA test were moving along good, and Tamara had been promoted to full-time assignment reporter. Our busy schedules affected our sex life in a positive way. Spontaneity in forbidden places at odd times kept the fire burning. With our lease coming up for renewal, we decided it was time for us to purchase our own home. We'd begun packing and opened escrow on a five-thousand-square-foot home in a gated community. I felt like a king being able to provide Tamara with the home of her choice and the liberty to decorate it as she saw fit without the lack of money being a hindrance.

I hadn't spoken to Randall, or at least he hadn't spoken to me since baptizing me with his spit. The first week, I called him repeatedly, without a response. I left voice messages, and even stopped by his job, only to learn he was no longer employed there. According to Carlton, the firm let Randall go after he pulled another disappearing act. He now worked for himself. Without my assistance, Randall opened his own business in the exact location he'd presented to me. His actions proved his motive to use me, but I refused to accept that Randall's selfishness was ebbed in his heart. It was easier to blame the cocaine.

The few times Randall did bother showing up to Sunday dinner at Mama's, he'd speak to everyone except me and Tamara. He even held rare conversation with his daughters, although most of it was centered around watching out for selfish people. Mama and Carlton ignored his behavior. Tamara disregarded his antics. I was hurt, but knew I'd made the right decision. Randall had lost more weight and his nose constantly ran, signs of prolonged cocaine use. He'd also developed a sense of paranoia, claiming the family formed a conspiracy to keep him down.

I'd idolized Randall and considered him the male head of the family for so long, I didn't notice when the pendulum began swinging in another direction. Subtly, or maybe it had been this way for a while and I hadn't noticed, Carlton and Mama held our family together with me playing a minor role. Reverence once lavished on Randall transformed into caring for his daughters. Mama contributed financially whenever Randall slacked in child support, which was increasing. Carlton and I did our best to fill the paternal void in Randi and Kendall's lives. We attended school performances, field trips and spent as much time with them as our busy lives allowed. The girls routinely hugged their uncles, but reserved an obligatory "hello" for their father.

I used verstehen, a term I'd learned in my Sociology 101 class, to place myself in Randall's position in order to understand his behavior. Randall's influence in the family was lost, and his daughters didn't idolize him. I doubt if Randi and Kendall respected him. Carlton and I had wives who adored us. Randall lived alone without anyone to share his life. Strange and temporary sex partners yielded pseudo-relationships. I honestly felt sorry for my brother. As the Christian, I had to make the first move to eliminate the strain on our relationship.

Randall hadn't answered my calls, or responded to numerous voicemails in months, so I dropped by his condo one evening unannounced after working out at the gym. Instead of his old BMW, a new black BMW with dealer tags was parked in his stall. Business must be good if Randall could afford the ultimate driving machine, I rationalized.

I half-expected my brother to slam the door in my face, but he didn't. Randall answered with a smile on his face and a woman tucked beneath his arm. It was the same woman from that fateful limo ride the night before my wedding. The woman he'd dangled in my face at the reception. I was wearing shorts and a T-shirt, but my body temperature spiked higher than it had on the elliptical trainer minutes earlier. What was she doing here? Were they a couple? Randall never kept a woman around for longer than six weeks. He appeared sober.

"Well, I'll be. The little half-breed freckled mistake my mother brought home from the hospital is here. What brings you amongst the commoners?"

If the sneer on his face were any indication, this would be a brief visit. I forced my eyes from the woman proudly advertising her assets and locked eyes with my brother. "Randall, I was hoping you and I could talk," I stuttered.

"Unless you got my money, we don't have nothing to talk about."

"Randall, don't be like that," the woman said, slapping his arm. "That's your baby brother. He's family."

The hardened expression on his face softened, then transformed into a smile. "Excuse me. Where are my manners? Come on in, little bro." He stepped aside for me to enter. "Like Jordyn said, we're family, and it's not like you and Jordyn don't *know* each other."

Jordyn. The woman who could destroy my marriage now had a name. How well she knew me didn't matter, because I still couldn't remember her touch or smell. Unlike at the reception, today Jordyn didn't giggle uncontrollably, but she did have a welcoming smile, not at all embarrassed by our first meeting.

I followed behind Randall to the sofa with hopes that maybe my brother had finally found someone special to share his life with. Although the thought of me having had sex with Jordyn was odd. Evidence of a woman's presence was sprinkled throughout the living room from the color-coordinated throw pillows to the freshly cut flowers and jasmine-fragranced burning candles. Randall also had a new flat screen TV and surround sound system. As soon as I sat down, Jordyn played the role of the woman of the house and offered me something to drink.

"I was just about to make some smoothies, would you like one?" she asked from behind the kitchen counter.

"Jordyn makes the best smoothies. Better than Jamba Juice," Randall said when I hesitated.

"Sure, but no alcohol," I accepted, thinking maybe Randall was ready to put the past behind us, and re-establish our bond.

"Of course, we wouldn't give the golden child alcohol." Randall smirked, as if he hadn't used alcohol to manipulate me in the past.

Before sitting down on the couch, I had to be clear. I was not there for a repeat performance. "There's nothing golden about me. I've simply made the choice to abstain from alcohol. And drugs," I added firmly.

Randall's dark eyes scrutinized me from head to toe, until the blender sounded. "So what's up? Everything good with Mama and my girls?"

"Huh?" Now I knew Randall had cut back on the white lines. He'd never asked about his daughters before. "Mama's fine and so are Randi and Kendall."

"I've been meaning to thank you and Mama for putting some money up for them. I want my girls to attend the best schools without money being a problem. As soon as the business stabilizes, I'm gonna set some money back to."

My chest pounded with pride, hearing my brother, for the first time, accept responsibility for his daughters. I wanted to say how proud I was, but inwardly I was thanking God for touching Randall's heart. My pleasure must have shown on my face, because his next statement confirmed for me the goodness I'd always known was in Randall's heart.

"It may not seem like it, but I do love my kids. I know I haven't been the best father, but all that's going to change. I have to teach my girls about life, and what to expect from these low-down street dudes. My girls deserve to be treated with the utmost respect, and the only way they'll know what to look for is if I teach them. I appreciate you and Carlton for standing in, but it's time I stepped up to the plate."

In other words, Randall didn't want his girls to reap the seeds he'd sown. Whatever the motive was, I didn't care. My brother was finally settling down.

"That's wonderful, man. I knew you had it in you." I complimented him just as Jordyn placed a tray with two smoothies topped with whipped cream on the coffee table. Randall and I reached for a drink at the same time. "This looks good, Jordyn," I complimented my host holding up the tumbler. I can't wait to taste it." That's when Jordyn realized she'd forgotten to include a straw in my glass.

"Oops. Let me get you a straw." She turned on her heels and hurried back into the kitchen. She returned sipping her smoothie and handed me the straw. "I'll leave you brothers alone so you can talk family business."

"Babe," Randall called as she turned to leave. "It's good as always. Thanks." He winked and I nearly choked on the fruity substance. Did my brother just show genuine appreciation to a woman? Miracles never ceased.

As happy as I was, one question still needed to be asked. There was no way to minimize the elephant in the room, so I just blurted it out and prepared for the backlash. "You look and sound good. Does this mean you're in rehab?"

"Naw, man," he said, with more cool than I anticipated. "I told you, I was only a recreational user. I stopped doing lines when I opened my office. I'm my own boss. I have to be at the top of my game, or else I don't make money," he added after a long drag from the straw.

I took a big gulp and let the cool liquid chill my insides, giving me courage to complete my mission. "You know I would have given you the money, if you weren't using. I hope we can put this behind us and be brothers again."

The cocky sneer returned. "Don't worry about it. You know me; I always have a backup plan. I'll get my money one way or another. It may take a while longer and I may have to work harder, but trust me, I'll get my money."

That's the Randall I knew—determined to make something happen in his favor. I just prayed he didn't leave casualties in the process.

With my free hand, I picked up a decorative pillow and threw it at him. "Looks like you and Jordyn are serious?"

"You could say that," he admitted, after using his straw to spoon whipped cream. "I fed her dinner one night and now she won't go home? If I'd known she'd hang around, I would have fed her fried chicken instead of lobster."

I joined in his laughter, but knew there was more to the story. Randall liked Jordyn more than he wanted to admit. The mere fact that he'd fed her dinner in his home, and gave her free reign of his castle spoke volumes.

I nursed the remainder of my drink, listening to Randall jokingly complain about having to leave the toilet seat down and having to endure frilly girly things around his bachelor pad. I experienced the same adjustments with Tamara. I suspected Randall enjoyed the changes just as much as I had.

I sat the empty tumbler on the tray and leaned back on the couch completely satisfied, physically and emotionally.

So relaxed, I didn't move when Randall suggested we watch the latest action thriller on demand. Tamara was covering a story and wouldn't be home until later, so I wasn't in any rush to get home, besides it felt good to be around the sober Randall. The adrenaline from my earlier workout and the anxiety of visiting my brother completely dissipated, rendering me completely exhausted. I dozed off before the movie plot could unravel.

I woke up to the closing credits with what felt like a hangover. Since I hadn't had any alcohol, I attributed the lightheadedness to my sleeping position—my head hung over the arm of the couch. I slipped my sandals on, not remembering when I'd removed them. Once I gathered my bearings and checked my watch, I called for Randall, who was missing in action. The movie lasted longer than expected. Tamara was probably home by now and looking for me. The vibration of my cell phone against the coffee table proved my assumption. I had two missed calls and a text message from my wife. To ease my wife's concern, I texted I was at Randall's and would be home shortly. I stood and clipped the cell phone to its holder on my waist, unable to recall why or when I'd placed it on the coffee table.

"Randall," I called out again, toward the direction of his bedroom. "I'm heading out. Hope to see you at Sunday dinner." I assumed Randall and Jordyn were preoccupied. Randall proved me correct when he stuck his shirtless body halfway through his bedroom door and dismissed me.

"You'll be seeing me real soon, lil bro." His snide expression unsettled me, but I attributed the uneasiness to the light case of nausea I now had. "Lock the door on your way out."

The bedroom door slammed before I could tell him to give my regards to Jordyn.

I'll never forget the next morning. Tamara woke me from a sound sleep, straddling my shirtless body with tears streaming down her face. My heart lurched, fearing my past sins had been discovered. In my mind, I manufactured answers that would exonerate me. Just when I had a story formulated, I noticed the full smile dividing her face. My baby was happy about something. We hadn't had a chance to talk last night; she was already asleep when I arrived.

"What's up? Did you get promoted to morning anchor?" I assumed her happiness was work-related.

"Even better, daddy," she said, after leaning forward and kissing my nose and pinching my cheek. Something she did when she found me adorable.

I squeezed her rear end. "It must be big for you to call me daddy. I like it, but don't slip and call me that around Judge Jackson; he might get offended. I can't wait to hear what's got you all excited at," I paused and glanced at the alarm clock on the nightstand, "six a.m. on a Saturday."

"Well," she started, then stopped and leaned upright and took my hands. "I'm usually responsible, but this taking a pill every day thing is new to me. So I missed one, or two, here and there." Her face twisted. "Actually, when my assignment changed, I think I may have missed a whole week. So the pills didn't work." She shrugged.

My baby was so cute, admitting she was fallible. Why this made her happy, I didn't know. She was still perfect for me. "Just take your vitamins when you remember." The solution was simple; no need for dramatics. "You're young and healthy, missing a few days won't produce any long-term effects."

"Daddy, you're not nearly as naïve as I am about these matters," she said, arching her left brow. "If you are, our baby is in serious trouble."

"What baby?" No sooner had the two words left my mouth, the fog cleared the precise second Tamara placed my hands against her flat, but firm abdomen. It wasn't multivitamins she'd forgotten to take, but her birth control pills.

"Our baby," she whispered. "I'm pregnant."

I wanted to scream for joy, or run around the room. My mind raced and my heart sang. Yet, all I could physically manage was to press her body against mine and bury my face in her hair. My angel was carrying my child, and she was happy about it. Surely, she would love me forever now. No words were necessary, as our bare bodies and tears mingled and created a perfect symphony.

CHAPTER 14

Happy Anniversary

TURNS OUT, TAMARA had forgotten more pills than she remembered. Three days after the big announcement, I accompanied her to the doctor and we learned Tamara was ten weeks pregnant. She thought irregular periods was a side effect of the birth control pill and didn't question missing her period. Other than slightly larger breasts, she didn't look pregnant. Two or ten weeks, I didn't care as long as our baby was healthy. I wasn't even rooting for a son; I just wanted a child with Tamara.

With our first anniversary being just a week away, we'd planned a family gathering at my in-laws' to commemorate the occasion. Since our place was littered with moving boxes, we decided to wait until then to share our good news with the family. I had to limit my communication to text and email, afraid I would spoil the surprise. Mama accused me of avoiding her, and I was, but all would be forgiven once she learned about the baby. Tamara searched frantically to create the perfect baby announcement, finally settling on taping a simulated breaking news story at the television station to play after dinner and right before dancing.

Our anniversary dinner was one of the rare occasions I recall feeling complete happiness. I had a wife who adored me, and a baby on the way. In a few weeks, we'd move into our new home. My career plans were on schedule and money was not a problem. Our families blended well, Tamara and I both loved our in-laws. Mama finally had a daughter in Tamara and the Jacksons considered me a son. Carlton and Tamara addressed one another as brother and sister, as did Monica and I. An outsider may have considered my life privileged all along, but from my perspective, my life was just coming together. My inner desire for acceptance was finally fulfilled.

The clear sky was perfect for the outdoor affair and the floral combinations outlining the landscape seasoned the air. As always, Tamara perched beside me. We looked perfect in our matching white linen outfits. Her mother literally had to pry Tamara away from me to get her to join the women on the gazebo. I watched her pout off thinking how miraculous it was for her to love me so much.

"I'm pathetic, I know. But I can't help it." I continued staring in her direction.

"She's your wife, it's supposed to be that way," my brother assured me.

"I guess you're right." I shook from my trance and focused on Carlton. Some things never change. Love, family, and success hadn't ruined my brother. He still looked like a geek with those rimmed glasses. I'd come to love and appreciate the geek. If I were completely truthful, that love and appreciation had grown beyond my idolization of Randall.

"How do you really feel?" he leaned in and whispered.

I had slipped and told him about the baby the day before. "Happy," I started to say, but Carlton interrupted.

"I can't believe he made it."

I turned toward the gate, and sure enough, there was Randall with Jordyn on his arm carrying a bright green gift bag. The pair was dressed in color-coordinated clothing. Both appeared sober. Although I was elated my brother thought enough of me to attend my anniversary celebration, his presence set me on edge. Our brief conversations since my impromptu visit were cordial, but superficial. I'd sent him the digital invitation out of courtesy without expecting him to actually show up. Especially, not with the same woman he'd brought drunk to the wedding reception.

From the gazebo, Mama must have sensed her son's presence, because she made a beeline to him before Carlton and I could take a step. I'm sure Mama's words weren't tempered, but they appeared to have been effective. Randall smiled and hugged Mama, then Mama shook Jordyn's hand. I released the breath I'd been holding when Mama took Jordyn by the hand and started for the gazebo. As expected, Randall conducted a thorough visual inspection of the Jacksons' backyard before strolling over to where Carlton and I stood.

"Happy Anniversary, man!" Randall slapped my shoulder, nearly causing me to spill my cider. "Didn't think you'd make it, but you did. Enjoy it now, because tomorrow's not promised."

If Randall meant to be sincere, the snide expression belied him. Randall was up to something. My stomach knotted.

He turned to Carlton. "What's up, geek? How's mini-geek doing?"

Carlton hated Randall referencing his son as mini-geek, and his loaded response conveyed it. "My son is fairing much better than your fatherless daughters."

Randall dismissed Carlton's rebuke by flipping Carlton off. "Don't worry about my girls. I'll have plenty of time to play the daddy game after my business blows up, if I feel like it."

"How is business?" I asked, lifting the glass to my lips.

"It'd be a lot better, if you'd convince your father-in-law to give me a chance to manage his money."

The gold liquid missed my mouth and landed on my white linen shirt. "Excuse me?" My heart sank. Randall wasn't there for me at all. He hadn't changed. His supposed epiphany from a few days ago was an act. He was looking for a new victim. I would not stand by and allow my brother to take advantage of my family. But I didn't know how to convey that without causing a scene.

Carlton came to my rescue. "Dude, you need to get off that stuff. You have really lost your mind if you think Alex is going to recommend you to his in-laws. What's worse, you think Judge Jackson is blind and stupid."

"I'm not high," Randall responded more calmly than I expected. His hand swept the yard. "Everyone here has more money than me, even Mama. All of us weren't born with a silver spoon dipped in crude oil. I'm just saying, share the wealth."

The root of Randall's problem reared its ugly head. Despite the motivating speech on his couch, Randall was jealous of my father's provisions. This wasn't a new revelation. I was just now allowing my heart to accept the truth: Randall cared more about money than about me. Even more sobering, Randall wouldn't rest until he got his piece of the pie. Although the truth saddened me, I couldn't help but wonder how far my brother would go to satisfy his greed.

"Money isn't everything." Carlton offered. "One day you'll realize money has very little value in the grand scheme of things. At least, I pray you will." He nodded toward the men surrounding Judge Jackson. "Come on, let's join the fellas."

I followed behind, thankful for the reprieve. I didn't have to look behind me to know Randall was coming and would attempt to network for new business. I didn't worry about the Jacksons being taking advantage off. The men in the Jackson family were professionals, mostly lawyers who were used to double-talk and manipulation.

I spent the evening feasting on good food and family, and an occasional dance with my wife. Being happily married, financially secure, and expecting my first child made me happy, but I was not complete. Oddly, amidst the fellowship, I had a longing for my father. I don't remember him, but I wanted his presence to share in my joy. For the first time in my life, I wanted my father's approval. Like always, I suppressed my emotional turmoil and focused on the people around me. My father-in-law's boisterous laughter caught my attention. I listened to him tell legal jokes and laughed until the pain in my heart numbed.

Just before dessert was served, and after Tamara's grandfather toasted us, Tamara decided it was time to make the big announcement. I expected my wife to give a mini-speech, or a dramatic lead-in to the tape she'd prepared. Instead, she set her glass down, threw her hands in the air, and yelled, "We're pregnant!" The tape totally forgotten, I'd never seen her so excited before. She was literally glowing. She already loved our baby.

I didn't have long to marvel before the women bombarded her with hugs and questions of how far along she was. My father-in-law grabbed me in a bear hug, while pats on the shoulder and congratulatory remarks echoed from the other men. No sooner had Judge Jackson released me, did my big brother encase me in a vice-grip hug. Carlton was privy to our secret, yet his enthusiasm touched me. When Carlton stepped aside, I expected to fall into Randall's open arms. Instead of a hug or high-five, Randall's eyes were cold, almost lifeless. Then without uttering one word, he turned and walked away.

My mother's warm arms pulled me to her, both congratulating me and comforting me after Randall's snub. "Alex, don't worry about him. God has blessed you with a wonderful wife, and you're going to be a great father. Don't let no one make you feel ashamed of God's blessings."

I returned my mother's embrace, and out of my peripheral vision observed Randall speak to Jordyn and then start for the exit without her. Jordyn had to run to catch him before he exited the gate. I didn't have the time or focus to dwell on Randall's behavior; my wife wanted to dance. Tamara and our unborn child took precedence over Randall's mood swings. Randall was no longer the center of my world. A reality I was willing to accept, now that I was starting a family of my own.

When Tamara and I finally made it home that night, I thought we'd fall out from exhaustion. I looked forward to falling asleep with her tucked underneath my arm. Whereas I was tired from dancing, Tamara had a burst of energy and decided eleven-thirty at night was the perfect time to exchange anniversary gifts—something we had decided not to do.

"I know we decided the new house would be our gift, but I changed my mind," she announced and retrieved a rectangular frame from under our bed. "Since the first anniversary represents paper, I wrote and framed this for you." My heart doubled in size, listening to her read precious words of love and adoration. The sealing kiss expressed her sincerity and unconditional love. Desire replaced exhaustion as my wife's love removed all doubts, insecurities, and fears. Her touch and warmth erased rejection and transported me to a place of kingship. I fell asleep resting in her bosom, believing there wasn't anything I couldn't do.

◆━◆

At first, I thought an intruder had invaded the townhouse. I heard Tamara scream, then came crushing blows to my head. I bolted upright, vigorously shaking myself awake. I needed to protect Tamara, but before I could get my bearings, a slap across my face made me dizzy and sent me reeling sideways and onto the floor. My bare bottom plopping on the carpet and grogginess placed me at a disadvantage, but I had to regroup and protect Tamara—whose screams were getting louder—from whatever evil had entered our home. I managed to get on my knees and brace myself against the bed, only to be met with another punch across my jaw before I could stand. The punch sobered me, because before I squinted, my attacker's face came into full focus. A stranger had not entered my home and attacked my wife. Quite the contrary, my wife was attacking me. My ears tuned up. Tamara's screams weren't from fear. Raw anger fueled every curse word and derogatory name she hurled at me. Oblivious to what turned my angel into a raging maniac, I jumped up and attempted to calm her down.

I reached for her. "Baby, what's the matter?"

She slapped my hands away. "Don't touch me! How dare you stand there and act like you're not a dog and a liar!"

I could feel my face beginning to swell, but I ignored it. I had to find out what had set Tamara off. My last conscious thought was of her exploding beneath me. What happened? Did she have a bad dream? I was dumb enough to ask.

"I wish I was dreaming then I wouldn't have to look at you. My whole life with you has been nothing but a nightmare. Nothing but lies. You're nothing but a sorry..."

I waited for her to complete the string of expletives without interruption. Her words hurt, but I was amazed my saved and sanctified wife knew such foul language, and I needed to put my pajama bottoms on just in case she decided to aim below the waist.

"Baby, calm down and tell me what's the matter?" I pleaded, after she snatched the pajamas from me and threw them across the room.

"What's the matter with me?" She pointed at her chest and looked at me as if I had two heads. "The question is, what's the matter with your trifling behind? You had the nerve to parade your trick on the side in front of me, and my family at our anniversary party. And the broad had the nerve to pretend to want to get to know me. Talking about she would love to hang out with me sometime. Even had the audacity to give me an anniversary gift from her and Randall." She threw the bright-green gift bag I'd seen Jordyn holding hours earlier in my face. "Acting like we were going to be sisters-in-law. So you and Randall share women, huh? That's why he's always checking me out. He's waiting for his turn?"

Tamara's ranting continued, accompanied by neck-rolling, but my heart dropped the second I heard Randall's name. What had he done? The gift bag was empty, but I had a good idea what the contents were, some form of evidence of what happened the night before the wedding. I couldn't lie my way out of this, especially if the evidence included pictures.

"I can explain," I offered, praying I was stuck in a bad dream, and would wake up soon.

She stepped away from me, as if being near me repulsed her. "Explain? You don't need to explain anything. The little movie you and your freak made says it all!"

"What? Movie? Huh?" She slapped me again, erasing all hope that this episode wasn't real.

"Don't play stupid with me! I admit you put on an outstanding act to fool me. I may have been naïve, but I'm certainly not blind!" She stomped over to the television and pointed at the screen. "That's your pale behind! Trust me, I know."

I don't know why I didn't notice the TV playing before. I wish I hadn't. At that moment, I hated television and DVD players. I hated myself. There I was on the screen in the starring role naked as I now stood, having sex with Jordyn and doing things I held sacred for my wife. I couldn't remember one second of the encounter, but based on my sated expression in the still pictures, I enjoyed the experience.

I slumped on the bed, wishing I could disappear, or at least hide. But I couldn't hide. I couldn't lie my way out. Carlton couldn't fix this. I had to face the music, and pray Tamara would grant me some mercy. Shame and guilt prevented me from holding eye contact. Fear of her leaving kept me praying, rather pleading with God to fix my circumstance.

"It wasn't my fault," I stammered. "Randall took me out the night before the wedding and got me drunk. I don't even remember what happened. I swear I never met Jordyn before that night. I swear I haven't been with her since."

"You can't stop lying! Can you? Do you even know the truth? You don't drink, at least not with me." She paused before pointing back at the screen. "The hand that's squeezing her behind has your wedding ring on it!"

"No. It can't be. I promise I haven't cheated since we've been married. I stopped everything—the swing houses, drinking and smoking weed—once we got engaged."

"But you did before."

Her voice was so soft, I barely heard her. I realized then I'd given too much information. Tamara's anger dissipated before my eyes. Each second she stared at me, revealed a different emotion. Shock led to confusion. Confusion transitioned to pain so great, my wife collapsed on the bed, wailing with her face buried in her hands.

"Oh, God! My whole life with you has been a lie. I saved myself for you, and you did nothing but lie to me. The whole time you lied and played me for a fool. Everything was a lie. You never cared about me."

Her sobs broke my heart, but I couldn't stand having her believe I didn't care. Tamara was my love, my angel. I reached for her and instinctively she cringed.

"Don't touch me. Don't ever touch me again."

I don't know how I remained standing with my world crashing down, but I did. Completely exposed, both literally and physically,

I pleaded my case. "Baby, that's not true. I love you. It's just that Randall felt neglected once we started dating. I didn't want him to think I had replaced him, so I went out with him a few times, that's all. None of it meant anything. I swear. I never did coke, just a few joints here and there. Then the night before the wedding, he showed up in a limo. I didn't want to hurt his feelings, so I went out with him. He had already been insinuating Carlton and I looked down on him because he wasn't in church, and neglected his daughters. I didn't want to disappoint him. I had a few drinks, but that's all I remember. I woke up the next day barely in time to make the wedding." I stopped long enough to breathe, hoping she'd understand, or at least stop crying. I couldn't stand hearing her cry.

"Disappoint Randall?" Her head shook vigorously, like she was trying to gather her thoughts. "You didn't want to disappoint Randall? This is not about Randall. He didn't make a commitment to me; you did. Randall didn't stalk me at Starbucks, and then date me for two years." She pointed at my chest. "That was you. Randall didn't confess his undying love for me under my parents' gazebo. Randall didn't ask my father for my hand in marriage. You did. You're the one who vowed to love, honor and cherish only me until the day you die. Randall had nothing to do with that. So don't use him as an excuse. Breaking your commitment to me, if there ever really was one, was your choice." She pointed back at the screen. "I don't see a gun pointed at your head. You look downright happy to me."

"No!" I couldn't look at the screen, once was enough. "That's not the real me. I was trying to keep Randall happy. I—"

"If keeping Randall happy means so much to you, then marry him!" she yelled in my face, and then stormed into the bathroom.

Now that I had time to cover myself, clothes were no longer a priority. I had to make Tamara understand. "Tamara, I'm so sorry for hurting you. Please forgive me. We can move past this," I begged from the doorway. Then I threw what I considered my trump card that never failed. "Come on, let's pray about it."

The joke was on me. My emotional stature shrunk with every sadistic giggle that poured from Tamara.

"Oh, you want to *pray* now? Did you pray before you screwed Jordyn? Did you check with Randall first? The idea of you praying might disappoint him."

I didn't have legitimate answers, so I fumbled for words. I couldn't even remember any of Randall's master player lines.

"Stop! I can't take any more of this. I can't stand the sight of you, and your voice is driving me crazy. I have to get out of here before I kill you."

"Where are you going?"

A coldness I'd never felt permeated from her, gripped and paralyzed me. "As far away from you as I can."

I fell back against the doorframe as she brushed past me. Anxiety took over, causing me to hyperventilate. My cheeks burned. My body ached. Beads of sweat lined my forehead. My blood flowed and my heart pulsated, but I was dying. A part of me died with every item Tamara packed. What little pride remained evaporated the moment she grabbed her keys and started for the door.

"Please don't leave me," I begged.

"Call Randall. I'm sure he and Jordyn will keep you company," she barked, without missing a step.

The front door slammed and just like that, my happiness was gone.

The Whole Truth, And Nothing but the Truth

MY WORLD RESIDED in an utter state of chaos. Crying and begging God to change Tamara's mind hadn't brought my wife home. For practically thirty-six hours, the only things I'd been able to do effectively were pace from one room to another, and blow up Tamara's cell phone. Neither yielded positive results. The constant pacing between empty rooms and around boxes filled with the remnants of my once-happy life, depressed me. Tamara's avoidance of my calls worried me at first, but by day four, her rejection infuriated me. My messages altered between apologetic and anger. I was her husband, and I had every right to know her whereabouts. She was carrying my child. *The baby*. Anxiety mixed with fear, and possibly guilt pounded my chest. Would Tamara keep the

183

baby now that she knew the truth, or at least some of the truth about me? She said she wanted to kill me. Did that include the baby? Tamara didn't need my money, or my name for success. Would she wash her hands of me completely? Those questions and more sent me into another round of tears and pleas for God to fix my circumstances and to show Tamara how to forgive me. In spite of my lies, I believed my marriage could be saved. After all, I had been faithful to our marriage bed. I don't know how my wedding ring got in that DVD. I'd figure it out later. First, I needed to find my wife.

Pushing my fear aside, I summoned the courage to phone my mother-in-law. Tamara and her mother were close. If anyone knew where Tamara was hiding, it was Mrs. Jackson. The million-dollar question was, would she tell me. I didn't doubt for a second Tamara shared my deception with her parents. I didn't want to hear the angry words, or possibly feel the fists Judge Jackson would throw at me, but I had to know if Tamara was alright and if she still carried my child.

"Hello, Alexander," Mrs. Jackson answered on the second ring, confirming what I suspected. My mother-in-law always addressed me as "son".

I swallowed what little pride remained. "Hello, Mrs. Jackson. Um—"

She cut me off. "Alexander, I'm sure you're calling for Tamara. She's not here. I suggest you try her cell phone."

"I've been calling for three days, but she won't answer," I whined. "I just want to make sure she's okay and—"

She cut me off again. "Then I suggest you give her some time. She's dealing with a lot right now. She knows where you are.

When she's ready, she'll contact you. I'm praying for the two of you. Have a good evening."

The line went dead before I could plead my case.

My mother-in-law was right about one thing: Tamara was dealing with a lot. She had given me nothing but unconditional love and support. I repaid her with lies and deceit. I retired the demanding husband role and gave her the space she needed in a text message:

You don't have to tell me where you are, and you don't have to come back now. Just let me know you and the baby are fine. Luv you.

Although I prayed she'd respond, when my hand vibrated ten minutes later, I jumped.

She didn't greet me with an endearing term, nor did she ask how I was doing. She kept it short and simple enough for me to get the message to leave her alone.

Watch the 5 o'clock news

The screen on my iPhone said I had three hours to wait before I'd be able to see my love. It might as well have been three days. I chuckled at the irony of it. My love affair began with me obsessing over her on CalTV. We're married and expecting a child, and I'm still slobbering at the mouth at the thought of seeing her on screen.

I punched in the number of the other person I'd been calling to no avail for three days. Randall. Just like with Tamara, all I got was voicemail. Unlike with Tamara, I cursed Randall out on voicemail for passing that DVD off as an anniversary gift to my wife. I told him in no uncertain terms that thanks to him, my wife had left me. He didn't have to destroy my marriage. He and Jordyn were happy. They didn't have to ruin my life by bringing up my dirt—dirt that he created. All my life I tried to please him and live up to his standards, this betrayal was uncalled for. If I wasn't afraid of Tamara coming back, and missing her, I would have gone to his place and confronted him and Jordyn.

After failing to rationalize Randall's behavior, I entertained the idea that maybe he was snorting again. That would certainly explain his reaction to our announcement about the baby. Cocaine would impede sound thinking. I wanted to believe the best about my brother, but the words Carlton spoke to me on my wedding day haunted me. "Randall only cares about himself," Carlton attempted to point out, but I didn't fully understand, and honestly, I wasn't ready to face the truth now.

By four fifty-five, I had showered, shaved, and changed into clean clothing. Tamara wasn't physically present, yet I didn't think three-day-old funk and stubble was befitting. Her mere image deserved the best. A breath lounged in my throat during the newscast's lead-in stories. I didn't completely exhale until Tamara appeared on screen and announced she was filling in for the regular anchor.

My angel's ebony face glowed from the extra makeup required for the television cameras and lights. Hair I longed to touch and smell flowed loosely past her shoulders. The color on her lips mirrored the paint on her fingernails and the fabric of her dress. The dress that housed her enlarged breasts had my mouth salivating. My ego swelled, knowing that while hundreds, maybe thousands, of men watched my wife at that moment, I was the only one granted the priviledge to feast on her treasure. Tamara greeted the Bay Area, and I got aroused with every gesticulation of her lips. A small plane crashed into a residential home, a traffic accident had Interstate 80 backed up for miles, and the stock market was tumbling, but none of that mattered. Tamara was back, at least her image was. As beautiful as she was, I could see the sadness in her eyes past the brilliant smile. She put up a good performance for the camera, but inside my wife was hurting.

Sobriety cooled my libido and reality returned. The center of my world wasn't speaking to me beyond the television. I didn't know if Tamara would divorce me, or not. What if her projected image was all I had left? I half-listened to the rest of the newscast, inwardly praying she'd come home.

"And I'm Tamara Bennett. Have a good evening." And just like that, she was gone.

You look nice. I miss you. How are you feeling? I texted and waited in vain for an answer.

Three days later, when Carlton stopped by, I was still waiting. I'd called him, because honestly, I didn't know what else to do. Praying and begging God to change Tamara's mind hadn't worked. Honestly, I was tired of praying. Carlton and Tamara were friends; maybe he could talk some sense into her.

"Are you serious? They did what?" he exclaimed, after I poured out the details of Randall and Jordyn's feature film. "The real question is, what were you doing hanging with them in the first place?"

In indignation, I pounded my fist into the palm of my hand. "Why doesn't anyone believe me? That was the night before the wedding. I haven't been with Jordyn since."

"Then how did your wedding ring get on tape?"

I hated that I shared that little piece of information. "I don't know! Stop trying to make this my fault. I didn't do anything. This is all Randall's fault. Stop worrying about the details, and go talk to Tamara for me." I didn't normally yell at my brother, but I was desperate. "She trusts you; she'll listen. Tell her I didn't cheat on her. Tell her it was all Randall's idea."

Carlton's stare penetrated my resolve, but his words confused me. "If you keep telling yourself this is all Randall's fault, you just might succeed in not taking responsibility for your actions."

"Now you're turning on me?" I refused to believe Carlton didn't take my side. "You know Randall set me up. Don't you remember how jacked up I was and almost missed the wedding?"

Carlton removed his glasses, rubbed his forehead, and replaced the frames. After slapping his knees, he stood and looked out the bay window. "Maybe this is a good thing. This has been going on too long."

"What?" I jumped to my feet ready to pounce on my brother. "How is Randall ruining my life a good thing? All my life, he has done nothing but take advantage of me. Everything, from using me to clean the house to spending my allowance on strip clubs, and getting drunk."

"And yet, you keep going back," he interrupted, turning around.

"Huh?" I had no idea where the geek was going with this.

"Alex, it's time for you to grow up and take responsibility for your actions."

For the first time ever, I yelled at my older brother. "I have taken responsibility. I told Tamara the truth about how I met Jordyn. So don't be judging—"

"Only because you got caught," he interrupted again.

I slumped down, totally deflated. The truth hurt.

"Alex, no one is judging you, but you need to be honest with yourself. True, what Randall did was foul, but he only did what you allowed him to do. You just said yourself, Randall has been manipulating and using you all of your life. You know he's selfish, yet you continue to place yourself in a position to be used. You're too busy playing the victim, to admit you're allowing him to use you."

"I am the victim here!"

"No, you're not." He remained calm. "You are an accomplice."

"What the—"

The geek had the audacity to raise his open palm to silence me. It worked.

"Hear me out."

My jaws flexed and my chest heaved, but I didn't utter a word.

"After you committed to Tamara, you still participated in sexcapades with Randall. You continued to place yourself in circumstances in which you knew you were vulnerable and likely to fall. You lied to Tamara to please Randall. When I helped you on your wedding day, I thought you were done. At least I prayed you were. He showed up at your wedding itching to tell your new wife and anyone who'd listen about your indiscretion. Our brother has shown you his true colors time and time again, but you refuse to accept the truth. Randall is a greedy lion that you keep feeding. The question you need to search deep inside for an answer to, is why. Why can't you tell him no and stay away from him? He only comes by or calls when he wants something? Why do you keep allowing him to use you? Why is it so important for you to please him?"

Carlton's words slapped me so hard, my head reeled. I didn't have an answer to any of those questions. What's worse, he spoke a truth I could no longer deny. Randall controlled my life.

"I don't know," I admitted. "I'll work on that, but please, you have to talk to Tamara for me. I swear I didn't break my marriage vows. I love her. She's all I have." Anger and pride dissipated, leaving a trail of tears I didn't bother hiding.

Carlton stood over me, shaking his head. Finally, after what seemed like forever, he ordered, "Let me see the video."

"What? How is watching that going to bring Tamara back?"

"Stop whining and go get it," Carlton ordered. "Trust me, I don't want to see you in action, but maybe we can figure out if the recording was chopped, since you insist that was before the wedding. Not that it clears you, but it's a start."

He had a point, so I slouched into the bedroom, maneuvering around boxes. The DVD was still in the player. As I carried it into the living room, I fought the urge to break the shiny circle in half, but it was the only chance I had for some form of redemption.

I inserted the DVD and pressed the play button, then turned my back. I still couldn't bring myself to view my shame.

"I thought you said you and Jordyn got busy in the limo before the wedding?"

"We did." I whirled around, ready to state my position once again, but one glimpse at the screen and I couldn't. The action playing back at me wasn't set in a limo. The movie set was Randall's place, on the couch with the decorative pillows. "Oh, no!" I moaned, burying my head in my hands.

"That's Randall's living room," Carlton confirmed. "When were you last there, and was Jordyn there?"

I slumped on the couch, totally defeated.

"What happened? Were you drinking, smoking?"

Carlton wanted answers, but the pain in my chest rendered me speechless. I felt my head moving from side to side, more to shake the weight of the truth than answer Carlton. Everything made sense now about my last visit with Randall—the nausea, my missing shoes, cell phone, and memory loss. Randall had Jordyn drug my smoothie and then taped me having sex, then gave it to my wife on our anniversary. What kind of person would do that? What had I done to make my brother hate me that much? I don't know if I used a condom, and I came home and had sex with Tamara the next morning. I could have given her a sexually transmitted disease. Randall didn't care.

"He drugged me." Heavy tears lapped at my chin when I finished explaining my visit with Randall. I had went there to make things right, and he preyed on me. It wasn't the first time, but this time hurt the most. "Why?" I asked the rhetorical question aloud.

Carlton turned off the DVD and sat across from me. His expression had changed from unbelief to compassion, but I had a feeling I wasn't going to like what he had to say. "Alex, what our brother did was wrong, hands down, but, you shouldn't have been there in the first place. Randall had stopped speaking to you after you didn't give him the money for his business. Why did you go after him? Randall cared only about himself before the drug use, and his self-centeredness has only gotten worst since. You know this, but you refuse to accept him for who he is.

"I can't talk to Tamara, and neither should you. It's way past time for you to talk to God about your relationship with Randall. You need to be honest and admit your role in Randall's abuse. And, you need to stop straddling the fence with God. In some ways, I think you've made Randall your God. You don't have to tell me, but just think about how many times you've transgressed against God to make Randall happy. Now, you want to blame him for decisions you made. It's time for you to be accountable and take responsibility for your life. You need to come clean and stop playing the role of victim. Until you get right with God, you don't have a chance with Tamara. She's God's daughter, and He's not going to allow you to continue taking advantage of the gift He gave you and then blame Randall. We have to love our brother, but you need to seek God on *how* to love Randall. Sometimes the best love is expressed in distance."

For the first time, I completely *heard* my brother. My walls of denial collapsed with my broken heart. I thought I had grown into my own man, only to learn I was nothing but a grown puppet. Thanks to the blind faith I'd placed in Randall, my marriage was over, just as he wanted. I played right into his hands.

"I'll be praying for you, like always, but the change has to come from within you. Randall is not going to change until he opens his heart to God. That may, or may not happen since Randall feels entitled, a trait he inherited from our father." He pointed at my chest. "You can change once you find your self-worth in God, and stop using Randall as a measuring stick."

Carlton's voice boomed over the pounding in my head and reached my aching heart. I wanted to scream out, but my jaws locked as previous conversations replayed in my mind. Every warning from Carlton and my mother recycled as if on automatic repeat. I heard my front door close, but didn't move to lock the door. My naiveté, no my stupidity, had cost me more than Tamara. A part of me died that afternoon. I unconditionally loved my brother. He was my idol, my mentor, but my brother didn't love me. A truth I could no longer deny or justify.

I don't know how long I sat on that couch, silently crying as I regurgitated every negative comment Randall made about my skin color, height, and sexual ability. That horrible day at seven years old, and the humiliation in front of strangers at strip clubs, constant rejection, and the ultimate disrespect of my wife; all of it bombarded my spirit and rested on my chest. I thought I'd pass out from the pressure. The deepest breaths yielded no relief, and to be honest, I didn't want air to fill my lungs. I wanted to die rather than confront the truths Carlton's rebuke revealed. In addition to Randall controlling my life, I'd also made him my God. I placed more validity in Randall's happiness than I did in God's word. I'd never completely surrendered to God, only perpetrated enough to get Tamara and to satisfy Mama. I read the Bible and prayed, but I didn't invest my heart. I'd used God the way Randall used me: to get things. The shame of it all was too much for me to bear. I dropped my head and let tears mingled with snot soak my shirt.

A shadow covered the opposite side of the living room, an indication the sun was setting, when the whimpering started. Soon the whimpers became sobs that shook me so hard, I fell to the floor on my knees. I didn't attempt to stop the horrible noises coming from the pit of my soul, nor did I stop my body from falling completely on the floor. No effort was made to protect the carpet from my bodily secretions of tears, snot and slobber.

"Oh, God I'm sorry!" I yelled between heaves. I lay with my face kissing the carpet, repenting for every deceptive act. The lies, the drugs, the strange women, all of it. And for the first time, I repented knowing I would not return down that path. I cried some, then prayed some and cried and prayed some more. I admitted my insecurities and perceived inadequacies, and asked God to show me who I was outside of Randall and Tamara. I came clean about my fear of being alone and fatherhood and asked God to heal me of the fear of abandonment that hovered over me. As the room grew dark, I lifted my hands in total surrender to God's will for my life. Confessing my brokenness, and disrobing my soul before God was so intense, my body trembled, but I had to figuratively and spiritually let go of every controlling force over my life. I needed a miracle and the only way for total deliverance was for God to take complete control. I couldn't handle this on my own, the pain was too great, and frankly I didn't know how or what to do to make my life whole. My entire life was a cycle of trying to please people—Mama, Randall, Tamara, the Jacksons, professors, everyone—and trying to fit in. I honestly didn't know who I was unless someone told me. I'd become a chameleon, transforming to every whim and mood swing of the individuals I sought my value in. My day of reckoning had come, it was time for me to completely trust God, and not use Him as my fix-it man.

Except for the illumination from the streetlight, darkness filled the townhouse when my cries ceased and I garnered the strength to stand. Physically, I was the same. Spiritually, I felt different, lighter like weights had been removed from my soul. I wasn't completely free, but inside I knew I was different, and total freedom was near. Ironically, the streetlight offered me assurance. Regardless of the darkness, one flicker of light erases the darkness and provides direction. Darkness overshadowed my life, now, but I'd just opened my heart to the Light of the World. All I had to do was listen, follow, and allow Him to guide me from darkness into His light and truth.

The clock on the stove read: 1:57. I chuckled. I had finally experienced what I'd heard church folks term *a midnight experience.* "Although, it's still dark outside, midnight marks the start of a new day," I recalled the pastor saying. My new day had finally come.

———◆◆◆◆◆———

I spent the next two days reading the Bible, praying and preparing to transition into our new home. I opted for a satellite worship music station in lieu of the television. I stayed spiritually centered and worked. I didn't talk on the phone, or surf the Internet. I was on a mission. The movers were due tomorrow. Dishes had to be wrapped and closets cleared. I doubted Tamara would join me in the home she'd chosen. I hadn't heard from her. I continued texting her once daily to see how she was feeling. Since my midnight experience, rejection's sting had lost some of its potency. I prayed for her healing and took the focus off my pain.

I'd just stepped from the guest bathroom, carrying a box into the living room when the front door opened. Tamara stepped in, carrying the same bags she'd left with ten days prior. Her hair was pulled back into a ponytail, her face void of makeup except for lipstick. The jeans and sweater hugged her tighter than I remembered. My angel had returned in my presence, but not in my arms. No cheerful smile, or glow, only a solemn facial expression greeted me. Her stare bore into me, but her words came slow.

"Hello, Alexander," she said, after a visual inspection of the living room.

I let the box fall from my arms, not caring if the contents were fragile, and started for her. My stomach knotted when she stepped back and raised her palms. She didn't have to audibly voice her desire for me not to touch her. She conveyed the message loud and clear when she left the bags at the door and sat in the recliner and crossed her legs and folded her arms. Too happy to see her again, I let the rejection pass. I deserved it and more.

I sat adjacent to her on the couch. "How are you feeling? How's the baby?"

"We're fine."

The dry answer didn't deter me. "Can I get you something? There's not much here, but I can order you something. What would you like?"

The coldness in her eyes shook me. "The truth. For once, I want truth from you."

I flinched at the blunt request, not sure of its meaning. "What do you want to know?" I posed the question intent on being totally honest and facing the consequences.

"First, I want to know why? Why did you lie to me and deceive me? Why did you choose me to create this illusion of life with? I didn't chase you, or pressure you into a relationship. My life was content before I met you; why did you disrupt it? Why did you attend church with me, and pretend to receive the Lord? I am not your judge; you didn't have to play me for a fool. We didn't have to get involved. We certainly didn't have to get married. You knew I was a virgin, saving myself for my husband. Why did you manipulate me out of my virtue?" Her voice broke and her arms fell, but she continued as if rambling. "From the beginning, I gave you my best. I trusted you with my heart. I never denied you. I loved you with my soul. Why? Why did you…I just want the truth. I need to make some sense of this mess that's become my life. I'm married to you and pregnant with your child, but I don't *know* you."

Tearful pleading eyes caused my heart to constrict. Being the source of her pain, the only comfort I could offer was the truth, which would lead to more pain and more questions, but I had to come clean, so both of us could heal.

"I am sorry I hurt you. This may not make sense, but I love you. Honestly, I do. From the first time I laid eyes on you, I loved your aura. Once I got to know you, I fell in love with your spirit. I never meant to hurt you, but I did because, although I love you, I don't know how to receive love, or how to give love. I've been in denial about my insecurities, and how driven I was because of them. I'm not blaming Randall for my actions, but he used my insecurities to manipulate me into doing things I knew were wrong. It's always been that way."

"What insecurities?"

By her confused expression, my wife had no idea of what I was talking about. I'd hid myself well. I inwardly prayed the urge to lie away, and pressed forward. "For as long as I can remember, I've been trying to find where and how I fit into the world. As a child, no one but Mama loved me, or at least I thought no one cared." After a deep breath, for the first time I opened up and shared the details of my childhood. I started by admitting my fear of abandonment, that I blamed my father for dying and not being there for me. I traced my fear of rejection back to all the times my brothers and classmates made fun of me because of my lack of melanin. I recalled vividly the bathroom beat down. I shared my fascination with masturbation from age nine and the experience with the girl with the long braids. I came clean about drinking, and recreational marijuana use, the strip clubs, and the real reason I couldn't consummate our marriage until we got to Paris.

"To be completely honest, I never thought I was good enough for you. Like you said, you don't need me to feel good about yourself. You came from a good family, and eluded confidence. You were so beautiful and focused; *I needed you* to validate me. You're my angel, but I've always feared one day you'd wake up and realize I'm not good enough and leave me. Tamara, you and the baby are my everything, but I don't know how to trust our love. You give love so completely and freely, at times it doesn't seem real."

Her lips moved to speak, then closed.

"As for Randall, I've always idolized him. Growing up, Randall was the closest thing I had to a father. I went a step beyond pseudo fatherhood; Randall became my god. He was everything I thought I should be—popular, tall, strong, and revered by the neighborhood kids. What he said was law. Everyone, including Carlton, obeyed him. His authority made him cool. I wanted to be just like him—talk like him, dress like him, walk like him; everything. But all he ever did was drill into me how inferior I was." I paused, to rein in the emotions threatening to escape. Removing the scabs from old wounds hurt. Forty-eight hours of crying and confessing hadn't changed that. "Randall's influence in my life exceeded that of my mother. Whatever Randall said do, I did. I had to have his approval at all costs. As a grown man, that should have changed, but really, it didn't. Once we started dating, my devotion changed, somewhat, but not completely. Guilt consumed me whenever I disappointed Randall by spending time with you. Being with you disrupted his unlimited access to my time. Not that he valued hanging with me, but having me tag along meant free partying for him. I always paid for everything, and when I couldn't or objected, he'd openly taunt me until I did. Randall's opinion of me meant so much, I had sex with multiple strangers to fit into his world." I looked her straight in the eyes when I made the next statement. I wanted her to fully understand my reason for cheating had nothing to do with inadequacies on her part. "The only reason I cheated during our courtship was to pacify my brother. It had nothing to do with you. I was faithful to our marriage vows until I went to visit Randall a few weeks ago. I don't remember everything that happened, but Randall and Jordyn drugged me. I would have never cheated had I been alert."

"Why would he do that?" The question came in a faint whisper. "He's selfish and arrogant, but..."

"My guess is, he's still upset with me for not giving him the money to start his business. Randall has always considered my money his money, and up until that point, I always yielded. I always yielded," I repeated, as the truth of our one-sided relationship resonated deeper in my spirit. I hurried to the kitchen and looked out the garden window to keep from breaking down in front of Tamara.

For what seemed like eternity, the only sound in the townhouse was my heavy labored breaths. I had regurgitated my pitiful existence to God and to my wife. I felt better, but not free. Something was missing, but I couldn't pinpoint what. Clarity would come now that I'd embraced the truth.

With forced courage, I leaned against the sink and faced Tamara, praying her answer to my question wouldn't bring me to my knees. "The movers are coming tomorrow. Will you be moving into our new home with me, or are you going to file for divorce? Do you believe me?"

She made no effort to hide the trail of tears staining her cheeks, or the pain and confusion veiling her face. I handed her a paper towel from the counter. With every second that passed, my hope dwindled.

"I don't know," she whispered, looking lost. "I don't know you," she continued, after looking around the room. "The person you just described is not the person I married. I'm not sure I want to know you, and yet somehow I love you. It's weird. I don't like you, but I love you." She lowered her head, and rubbed her forehead. "With my hormones and your drama, I'm too emotional to make a permanent decision. Besides, I no longer trust my own judgement. I don't trust you. I don't know what's going to become of us. I don't know if there is still an 'us'. If I decide to, I won't file for divorce until after the baby is born. Beyond that, I don't know anything."

Only a shell remained of my confident and purpose-driven wife. I had to do something to restore her. "Perhaps we can pray for direction and healing?" I suggested with an outstretched hand that she ignored.

"I don't think so." Her head shook vigorously, almost defiantly. "God and I aren't exactly on speaking terms right now. Praying to Him is what got me into this mess. The only reason I allowed my heart to get involved with you, was because, He assured me you were the one. I prayed every day about you, and how you fit into my life. I had to know if you were a reason, a season, or a lifetime connection. He filled my head with dreams of us growing old together. Scriptures pointing to you, or so I thought, dropped in my spirit." She was rambling, but I needed to hear, for it gave me hope. "I saw the goodness in your heart. I was faithful to God. How did I get here? Why am I here?" Her hands flew up in surrender. "I can't figure this out now, and I've cried too many tears over this. When it doesn't hurt so much, I'll pray again. I have to focus on something else, before I go crazy." She stood with her hands on her hips. "What's left to pack?"

And just like that we settled into packing the remnants of our once-happy home.

No Honor Amongst Thieves

B Y LATE AFTERNOON the townhouse was packed. Boxes were labeled for the movers and only the bare necessities and the television remained accessible. Tamara confirmed turnoff and start dates with the utility companies and the cleaning service. We worked well together, but didn't talk much. However, Tamara's actions spoke volumes and gave me reason to believe reconciliation was an option. She separated our personal items, but kept our common belongings together. Neither did she label the box containing the love notes and mementoes I'd given her over the course of our relationship, junk. As I removed our wedding portrait from the mantle, a whimper escaped her lips. I sat the picture down and attempted to comfort her, but she slapped my hand away and turned her back to me. The fact that she didn't throw the picture across the room, softened the rejection. I gave her the space she needed until I saw her rubbing her stomach. She looked tired and hadn't eaten anything since her arrival.

"I'm going to order food from the restaurant down the street. Do you want a short or full stack of pancakes?" At least, I could provide some pleasure in the form of her favorite food.

"Thai would be better, and make it slightly spicy." She rattled off a list of Thai food entrées that left me scratching my head. Tamara rarely ate Thai food, and even then limited it to a noodle dish, and wasn't keen on spicy food. "I've acquired a taste for Thai, must be the baby." She shrugged her shoulders, then grabbed her purse, sending me a message I refused to accept.

I left her counting out bills, sending a message of my own. Tamara may not need me, nor my money, but for now, she was my wife and my baby was growing inside her. Tamara and the baby were my responsibility. Anger and hurt couldn't change that.

"Go ahead," I acquiesced, later when we reached for the last chicken satay skewer at the same time. We, mainly Tamara, had devoured a smorgasbord of entrées. I never thought I'd see the day when my wife ingested more food than I did, but now she was eating for two. During the meal, I started to inquire about the baby, but her distant and somber mood didn't invite conversation. I disposed of the trash and placed the scraps of leftovers into the refrigerator, not knowing what to do next. Cuddling, which was our routine after dinner, was out of the question. I settled on the evening news.

"You did a great job filling in as anchor, but then I knew you would. You excel in everything you set your mind to." The compliment was sincere, but my credibility was nil.

The smirking followed by eye-rolling was new. "Everything, except in selecting a husband."

My breath hung in my throat as I absorbed the blow. My worst fear had come upon me; my wife viewed me as a failure. I collapsed on the couch and aimed the remote at the screen to suppress the pain. She remained at the kitchen table.

The doorbell sounded somewhere between the weather and sports report. She jerked around. "Are you expecting company?" It wasn't a question, but an insinuation.

"No, but it might be Carlton." I walked to the door, praying my brother was on the other side of the door. Carlton could validate my idolization and Randall's abuse. To my misfortune, the uninvited visitor wasn't my brother, but my nemesis.

"So your trick is making house calls now?" Tamara lashed out.

No answer came. Jordyn's presence knocked the wind out of me.

"I get your anger, but don't take it personal, it's just business," Jordyn explained, casually removing her sunglasses and stepping into the townhouse.

"Business," I stuttered and Tamara cursed.

"Calm down. I can explain, but enough with the name-calling," she said, pointing a finger at Tamara.

"How dare you come up in my house and tell me what to do!" Tamara lunged forward. I grabbed her from behind just before she pounced on Jordyn. Something else I discovered about my wife: She wasn't afraid to fight to protect what was hers.

She struggled to get free, but my grip wouldn't budge. "You're protecting this broad over me?" she snarled.

"No, I'm protecting our baby," I stated firmly in her ear.

She huffed and puffed, but settled down.

"Sorry for the trouble, but like I said, it wasn't personal. Randall and I had a business arrangement. "You," she said pointing at my chest, "were just a pawn in our game. Hopefully, the two of you can get past this and move on, because nothing happened."

I released Tamara and restrained myself from attacking Jordyn. What did she mean by a "business arrangement"? My life had been destroyed over some hair-brain business deal? "What are you talking about and why are you here?"

Jordyn confirmed what my heart already knew. "I loaned Randall the money to start his business. He was supposed to pay me back in installments, but then he got the idea that screwing me was part of the repayment plan. He also got confused and gave most of my money to the coke man. What Randall didn't know was, I don't play about my money. I took out a second mortgage on my rental property to help him. When I threatened to repossess the BMW, since it's in my name, he promised to get the money from you. That's why we slipped you some X when you came by. At first, I thought it was to blackmail you. I didn't realize Randall wanted to destroy your marriage until the day of the party. That's when he told me to pass the DVD off as a gift to your wife." She directed her attention to Tamara, whose mouth hung opened. "Just so you know, Alex and I never had sex. I don't do brothers. It was all staged for the purpose of shaking Alex down. It was all Randall's idea, and I went along with it because I wanted my money." She turned back to me. "The night before the wedding is another story. You got busy with both of those hoochies, and then zonked out. The alcohol and X combination may have been too much," she added matter-of-factly.

"I can't believe this," Tamara murmured. "This is insane."

I had to turn away. Jordyn's confession removed all lingering hope that Randall cared about me.

"There's something else you need to know," Jordyn continued. "I stopped trusting Randall when he snorted my money, so I left the camera running while I showered after we filmed you at the house. He must have been too high to notice the red light illuminating from the tripod. Or maybe he thought he could trust me with his dirty secret. Whatever the case," she reached into her purse and pulled out a DVD, "you need to see this. I think you should know what Randall has really done to you. Don't get it twisted. I think it's unfair what he did, but I'm giving you this as partial payback for him snorting my money. I repossessed the BMW this morning. When I get through with him, Randall will be sleeping on the streets," she vowed.

I turned and stared at the DVD, wanting nothing to do with it. "I don't want to know. I've heard enough. I can't take any more." A critical piece to my life was missing, and I dreaded that the metal disk contained the missing link to my total freedom. Yet, deliverance terrified me. With raised palms, I back-peddled into the kitchen.

"Suit yourself." She tossed the DVD on the counter. "Don't say I didn't warn you. One look and I moved back into my house."

"It's been interesting, but you should leave now," Tamara ordered, opening the door.

Jordyn offered some advice as she walked through the threshold. "Alex, you're a good guy, but naivety will destroy you, if you don't face reality soon."

I like to think the door slipped from Tamara's hand, but I know she meant to slam it. I also knew she would play the DVD. My wife was a journalist and trained to get the facts. Now that she had the facts about the pictures being staged, would she believe me? I paced the kitchen, praying, for what, I really didn't know. Tamara fetched the DVD player from a box and reconnected it to the TV.

Tamara's shrill cry pierced my ears. "Oh my, God!"

I bolted toward the screen, drawn like a magnet to what I didn't want to see, but needed to know.

"No!" Tamara cried again.

Unlike the previous DVD with still shots, this production contained live action, uncut and raw. An undeniable image fondled my unconscious naked body and then performed oral sex on me. The person I'd loved and idolized, and wanted to be was live and in color, violating me. Randall.

A sudden burning and searing sensation took over my body, and I jolted around. I wanted to run away, but didn't know which way to go. The room was spinning too fast. Or was it my head? The pounding in my head synchronized with gagging, caused me to double over in agony. I staggered to the garbage can and regurgitated every ounce of the Thai food, followed by a bitter green substance. The dizziness threw my aim off, and half ended up on the floor. I needed to clean up the mess, but the world kept spinning. Images and voices from the past raged war inside my head, fighting against my will to come forth. Too depleted to fight the truth, finally I released the reins of denial and fantasy once and for all. The world didn't stop spinning and the burning didn't subside until my dazed body fell to the floor.

The vomit's stench violated my nose and my left hand rested in the slimy substance, but I couldn't move. Emotions joined the antiquated images and voices and rendered me paralyzed. Like all those years ago, I opened my mouth to call for my mother, only this time no sound came out.

"Alex! Alex!"

A female's voice was calling my name. I wanted to leave the ancient world inside my mind and respond, but its grip was too tight. Then the shaking started.

"Babe, answer me!"

Babe. The voice resonated. It belonged to my angel; I had forgotten she was there. I blinked my eyes rapidly until Tamara came into focus, relieved I wasn't having convulsions. She was trying to shake me back to the present.

"Alex, talk to me!"

"I remember. I remember it all," I said, faintly with my eyes transfixed on the now-black TV screen.

Firm hands turned my face until our eyes met. She was kneeling in front of me. "What do you remember? Tell me what's going on in your head?"

"The summer I when was ten years old." I couldn't stall; I had to get the voices and images out of my head. "Carlton was away at some science camp internship for the summer. Randall watched me during the day while Mama worked. He'd just graduated high school and was starting college in the fall. He hated me cramping his style. He wanted to hang with his friends and party, but Mama commanded him to babysit me. Uninterrupted time with my big brother, I thought I was in heaven, even though it meant I'd have to complete all the chores. Several days into the stint, something happened." The shaking returned, only this time Tamara wasn't the cause. "Randall yelled at and ordered me around all the time. That day wasn't any different, but he was different. I didn't want him to do it, but he was in charge. And, and," I began stuttering.

Tamara's palms pressed into my cheeks. "Alex, slow down and tell me what happened."

My head hung, as I recounted how Randall performed the same acts on the DVD years ago on me, and forbade me to tell anyone. If I did, he would never speak to me again after he beat my half-white…" I couldn't complete the expletive term he'd labeled me. "I didn't want him to hate me. It was my summer of torture. I knew what he was doing was wrong. He should not do to me what he forced girls to do to him. We were brothers. The emotional trauma and physical stimulation mixed my brain into mush. Randall seemed to like touching me and putting his mouth on me. He did it a lot. I cried, but he never stopped. The day I refused and threatened to tell Mama, he punched me in the face, and then locked me out the house without food until just before Mama came home. After that, I stopped crying. I'd squeeze my eyes shut and pretend it wasn't happening. He molested me until Carlton returned from camp. Then he acted as if he didn't know I was alive. He pretended it didn't happen, but I went a step further and willed the memories from my mind. But it did happen. It really happened. Oh, God! It's still happening!" The rambling continued as the memories shed light on Randall's behavior. "That's why he didn't want me to get married. It's about more than the money. He has some twisted idea he owns me." Sobs poured from me, as I considered all the times Randall could have had the chance to violate me—the alcohol and swing clubs. Did he? Was I blocking out something else? I racked my brain, recalling the time I caught him watching me at the swing club, but nothing else surfaced.

His repetitive references to the size of my manhood served a dual purpose—to degrade me, and hide his desire. My brother was sick and confused. If he desired men, why didn't he come out the closet, instead of degrading women and mistreating his daughters? We wouldn't love him any less. Was he using drugs and alcohol to anesthetize his true struggle?

When the sobs quieted, Tamara offered me a paper towel, but no words. Our eyes met for a brief second, before she began cleaning my vomit. Both her hands and lips quivered. I wondered about her thoughts. Did she think any less of me? Somehow, I didn't think that was possible; she already viewed me as a failure.

"Go get cleaned up." The soft order came just before she dumped paper towels into the trash. She turned away from me, but not fast enough. I saw the pain and tears she tried to conceal. I wanted to say something, but what? Maybe after a hot shower my thoughts would unravel and I'd be able to form words and sentences.

Amazingly, my steps toward the bathroom were steady. My head felt weighted down, but my legs were light. The hot water pellets massaged my tired muscles and internal aches. The pounding in my chest slowed with each heave. The steam seeped into my pours, clearing the mass of thoughts from my head, providing a resemblance of peace. The chains of bondage were loosening with each scrub. Sadness, anger and hurt remained, but I also sensed a new emotion: freedom. Tentacles of fear assaulted my spirit, releasing anxieties of the unknown in an attempt to sabotage my journey to total deliverance. Instead of yielding, for the first time I fought back with prayers for strength. I washed and prayed, prayed and washed until the hot water ran cold.

"That's it." The revelation came after I'd turned the faucet off and reached for the towel. The source of my anxieties, the reason I feared being left alone and not accepted—Randall. Whereas Mama spoiled me, Randall, being the male I admired, was where I defined my value. I'd been measuring my worth by someone who refused to accept, or didn't know his own identity. I needed to call Carlton and apologize for all the times I brushed off his advice and warnings. I also needed to thank him for having the guts to call me out and force me to face reality and take responsibility for my actions. He rebuked my victim mentality, and pushed me onto the road to recovery. I loved the geek, but doubted if I ever told him. Carlton once accused me of loving Randall more, and he was right. Yet Carlton loved me in spite of that fact. The acceptance I sought was right in front of me all along.

Tamara startled me when I stepped into the bedroom from the bathroom, wearing a towel draped around my waist. She sat on the edge of the bed, rocking back and forth with her eyes closed and lips moving. My angel was praying. "Thank you, Jesus," I mouthed. The boycott against God was over. I tiptoed around the room, trying not to disturb her.

"I don't know if I can take anymore, but I need to know exactly what I'm dealing with. Just how much swinging did you do at those swing clubs?" She asked the question as I stepped into sweats. "I've never understood the control Randall has over you. Now, I understand you were molested by him as a child, and as an adult for that matter. Just tell me, honestly, is Randall the only male you've had sexual relations with? Do you have any desire for, or are you attracted to men? If you do, it'll hurt, but it won't kill me. Just no more secrets and no more lies." Her voice trailed off, but her puffy eyes remained pierced.

Relief washed over me. Finally, questions I could answer with certainty. I sat beside her, wanting to take her hand, but didn't dare risk it. "I am not gay, or bisexual. I am not sexually attracted to men. Besides what Randall stole, I have not had any sexual relations with males." The image of Randall in action on the DVD flashed through my mind, leaving a bitter taste in my mouth. After swallowing hard, I continued. "I had multiple partners at the swing clubs, but they were all females and I always used condoms. None of it meant anything. It was just sex. I don't remember their names; that's how little they meant to me."

I was hoping for relief, but her expression changed to contempt. "Is that supposed to make me feel better? Knowing you violated our relationship for a meaningless freak show, demonstrates how little I mean to you. You had sex with two strangers, and less than twenty-four hours later, married me. You delayed consummation of our marriage for something that meant nothing? That's insane."

I wanted to argue my position, but now wasn't the time. Too much pain and anger lingered between us, and the line bordering my sanity was thinning by the second. Since I was the cause, I'd have to let her take the lead.

"I can't discuss this anymore. I'm going to sleep." She made the announcement, while removing the only blanket from our bed and taking both pillows. She stomped out of the room without so much as a "good night".

Leaving me alone to sleep on the bare mattress was her way of saying, "Stay away from me." I got the message loud and clear, absorbing the snub without complaining. I'd spent ten nights alone in bed, missing her. At least now we were under the same roof, for now anyway.

CHAPTER 17

Freedom is Never Free

I COULDN'T COMPREHEND IT, but I awoke the next day feeling refreshed and energized. I'd slept shirtless on a bare mattress, yet enjoyed the most restful sleep I'd had in years. I was up in time to walk down to the neighborhood cafe and pick up some breakfast for us before the movers arrived. My reward, a brief smile from my wife when she saw the stack of pancakes topped with fresh strawberries and bananas.

The move went fairly smooth. After learning about the baby, I hired a team to unpack and set up the house. All Tamara had to do was direct the team on where to place things. I stood out of the way, letting her run the show. I wanted her to be at ease in our home. I interjected only when she asked my opinion on something.

The team was on a break when the dam broke, spewing Tamara's emotions. "This is too much!" she cried. "This is a beautiful house. I love this house; it has everything I want. I'm pregnant after only being married a year. I have a career I love. I don't have to worry about money, or bills. I'm supposed to be happy, but I'm miserable!"

My heart ached for her. All I ever wanted was to keep her happy. I would have traded anything to see her smile again. "I'm sorry. I—"

"Yes, you…" She didn't finish the sentiment, but I filled in the blank. "Don't say that again. Just leave me alone. I need to think, and pray," she added in resignation.

I obeyed her command and found solace on the deck outside the master bedroom suite. Tamara wasn't the only one who needed to pray. Praying to God was the only thing that kept me sane. I also needed to call Carlton.

I remained there until dusk, hoping to find Tamara in a better mood. I found her sitting on the bed in one of the guest rooms, more like her room. I hadn't noticed earlier, but she'd chosen that room for her living quarters, and not the master bedroom.

"I will stay here, but this is the best I can do right now," she explained, almost apologetically, when she noticed me in the doorway.

My first thought was to complain and ask for how long, but wisdom glued my mouth shut. She'd agreed to stay—a baby step I had to accept. "No problem. What would you like for dinner?"

Relief washed over her, and she rattled off a list of Mexican food large enough to feed a small army. "And jalapeños on the side," she added, as an afterthought.

"It must be a boy." We shared a laugh, and then I went on a mission to feed my wife and unborn child.

———◆•❈•◆———

The first week in our new two-story home zoomed by in a blur as Tamara and I settled into a routine of eating together, exchanging few words, and sleeping apart. Daily visits from family and church members distracted us form dealing with our issues as a team. We both endured personal turmoil.

Instead of a housewarming gift, Carlton presented me with a "new birth" gift—a study Bible with my name engraved in gold letters. Over the phone, he'd both rejoiced with me over my sincere commitment to the Lord, and cried with me when I shared Randall's violation. He profusely apologized for not being there to protect me, then scolded me for not telling him back then. "None of this current mess would exist. I would have handled him," Carlton had vowed. Knowing what I know about him now, I believe my geeky brother would have. The second he stepped into my home, I bear-hugged him and told him I loved him. The glare from his lenses almost hid the tears in his eyes. He didn't need to return the sentiment; he'd been demonstrating his love for me all along.

Mama's joy over our home was short-lived after observing the interaction between Tamara and me. Tamara napping in the guest bedroom wasn't lost on her either. She demanded to know what was going on. I sat her down and attempted to explain, but she'd formed her own conclusions.

"Leave Randall out of your marriage!" she ordered, before I could explain. "I know Randall has something to do with why you and Tamara have separate bedrooms. That's why I didn't want him to come to the anniversary party, he's always stirring up mess. He's not happy and can't stand seeing anyone else happy. Fix whatever is wrong with your wife, and stay away from Randall! Love him from a distance." She stood and paced the length of the great room. "That's the only way I can love him, is from a distance. I chased him out of my house with a baseball bat the other day when I caught him in my house searching for my car keys. He told some lie about his car being in the shop, so he needed to borrow mine for two weeks. And the deadbeat had the audacity to ask me for the name of the brokerage managing the girls' college funds. That Negro ain't paid child support in months, he certainly isn't going to deposit into Randi and Kendall's education fund." She stopped abruptly. "Did I tell you someone 'stole' his office furniture? I am not stupid. His furniture was probably repossessed, or sold for drugs. He looked and smelled like he hadn't bathed in days. And why does his nose keep dripping?"

Mama and I both knew the answer to that question. It was a side effect of excessive cocaine use. "Maybe we should try an intervention, and get him back into treatment." As the suggestion left my lips, I knew the chances of getting Randall to commit would be impossible. Especially, now that he was reaping Jordyn's wrath.

Mama's neck twisted. "What do you mean back? That trifling child has blown my money twice on 'supposed' treatment programs. He is so much like his daddy, I wish I could give him a DNA transplant." She peered at me and gripped my shoulders. "Stay away from him. Love him, but don't allow him to drag you down. He will ruin your life, if you let him."

I determined then I would never tell Mama about that summer, nor the current indiscretion. Randall frustrated Mama, but she loved him. I couldn't destroy what love she had left. I was her love child. Knowing she'd failed to protect me from the predator within her house would break her heart.

"Baby, promise me, you'll make things right with Tamara. That woman loves you. Her sun sets and shines on your freckled face." She leaned in closer. "You only get that kind of love once in a lifetime, if at all. Trust me, I know. I would give anything to have one more day with your father. Promise me, you'll keep your family together. As the husband, it's your responsibility to band your house together by any means necessary."

"I'll do my best." I couldn't dwell on how badly I'd messed up. Going forward, I would fight for my family.

My in-laws visit yielded similar results. The Jacksons were cordial, but distant. My mother-in-law's smile didn't accompany her greeting. My father-in-law didn't offer a hug or handshake with his congratulatory remarks. My chest ached observing them tour the house with Tamara, and me tagging along a few steps behind. I was excluded from the interaction until Judge Jackson asked to speak with me privately. It didn't take divine intervention to know the conversation would be harsh and one-sided. I squared my shoulders, feigning courage, and led him into the room designated as my man cave. The door only partially closed before he dropped the gavel and rendered his judgment.

"Alexander, when you asked for my daughter's hand in marriage, I didn't hesitate granting my consent because you were sincere and I believed you loved my daughter. You were the first and only man Tamara praised more than me. Your father was a good man, and I saw that same goodness in you. I welcomed you as a son, never doubting you would cherish and honor my baby." He leaned into my personal space. "Don't make me regret trusting you with my daughter." He leaned back. "You're young. Most young men make stupid decisions. I certainly made my share, so I won't judge you, but let me be perfectly clear. I don't like seeing my baby girl miserable. Tamara and my wife won't give me the details, which is probably a good thing. So, I don't know exactly what you've done. I know you've hurt her deeply, but her love for you is deeper, otherwise, she wouldn't be here. Be the leader in your house and do whatever it takes to regain her trust and respect. It won't come easy, because I didn't raise my daughter to define her self-worth through a man. From the age she could comprehend, I taught her to value herself. It may take some time, but my daughter is more than worth the effort." The force of his index finger against my chest sent me off balance, causing me to brace myself. "Whatever the problems are, fix them! Or die trying!"

As abruptly as it began, Judge Jackson's court ended. At least now I knew he didn't hate me.

I didn't share the mandates from Mama and Judge Jackson with Tamara. Time for whining and passing the buck was over. Later that evening, I boldly stepped to the plate to redeem my marriage.

"Do you have a moment?" She was in the middle of laying out her clothes for her first day back at work. I had another five days of leave.

"What's up?" She didn't look up or turn around.

I stood in front of her, forcing her to make eye contact. "Tamara, it may not feel like it right now, but I do love you. If you move into our room, fine. If you don't, that's fine too. I just want you to know from this moment on, I'm going to do everything I can to restore our marriage and to regain your trust, and your forgiveness. If that means living in this house as roommates, I can do that. If that means not touching your soft body, or tasting your warm lips, I'll take my punishment. Just know, I'm not giving up on us. God gave you to me; you're my angel."

Her head shook, but not nearly as violently as before. "Please, don't."

"Also, I'm not faking anymore. I really have a relationship with the Lord now. I've accepted the fact that I can't do life without Him. My need for Him exceeds my desire for your love. The only way I can truly love you, is to discover my identity and learn to love myself through His eyes. In addition, I'd like us to resume praying together. If you don't want to pray, just listen, and I'll pray. I may fumble some, but I will fulfill the vows I made to you. All I ask is for grace and patience."

"I, but I…" Unable to form words, Tamara waved her hands in the air and stormed from the room. "Whatever, Alex," she called over her shoulder.

The doorbell chimed moments later. I hurried down the stairs to answer the door, but Tamara beat me to it.

"What are you doing here?" the cantankerous voice charged.

"I live here," Tamara shot back. "Why are you here?"

"Even after proof the little half-breed gigolo cheated on you, you're still here?" Randall's smirk reached my ears before I rounded the corner. "Well, what do you know, even sadity broads can't turn down money."

"That's enough, Randall," I roared from behind Tamara. "Not here, and not her." For a split second, Randall appeared startled by my rebuke. "Why are you here, certainly not to congratulate us?"

"Didn't know I needed a reason to see my little brother," he responded, after he recovered.

"Did you need an invitation to ruin our lives?"

"Tamara!" I interjected before my wife's head and neck started rolling. "Leave us. I need to speak to my brother alone."

Her head cocked at my uncharacteristic demand, but she honored the request.

I waited until I heard her trek up the stairs before setting Randall straight. His presence had thrown me off balance, and thrust me to confront my predator. I didn't believe I had the courage, and I found it difficult to look him in the eye. I wasn't ready, but I wasn't going to back down. Fervent prayer for strength ran through my head, and I, for the first time, saw and accepted my brother for the oppressor he was.

Randall looked much older than his thirty-six years. His clothing, although designer, looked worn and wrinkled. Discoloration and lesions sprinkled the skin on his forearms, face, and neck. His height no longer impressed or intimidated me. No longer on the pedestal I mounted him on, his stature seemed to shrink by the minute.

"I see you finally got her under control." He sauntered from the foyer, pausing in the living room, taking it all in, rubbing his chin and nodding his head before starting for the kitchen.

"That's far enough!" The force of my yell startled me. A volcano was brewing in the pit of my gut.

"What? I don't get a tour of our new home?"

Had my brother always been this stupid? The drug use must have destroyed some brain cells. After all, Randall had a degree.

"This is not your home! It's Tamara's and mine. How dare you waltz in here and act like what you and Jordyn did wasn't beyond foul? Tamara could have had a miscarriage from all this stress. Tamara left me behind that and may divorce me. Why, man? "Why did you do it?"

"I see she came back. Must be the money," he yelled in the direction of the staircase. "Look," he said, turning back to me, "you're mad now, but trust me, you'll thank me later. I didn't know there was a bun in the oven until your stuck-up wife announced it. It wouldn't have mattered anyway. I warned y'all this little arrangement wasn't going to last, but, y'all was too in 'love' to listen to me. Once the divorce is final, you can go back to being your own man. Tamara has done nothing but control you from day one."

"What?" I stuttered. Certainly, I hadn't heard him correctly. Who controlled me more than him?

"When you started dating her, you kicked the family to the curb. You stopped hanging out, and started going to church because *she* wanted you to know Jesus. You wouldn't give me the money to start my business, without checking with her. But you didn't have a problem shoveling out close to one million dollars of that oil money on this house. Don't deny it," he said, when I opened my mouth to ask how he knew what my house cost. "I researched the address on the Internet, and saw the sales history. You're living in this mini-mansion, and I can't even go into the kitchen for a glass of water?" He pointed at his chest. "I am your blood, not her. I've always tried to help you be the best. Okay, maybe my methods are a little rough, but you know I got your back. Tamara has proven she'll leave at the first sign of trouble. You should be thanking me for revealing her disloyalty." His back rested against the wall, his arms folded like he'd made valid points.

"And just how do you know the baby's yours? Broads pass babies off all the time to gullible brothers with money. What you need to do is let that skank walk and don't give her a dime until you get a DNA test. And you better get a good lawyer—"

"Stop it! Stop it! Stop it!" My inner volcano reached eruption status and I could no longer listen to his foolishness and manipulation. His arms fell as I stepped into his personal space. "For once tell the truth! This mess has nothing to do with Tamara. It's all about you. Always has been. You're mad because marrying Tamara elevated me from being your flunky and bottomless ATM. You're jealous of our relationship, that's why you sabotaged it. You want what we have, but don't know if you want it with a man or a woman. That's why you disrespect women and neglect your daughters. You sleep with strangers to validate your manhood, when in truth, you don't know what it means to be a man." I paused, forcing back my emotions. "You're right. You've always had my back, but that was so you could dig the knife in deeper. Did you have my best interest that summer you molested me?"

His already-ashen skin faded.

"Well, did you?" I pressed when his jaw dropped. "I remember you violating me every day until Carlton came back. You threatened and beat me when I complained. You had all the girls in the neighborhood, why did you target me? And the DVD, why did you do it then?"

"If you'd given me my money, I wouldn't have had to make the DVD. It's your fault I had to resort to X."

The involuntary flexion of my fists scared me. I wanted to punch some sense into him. "I don't owe you nothing, but I will offer you some free advice. Next time pick a loyal accomplice. Jordyn left the camera rolling while she showered. In retaliation for not paying your debt, she brought me a different DVD—one with you in the starring role." His lips moved to speak. "Don't bother lying. Tamara and I both saw it, and Carlton knows about it. I just want to know why? For once, tell the truth. As far as I can remember, I've done everything possible to please you, but all you do is manipulate and take advantage. Why?"

Randall took deliberate steps into my personal space. I didn't know if I should prepare for a fist across the jaw, or another wad of spit. I took two steps backward, preparing for both.

"You really want the truth? The truth is, I hated you before you were born, and every day since." His hot breath fanned my face with every syllable. "I hated your daddy for taking Mama away from my daddy."

His words hurt, but like always, I ignored the pain. "The way I heard it, after using Mama as a punching bag, your father left her to raise you and Carlton alone."

"He was coming back!" he roared. "He promised he would. He may have flaked on us a few times, but he promised he wouldn't beat us anymore and would get counseling. Mama didn't give him a chance. As soon as she met the great white hope, she divorced my dad, and married yours, because he was white and had money. Whitey was always showing off—buying us clothes, toys and taking us on trips my daddy couldn't afford. Then you came along and ruined everything. You were the perfect love child. From day one, Mama spoiled you with affection and adoration. Your daddy even rocked you to sleep, while me and Carlton never got to see our father."

I had to stop his rant. "So, you hated me, because my father stayed and yours left?"

"*Hated*? I never stopped hating you. I hate you, and your daddy. I was glad when he got popped. Thanks to him, you've never had to want, or work for anything. Everything has been handed to you on a silver platter." He waved in my face. "Look at you. You're twenty-seven years old, and have never worked a day in your life. Yet, you have two degrees you didn't pay for, live in a mini-mansion, drive a luxury vehicle, and a bank account that will never run dry, thanks to him. I've had to work extra hard for every little dime I get."

"I hated every second I had to watch you because Mama didn't want you outside alone. She let Carlton and I roam the street, but your bronzed feet barely touched the porch without her having a panic attack. Mama raised Carlton and me, but she loved you."

"That summer I enjoyed every second of watching you suffer. For once, you weren't so precious. You were so pathetic, crying like a wimp. I don't regret what I did back then. In fact, I don't regret anything I've ever done to you. Truth is, causing you pain makes me happy."

I turned my back, trying to reel in my emotions and maintain my sanity. I loved my brother in spite of everything. To hear he never cared for me was detrimental. I wanted so much to attribute his disposition to the drug use, but couldn't. The words sounded real. The truth hurt too much. Denial was more comfortable.

I turned back around. "You told me why you violated me as child. What about at your place? Why did you do it then? Were you high? I was unconscious, what joy did you gain from it then? Did you do it out of spite, or did you enjoy it?"

I waited for what seemed like an eternity for an answer, but none came. That moment, I began accepting the fact that my brother and I no longer had a relationship. My mentor and idol was lost forever.

"Randall, leave my home. Don't ever come back," I added, after he gasped. "I think its best we keep our distance. You're too toxic. Don't call me. Don't text, just stay away from me." My body trembled as the words left my lips. "That shouldn't be hard to do, since you hate me so much."

A morsel of hope wanted Randall to apologize, or say he didn't mean those statements until he began cursing me with a vengeance. It was as if all the resentment he'd harbored rushed to the surface and spewed in my face. He definitely hated me, the names he called me proved it. When he slammed the front door, he shattered what little self-esteem I had left and destroyed my spirit. I wanted to be free from the manipulation and control, but the pain of losing my brother was too much to bear. He hated me, but I loved him.

The pressure in my chest escalated to the point I wished for a heart attack to put me out of my misery. My emotions and will collided, and when I began to hyperventilate, I gave up and listened to the voices in my head. I couldn't continue living my pathetic life. I was a smart, rich spoiled mama's boy without an identity. Outside of my mother's arms, I didn't fit in anywhere. My wife couldn't stand to be in my presence and would probably leave me all alone in this big house. *Tamara, had she heard the exchange?* My life was over. My head shook violently, agreeing with the voices telling me not to wait and just end it now. I tugged my keys from my pocket and started for the front door in a daze.

"Alex, wait!" Tamara ran in front of me and pressed her back against the door. "Where are you going?"

The tears streaming down her cheeks confirmed she'd heard everything. I hung my head in shame. "I don't know. Out. I can't deal with this."

Tamara removed my cell phone from my waist clip. "Before you go, let me put my next prenatal appointment in your calendar. It's in three weeks. I'm having an ultrasound and there's a possibility we'll be able to tell the baby's sex."

I lifted my head and watched her add the details in my phone, all the while wondering had she lost her mind, or, was I the lone nutcase. After what had just transpired, why would she think about something so far away? "Sure. Whatever."

The second she replaced the phone, I reached around her and grabbed the doorknob. Her warm fingertips fanning my face prevented me from turning it. She maneuvered my head, forcing me to hold eye contact. "Alex, promise me you'll be there. I *need* you to be there." She held me longer, using her thumbs to wipe the tears that managed to escape, then turned and walked away.

I watched her back, thinking my angel hadn't lost her mind at all. In her subtle sweet way, she'd just given me a reason to live three more weeks.

CHAPTER 18

A Reason to Live

DARKNESS AND MISERY is what I remember most about the time between Randall's visit and Tamara's prenatal appointment. Those first days consisted of sleeping, staring at walls, more sleeping, counting down the days to my demise, and more sleeping. I didn't bathe, nor eat. Calls went unanswered and text messages unread. My desire for communication dissipated. I lost my will to pray, but hoped God would forgive me for committing suicide. I didn't leave the bedroom, and pretended to be asleep when Tamara checked on me after returning from work. I'd plan to stay in that room until the day of the appointment, then end it all. I wasn't sure which method of execution I'd choose, I just knew I wouldn't do it inside the house. I'd also planned to call my attorney and set up my will. Tamara, the baby, and my nieces and nephew would be well taken care of. It pained me to know I'd never see my child's face, but it had to be this way. I was useless with nothing to give. I also emailed my resignation letter to my job.

"Alexander, it stinks in here!" Tamara barged in on the third day without knocking and turned the lights on. "I don't care if you are asleep, you're getting out of that bed and taking a bath today." She started opening windows and shades.

I rolled onto my side. "I don't want to."

"I don't care." She yanked the covers back, stealing my warmth. "You're going to bathe, and then eat."

"You heard her. Now get up before fungus starts growing on you," Carlton ordered from the doorway.

I groaned. "What are you doing here?"

"I'm the muscle," he said, folding his arms. "Now get up, before I throw you over my shoulder and hose you off."

"You'd try it, wouldn't you?" I smirked.

"Please, Alex. You haven't uttered a complete sentence in three days. I'm worried about you." Tamara's tone, now less authoritative, sparked life within me. If she was worried, that meant she still cared.

I sat up, adjusting my eyes to the light. Sitting in the dark for three days made my eyes sensitive. Tamara walked into the bathroom, a moment later I heard the tub filling with water.

"She told me about Randall's visit." Carlton let the statement hang. I knew he wanted me to elaborate, but I didn't have the strength. "I'm sorry it came to this. You don't have to talk about it now, but you can't hibernate in here for the rest of your life."

"I know. Tamara has a prenatal appointment coming up, and I have to be there."

"That's right. Think of your family and move on."

I indeed planned to move on. "I'm looking forward to it." I attempted to stand, but got light-headed and fell backward. Before my bottom touched the bed, Carlton had me in a vice grip, holding me up.

"That's why you're taking a bath. You're too weak to stand." He steered me toward the bathroom. "Come on, before I pass out from your three-day-old stale breath."

I wanted to laugh, but walking took all of my energy. When I entered the bathroom, I also wanted to cry. Tamara had filled the tub with bubbles. A clean set of clothes, including my slippers were laid out on the chaise. Soft music played in the background and a soft vanilla scent filled the air. Tamara and I had shared many baths in this atmosphere. I'd found them soothing, but never considered taking one alone. Afterward, Tamara would favor me with a massage; no chance of that now.

"I think that's everything," Tamara said, handing me clean towels. "I expect to see you downstairs." She hurried out before I could thank her.

Carlton released his grip. "She's worried sick about you. I hope you realize how blessed you are."

"Yeah, she was my angel and I blew it. She doesn't trust me. She doesn't even like me."

"That may be true, but she also loves you. Hold on to that. Trust God to work out the details." He turned to leave. "In the meantime, wash your behind."

I pondered Carlton's words. I wanted to believe him, but after Randall's disclosure, I no longer believed I was worth loving. Even after I found clean linen on my bed after I showered, I doubted.

I fulfilled my wife's request and went downstairs.

"Have a seat. The soup is just about warm," Tamara called over her shoulder.

I obeyed. "Where's Carlton?"

"Monica was running late, so he had to pick the baby up from childcare."

"Thanks for changing the bed."

"No problem."

Tamara served me soup, followed by a meal from my favorite seafood restaurant without conversation. For the majority of the meal, a blank stare covered her face, but she never shared her thoughts.

"Since you provided the meal, I'll do the dishes," I offered.

"Thanks."

Just like that, we settled into a new daily routine. In the mornings, Tamara stopped in and reminded me of my commitment to prayer, then waited as I fumbled through a generic prayer. She'd then convey her wishes for dinner and small chores around the house—her subtle way of telling me to get out of bed. Her method worked. Every day, I complied and made sure dinner was on the table when she returned. She resumed bringing home fresh flowers and playing soft music. During dinner, she mentioned how nice it would be to have a rose garden. The next day, I was off to Home Depot to learn how to plant roses. I figured the garden would be a nice place to scatter my ashes.

As the days drew nearer, I secretly began packing my clothing and personal belongings. After finalizing my will, I began drafting farewell letters to each of my family members, including Randall. I told him, I forgave him. I had to, if there was any chance of avoiding hell fire. Carlton called every day to check on me, and I made sure I told him I loved him. I appreciated him for showing me what a true man does. I just didn't have the strength to follow his example.

The morning of the appointment, I removed the linen from my bed and folded the blankets. After showering and shaving, I neatly placed the toothbrush and razor into the box I'd been hiding underneath the sink. After packing my remaining toiletries, I dressed in a dark brown suit, cream dress shirt, and tie. Tamara liked me in brown, said it complemented my freckles.

I'd just finished tucking the pill bottle into the inside jacket pocket when Tamara's screams reached my ears.

"Alex! Alex!"

I rushed to her room, expecting to find her in danger or hurt. She was standing in hallway in front of her room, in her underwear, one hand holding her stomach and the other reaching out to me.

"Hurry up! You're going to miss it."

As always, I was clueless. "Miss what? Are you having the baby?"

"No, silly!" For the first time in weeks, genuine laughter flowed from her. "The baby moved. I felt a flutter, or something. It wasn't gas; I know it was the baby."

I had no idea what to say, or do. "Okay. Is that normal?"

She shot me a look that confirmed I was clueless. "Of course, it's normal. Give me your hand." She grabbed my hand and pressed it against the little bump. I didn't feel what she felt, but a lump formed in my throat. I hadn't touched her in over a month, nor had I seen her body. The warmth and the view instantly aroused me. Tamara didn't notice.

"Do you feel that?"

I wanted to redirect her hand and ask if she felt how much I needed her. I swallowed again, reminding myself in a few hours it wouldn't matter. "I don't feel movement, but your stomach is definitely hard."

"Well maybe next time." She pouted, before dropping my hand. "I'll be ready in a minute." After she stepped back inside the room and closed the door, guilt nudged my conscience. She was looking forward to something that wasn't going to happen.

Determined to end my suffering, I returned to my room to gather the envelope containing the letters to my family. I'd planned to mail it to my attorney after the appointment. From there, I took one last walk around our home. It truly was a magnificent home. Tamara had done an outstanding job of decorating. I prayed that one day she'd find someone to enjoy it with.

"I'm ready," she announced from the top of the staircase.

"I was thinking we could take separate cars," I suggested, as she made her way down. "I have plans after the appointment."

"Plans? Really? Oh, okay." She looked perplexed. "Since I have the day off, I assumed we could spend the afternoon shopping for the nursery. Oh well." She shrugged. "I've been looking online, and have an idea of what I like, but I think we should decide together. Maybe the weekend?"

"Sure," I answered, knowing the weekend would not come for me.

"Is it cold?" I asked later when the sonographer squeezed gel onto Tamara's stomach and she shivered.

"Yes." She reached for my hand. "I hope we can tell the sex. I'm so excited, one moment I want a boy, the next a girl. What do you want, Alex?" she asked while squeezing my hand.

Before I could answer, the baby's heartbeat boomed over the sonographic waves, and I jumped. I'd forgotten it sounded like swishing water. The rapid rhythmic sound both soothed and excited me. It was strong and full of life. I probably imagined it, but in the rhythmic beat, I heard the word "daddy".

"Look!" Tamara pointed to the 3-D screen. "There's the head." She asked the sonographer for confirmation. "Right?"

"Right."

I watched in amazement as the probe slowly moved over Tamara's lower abdomen.

"And there's the heart, the lungs, stomach, legs and arms." She stopped the anatomy lesson, and faced us. "Would you like to know the sex of your baby? Or, would you like to be surprised?"

"Tell us," I ordered, without giving Tamara a chance to respond.

"Please tell us," my wife added, when the sonographer hesitated.

"In that case, Mr. Bennett, I hope you're ready for junior. It's a girl."

Tamara gasped. "Oh my, God."

At that moment, I thought my heart would leap out of my chest. The idea I would be a father in a few months, suddenly became real to me. Before I saw her 3-D image and little extremities, she was an idea. Unlike the rest of my life, my baby girl was real and full of life. I wondered about her facial features and skin color. Would she have freckles like me, or smooth ebony skin like Tamara? Would she be tall, or short? Would she inherit my smart genes, or Tamara's organizational skills? There was only one way to find out the answers to those questions: I had to keep living. My daughter needed me.

Inwardly, I scolded myself for almost falling prey to Randall's final manipulation. I was on the verge of leaving my daughter unprotected and fatherless like his girls were, because of his devaluation of me. My baby girl deserved better than that. Like my father, materially I could leave my daughter the world, but she would still miss my presence. She would long for me, just like I longed for my father. I had to endure my pain and stay around for her.

Tamara shook me out of my epiphany. "Well, are you?"

"Huh?"

"I asked if you were happy about having a daughter."

Tamara was already shedding tears, so I stopped hiding and let mine flow. In spite of everything, this was a happy moment for us. I hadn't officially met my daughter, and already she saved my life, by giving me a reason to live. I rested my hand in the cold gel on Tamara's stomach. "Yes, I'm happy. I can't wait to meet her. I hope she's just like her mother." Tamara didn't verbally respond to the compliment. She didn't need to; placing her hand on mine communicated more than I deserved.

"I'll meet you at the house in an hour, then we can go shopping," I said, opening the door to Tamara's car.

Her face lit up. "Really? What about your plans?"

"I cancelled them. This is more important." Tension instantly left my shoulders. "I just have a quick stop to make, then I'm all yours."

She got my subtle message; her blush confirmed it. "I'll be waiting."

I waited until she drove off before trotting to my car. On the way, I tossed the full pill bottle into a trashcan. If I hurried, I could make the mid-day prayer session at the church. I had some serious repenting to do.

In addition to giving me a reason to live, our unborn daughter also ignited the restoration process in our marriage. After the prenatal appointment, Tamara and I began talking and spending time together on a regular basis. Most of the discussions centered on the baby, but at least the tension had decreased. We'd found common ground and worked as a team preparing for our new arrival—selecting nursery furniture and schemes, and the stressful task of selecting a name. We prayed daily for our daughter and resumed attending Sunday worship service together. Tamara allowed me to rub her stomach and talk to the baby as much as I desired. The intimate parts of her body remained off limits. I massaged her feet, propped pillows for her back in her favorite chair, ran countless errands to quench cravings, prepared for Lamaze classes. Since my presence no longer irritated her, I took the opportunity to court her again. We shared date nights, picnics in the park and strolls along the beach. Once we actually shared a dance with my arms cuddling her stomach from behind. There were moments I'd catch her staring at me, as if she wanted to say something, but wouldn't.

As her body expanded, Tamara's sex appeal magnified. Every day was sheer torture. I needed my wife beyond baby talk and platonic dates. Cold showers became my antidote. When cold pellets were on longer enough, the urge to masturbate reared its ugly head. My weapon was prayer, and most of the time I prevailed.

Finally, around the sixth month I witnessed and felt the baby kick. My elation overwhelmed me, and I wrapped Tamara in my arms and kissed her without thinking. I sobered when she didn't return the kiss, but took consolation in that she didn't push me away.

Even with prayer, meditation and attending the Men's Bible study, my faith wearied at times. Depression shadowed me daily. I avoided stressful situations and people, mainly Randall. I hadn't seen him since he slammed my door months ago. I erased every text he left without reading them, and blocked his number from calling my phone. Perhaps, he wanted to apologize, but my sanity couldn't take the chance. From Mama and Carlton, I learned Randall had been hospitalized after being discovered beaten behind a dumpster. Jordyn kept her word. Randall lost his condo and was supposedly living with a friend. Translation: an unsuspecting female. I prayed for him, but refused to go to him.

During my downtime, I obtained my CFA credentials and started the process of opening my non-profit community agency. I leased a building, solidified board members, and developed vision and mission statements. I hired office staff, created a curriculum, and marketed clients. My dreams of family and helping the community were transforming into reality, but complete contentment eluded me until Ramon entered the picture.

I burst into our home one afternoon, elated to share the news of solidifying a benefactor willing to purchase computers and budgeting software for clients to use at the agency. My joy evaporated when a forty-something-looking Latino I'd never seen before, stood in my den to greet me. Clean-shaven, he was dressed in a causal suit and loafers, with thick dark hair.

"You must be Alex. I've heard a lot about you. It's nice to finally meet you."

I didn't acknowledge his extended hand, nor return the greeting.

Tamara entered the room carrying a small tray of food and stood beside him, smiling nervously. Instantly, my anxiety took over. Was this man my replacement? Was Tamara leaving me for him?

"Alex, you're home."

Tamara wasn't one to stutter. I knew then my life was about to change. "What's going on?"

She placed the tray on the table then gestured toward the unwanted guest. "Alex, this is Ramon. We worked on several Psych projects together back at CAL. You may recall me mentioning his name once or twice?"

"No, I don't."

Her smile fell at my sharp answer. "I wanted you guys to meet and spend some time together."

What on earth was my wife trying to tell me? And why was Ramon smiling? "For what, Tamara?"

"He's a therapist and is currently working on his doctorate. He's also a Christian." The stuttering returned.

"So. And?"

"Ramon, eat some food," she ordered. "We'll be right back." She grabbed my arm and dragged me into the kitchen.

Self-preservation took over, and I attacked first. "You have some nerve bringing your boyfriend here?"

The nervous smile transformed into a hot glare. "Shut up, before you make me backslide and start cursing again. Ramon and I are just friends. I asked him to come here for you."

"For me?" I pointed at my chest; she had me twisted." I told you, I don't do men. That thing with Randall was one-sided. I was unconscious. I—"

"Stop it!" she ordered, grabbing my shoulders. "For once, step into reality and deal with your issues!" Her hands moved upward and cupped my cheeks. "Alex, you need some help." Her voice softened. "You can't keep living like this. Your eyes have lost their light. Your smile is lifeless."

I wasn't ready to agree, and I wanted her hands on me longer. "Living like what? All I do is work and come home and talk baby talk with you. I spend as much time as you'll allow with you. I'm trying to work on us, but I'm not so sure that's what you want. I've been trying my best to restore our marriage, but you haven't given me one sign that my efforts are working. And now you bring some guy home? What do you want?"

Coldness replaced her warmth as her hands fell from my cheeks to her side, exasperated. "Alex, what I want is for you to fully heal and let go of your baggage. I want you to start living."

I went on the defensive. "I'm working on it. I pray every day and read the Bible. I sit right beside you at church every Sunday. What more do you want from me?"

"Are you really working on it? Or, are you hiding again, going through the motions?" She leaned back, making her seventh-month pregnant belly bulge outward like a basketball. "Before you answer, I found the envelope you left in the backseat of your car."

"What envelope? And what were you doing snooping around in my car?"

"Snooping? Really, Alex? I'm not going to go there with you," she said, shaking her head vigorously. "I used your car to run to the grocery store. I'm glad I did; otherwise, I wouldn't have discovered your suicide notes."

My heart sank, mainly from embarrassment. I'd meant to discard those after the appointment months ago, but in my excitement, I'd forgotten. "That's in the past. I'm better now. All that Randall mess is over." I offered the explanation after turning my back to her.

She wobbled around me. "Is it really in the past? Is it really over? I don't think so," she said, shaking her head. "I think you're suppressing the hurt by focusing on the baby and medicating the pain with work."

Ouch! A physical slap would have stung less.

"I've been watching you ever since that night. Part of you died when Randall slammed that door. Sure, you walk around here with a smile on your face, but it's not relaxed. True, you have been working extremely hard to please me, but what about learning who you are, so you can please yourself? You still don't have any idea of who you are."

Now she was hitting below the belt.

"You're still depressed, because you're mourning the loss of the one-sided relationship with Randall. You've engulfed yourself into work, because you have no identity outside of being my husband, and soon, a father. You're terrified Randall's assessments of you are true. That's why you assumed Ramon is my man, although I sleep in this house with you every night. And," she paused and cupped my face again. "Reliving Randall's violation has caused you to question your sexuality. Don't deny it," she ordered when my heading began shaking. "Be honest. You're wondering if the love you have for your brother stems from the sexual contact. You can't rationalize why you tolerated the emotional abuse and justified his actions for so long."

My wife pulled back the scabs to wounds my spirit wanted to stay anesthetized. "What do you want from me?" I yelled, after yanking her hands away, then went on a rant. "I told you, I have issues I don't know how to handle. You don't know what it's like being me. I've been trying to fit in my entire life, and to please everyone. You don't know how many times I plead with God daily to show me who I am; to tell me why my brother refuses to love me; to make me good enough for you to forgive me and not leave. I have read every scripture on love in hopes of learning how to love without hurting," I added, pacing. "Yes, I'm unsure about many things. I lived a counterfeit life for so long, I'll admit, I now have a hard time deciphering what's real. I'm not gay, but yet, I question why Randall's insults about my manhood always drove me over the edge. Why did I hide that summer so deep in my psyche? I'm not sure if my mother really loves me, or if I'm just a substitute for the love she lost. You used to love me, but that was based on the lies and false image I fed you. The baby and work are the only things keeping me sane right now. They give me something to look forward to. At least my clients will thank me for making their lives better, and our daughter will need me. Beyond that, I have nothing." I took a deep breath, in hopes of loosening the tension in my chest. I hadn't meant to unload my baggage on her. My attempt as the strong leader in the home had failed.

"Alex, everything you're searching for, you already have. You just don't know it."

Warm fingertips fanned my face again, forcing me to make eye contact.

"That's exactly why you need counseling. Prayer is always good, but sometimes we need the aid of a trained professional to help us process the pain, and then let it go."

"You minored in Psych; why can't you help me? The mere sound of your voice calms me." Baring my soul to a stranger wasn't something I wanted to do.

"That's just it. I don't need you calm." Her hand pressed mine against her belly. "*We* need you healed and whole. And honestly, Alex, I'm not sure I trust you to be completely transparent with me. I would be more of a hindrance than a help. Besides, you need to forget about pleasing me and focus on you. Whether we remain married or not, we will share a daughter, who deserves two whole parents. Your goal should be to be the best man and father possible outside of me. You once said, I was your angel, yet you don't believe you're good enough for me. From the beginning, you've lived in fear that one day I'd desert you." She moved our hands to my chest, over my heart. "Search deep in here before you answer. Did you transfer the dependency and your self-value from Randall onto me?"

The question stumped me.

"If that's the case, depression will keep knocking and you'll remain in a vicious cycle. Alex, you're one of the smartest people I know. I've never doubted for a moment that you would accomplish anything you set out to do. To have survived the emotional and physical abuse you have sustained means you're a lot stronger than you think. And, despite deceiving me, you're a very caring person. I know that about you. Others know that, but *you* need to know that."

My heart and understanding began to open. I did need help. I was tired of running from the dark shadows. I needed the dark clouds to dissipate and make way for the sun's brilliance. My goal was to be the best man I could be, but first I needed one question answered. "Do you still love me?"

"Love isn't an issue for me. Of course, I love you; perhaps maybe too much." A soft stroke against my cheek accompanied the declaration. "It's love and a ton of prayer that has enabled me to look past your actions and forgive you. Intense counseling sessions didn't hurt either. I know the deception wasn't from the heart; you were driven by insecurity. I believe you love me, but you can't live for me. Now trust is another story. I'm trying, but I don't know if I'll ever trust you completely again. I'm not sure I can be married to a man I don't trust, but above all, I want you whole."

Regardless of my mental instability, I knew Tamara was my angel. Even in her pain, my wife loved me enough to push me to become a better person. I'd earn her trust if it was the last thing I did, but first, I needed to accept the help afforded me. I wrapped my arms around her, and when she didn't pull away, I leaned in and kissed her. She returned the kiss with more compassion than passion.

"Thank you, Mrs. Bennett," I whispered, after the short feast. "Come on. Reintroduce me to my new therapist."

CHAPTER 19

Self, Meet Me

"I AM LOVED AND I love myself. I am not perfect, but I am fearfully and wonderfully made. I am created in the image of God. My conception and appearance are exactly what God intended for my life. I am here for a purpose, and not by accident. With God's help, I will fulfill my purpose. My mistakes have been forgiven, and my past is over. I may have been victimized, but I am not a victim. My Heavenly Father's everlasting love makes me victorious."

It took a month of reciting the affirmations Ramon had me compile before I actually started believing them. Speaking positive about myself was a new experience. In the beginning, it sounded strange, vain rhetoric. Ramon assured me the words would eventually resonate in my spirit and encourage me. He was correct. I began seeing myself in a positive light and self-examination became less scrutinizing.

Ramon was the perfect therapist for me. He didn't present himself to know how to fix my life or as a know-it-all. His method was to lay the platform for me to open up about the incidences and influences that traumatized me and shaped my low opinion of myself, but he didn't stop there. Ramon became my "midwife", helping me give birth to the pain buried deep inside, and then walking me through the steps of acceptance and releasing the pain by combining clinical theories with Biblical principles. We met three days a week for an hour. Some days I'd talk most of the hour, other days, I'd cry. Most sessions were conducted in Ramon's office, but occasionally we'd meet on a local walking trail or gym. Regardless of the venue, I left every session feeling refreshed. The first month was hard, detoxing from my dependence on Tamara and Carlton and even Mama. Most days, I felt abandoned, but I pressed forward.

For the first time I visited my father's grave, alone. As a child, Mama used to take me to leave flowers on his birthday. I'd planned to stay just long enough to read the letter Ramon encouraged me to write, then leave, but after the first sentence the floodgates opened. Five little words—I wish you were here—laid the foundation for a deep soul purging. I spent hours sitting on the manicured lawn, leaning against my father's headstone pouring out my heartache. Since detaching from Randall, I discerned the hole in my soul. For so long I crammed Randall into that space, but even in death, my father's shoes were too big to fill. The setting sun had cast a shadow over the granite stone by the time I was able to stand. For the first time, I told him I loved him, and how proud I was to be his son. I believe his spirit in heaven heard me, because the shadow disappeared and the sun's rays warmed my back. I walked back to the car determined to make him proud.

Subtly, my confidence and demeanor began to change. I began squaring my shoulders and looking people in the eye again. As I reprogramed my mind and spirit, hatred for my pale skin and freckled-face transformed into appreciation. Self-love replaced self-loathing. For the first time ever I felt completely comfortable in my own skin. Ramon's "homework" assignments helped me to discover some likes and dislikes. He challenged me to try new activities and find contentment within. Much to my surprise, I soon discovered I really didn't care to play basketball. I'd only done so recreationally, because Randall had. Pool and golf were my forte. The assignment that stretched me the most was going places alone. I learned how to go out to dinner, visit museums, watch movies, and ride my bike alone and enjoy myself.

With Tamara's due date quickly approaching, I boldly took control of my home by adding affirmations and scriptures about being a successful husband and father. I stopped waiting for Tamara's permission and began showering her with affection at my discretion. If I wanted a kiss, I took one. If I needed to hold her, I did. When I felt like dancing, I'd turn on the sound system, take her by the hand, and dance. If she wasn't home, I danced solo and sang along with my favorite songs. She didn't resist my affections, but rather seemed to welcome them. Every morning I greeted her with, "Good morning, Mrs. Bennett," and at night saluted her with, "Sweet dreams, love," my way of sending a subliminal message that we would remain married until death. After work, therapy and homework, I came straight home and invested time into our relationship. As my desperation eased, so did the tension between us. She blushed more and scowled less and her laughter returned.

At night, I'd sit on her bed and rub her lower back until she fell asleep. On a few occasions, I treated myself and stayed the entire night cuddling her from behind. I knew I was regaining her trust when she didn't reprimand me. In fact, the closer her due date got, the more she clang to me. Whenever she experienced Braxton-Hicks contractions—false labor—she'd grab me and we'd practice the breathing techniques we'd learned in Lamaze class. Tamara grew more anxious every day about giving birth. She packed and unpacked her suitcase for the hospital at least three times, checked the Internet for any recalls on the crib and car seat we'd purchased, and second-guessed the nursery lay-out. I obliged her until I came home and found her on a ladder attempting to remove the Noah's Ark wallpaper she just had to have. I officially placed her in "timeout", and for the first time, I looked beyond the surface and made her tell me the source of her anxiety.

"I'm scared," she admitted, with an unfamiliar timidity.

"Of what?"

She uncharacteristically paced with flailing arms. "Everything, the whole delivery process. I could be in labor for days. What if I can't push her out? She might not want to nurse. What if she does and I can't produce enough milk? What if I can't get her on a schedule? What if I forget to change her and she gets a diaper rash? What about ear infections? And…stop laughing at me!" Her flailing hand slapped my shoulder.

"I can't help it. This panic mode is too cute."

"Cute is what got me pregnant. I need some real help here. In a few days, I'm going to be responsible for another human being."

Although I don't fault her for her response, I realized the night of our anniversary Tamara wasn't perfect. Watching her exaggerated fears play out before me now, helped me see my angel's humanity. For so long, I thought my wife was too good to be true. In actuality, Tamara had flaws and shortcomings just like me. The only difference, she wasn't afraid to show them.

"*We* will be responsible for our daughter," I corrected, while boldly, collecting her arms and drawing her as close to me as her protruding abdomen would allow.

"Yeah, but labor is on my own. You won't feel one iota of pain."

"Of course I will. Watching you suffer will be torture." I lifted my head before I gave into the urge to taste those pouty lips. Right now Tamara needed my assurance. Underlying the rant was her fear of being a good mother. With my thumb and forefinger, I lifted her face to meet mine. "I have complete confidence you'll be a great mother. There's not another woman on this earth I want to share this experience with. I won't physically feel your pain, but I'll be right there beside you every step of the way. When it gets hard, just lean on me; we're in this together. I'm going to take care of you."

"Promise?"

"I promise."

Her facial muscles transformed into a smile. "I'm going to hold you to that. Oh, and babe, it's good to hear you laughing again."

My heart nearly jumped inside my chest. I hadn't been "babe" in months. I celebrated with a kiss, which our unborn daughter's kick interrupted. We laughed, and I released her knowing another brick had been laid in her trust wall.

"Babe, huh? You're starting to like me."

She pinched my cheek. "Maybe."

Proof came six days later while we enjoyed Sunday dinner at my in-laws. The relationship with the Jacksons had somewhat been restored. Slowly, I moved from being tolerated to accepted again. At least I was included in conversations and Judge Jackson welcomed me back into his man cave.

After dinner, while Tamara engaged in conversation with her father, her water broke. Judge Jackson stood beside her, I was across the room, yet she called and reached for me. Not her father. Now wasn't the time for pride, but my chest swelled when he nodded his approval, stepped back, and called for my mother in-law.

Tamara's vice-grip and glossy eyes communicated everything her mouth couldn't. I wasn't a novelty or charity case. She loved and needed me, and I refused to let her down.

Our daughter took five and a half hours to make her debut into the world. I left my wife's side only to use the restroom. I'd never witnessed childbirth before, but I'm sure no woman looked as beautiful and poised as my wife had. Cries of agony never escaped her lips. She found a focal point and focused on the breathing techniques we learned in Lamaze. She squeezed me, and at times pounded my arm and shoulder, but never let the pain overtake her. She pushed on command and I prayed nonstop.

Precious Hailey came into the world at eight pounds and two ounces at 2:34 a.m. Everything about Hailey was perfect—her ten fingers and toes, full head of curly hair, and loud cry. I loved her so much, I was afraid to cut the umbilical cord. I didn't want to hurt my baby. Only after the doctor and nurses assured me Hailey wouldn't feel any pain, did I perform the ritual. At that moment, my life was perfect, but instead of celebrating, I broke down, thinking back to months prior when I nearly forfeited this moment. I had to turn my back as the medical team continued assessing my daughter.

"Aren't you glad, you stuck around?" Tamara's outstretched arms beckoned me back to her bedside.

I collapsed in the chair beside her bed and buried my face against her hospital gown, in awe. The instant her fingers stroked my hair, I knew for certain our marriage would be fully restored. My wife was human with faults, but she was my angel. In her subtle wisdom, she'd saved my life months ago by forcing me to connect with our unborn child, which renewed my will to live. Then she brought Ramon into my life, forcing me to discover myself. I loved her beyond expression, and I loved myself.

I wrapped my arms around her body, then leaned up and kissed her, not caring that tears dripped from my chin. "I love you. Thank you. Our daughter is beautiful, just like her mama." She smiled, but didn't speak. No words were needed. Her wiping my tears away communicated everything I needed to know.

CHAPTER 20

The Final Confrontation

THE FIRST MONTH of fatherhood went by in a blur. I had the strange notion that Tamara and I would be alone in adjusting to late-night feedings and changing diapers. I'd arranged my schedule at the office so I could work from home and care for my wife and daughter. The day before Tamara and the baby were discharged, I stocked the cabinets and refrigerator with all of Tamara's favorite items. I created daily meal plans and hired a housekeeper twice a week. All of my preparations were in vain thanks to Mama, my mother-in-law and endless visitors.

I'd expected Mama and my mother-in-law to swoon over Hailey, but I had no idea they'd take over my home. Mama started by tossing out my meal plan and then banning me from the kitchen. Mama Jackson moved into the guest room next to the nursery, and stayed there for a month. My mother camped out in another room. The grandmothers took turns tending to

Tamara and taking care of Hailey. My daughter was spoiled rotten in a matter of days, without any help from me. With Carlton, my sister-in-law, Monica, my nieces, Tamara's relatives and Judge Jackson dropping by at will, I barely got a chance to hold my baby. I had to sneak time in the middle of the night.

"Enjoy the break now," Carlton said, when I complained. "In a few weeks the novelty will wear off and you and Tamara will be running around like headless chickens while little Hailey rules the house."

I snickered. "I can't wait."

In addition to not being able to enjoy uninterrupted time with my daughter, my bed remained empty. Despite the strides we'd made, Tamara chose to return to her room instead of joining me in the master bedroom. I didn't pressure her about it. I took Carlton's advice and enjoyed what quiet moments I could with her. Tamara loved me. She just didn't trust her own judgment anymore. When my wife fully returned to me, I wanted it to be of her own volition.

Since my services at home weren't needed, I resumed my sessions with Ramon sooner and returned to the office after the third week.

Financial Freedom Institute, the name of my non-profit, was growing phenomenally. The weekly classes were filled to capacity with a waiting list thanks to newspaper ads, PSA radio spots, and door-to-door knocking. In addition to helping families rise from the stronghold of debt, I was also providing finance students from local colleges a chance to fulfill internship and community service requirements. The resource lab was completely furnished with computers and software for the clients who didn't have home access to computers to complete the weekly assignments.

Our curriculum made the lessons fun and took the stress out of financial responsibility. My first day back, a client hugged me, excited she'd met her monthly goal. I was on cloud nine, until my cell phone went off.

Randall had been calling me daily since Hailey's birth. How he managed to get my new number was a mystery until my receptionist informed me my brother had been stopping by to see me. Her blushing told me my manipulative brother hadn't lost his touch. I firmly informed the unsuspecting young woman she was not to give my cell number to anyone, if she planned to continue working for the institute. Her nervous apology gave me cause to wonder if my brother conned her out of more than my cell number.

I never answered his calls, nor did I play his voicemails. Randall wasn't calling to apologize or congratulate me. He wanted money. According to Carlton, Randall's last conquest didn't last long—the young woman had put him out. Randall was living on the street when he wasn't hibernating in some drug house. Rumors from the old neighborhood suggested Randall was prostituting himself to support his drug habit. In his desperation, Randall attempted to steal Carlton's car, after Carlton refused to give him money. Fortunately, Carlton had GPS installed in the car and a disabling device. Randall didn't make it out of the subdivision before the car stalled. Now he was bothering me, probably because he was no longer allowed in Mama's house after stealing her flat screen TV.

June 16th started like any other day. I arose at 6:00 a.m. After prayer, meditation and journal writing—another homework assignment—I showered. Before descending downstairs to brew coffee, I stopped in the nursery to spend time with my daughter.

Her empty crib brought a smile to my face, because that meant Hailey was in Tamara's room. I'd get some private time with my wife and child. After a slight tap on the door, I eased into Tamara's room. My assumption proved right. Hailey was tucked underneath Tamara's arm, nursing.

I sauntered to the bed and greeted my wife with a kiss. "Good morning, sunshine."

"Why are you so happy this morning?"

"Other than loving life, I'm hoping today's the day your mother goes home." My mother vacated a few days prior, only to call every hour to check on Hailey.

"Me too," she whispered, as if her mother was in the room. "I appreciate the help, but I think we can handle it now. It's been a whole month for goodness' sake."

I laughed aloud, causing Hailey's head to move. "You're the woman of the house, and her daughter. I'll leave it up to you to tell her to go home."

"Are you kidding? I've been throwing hints for days."

"You'll figure it out." I leaned in and kissed my daughter. "Just like you'll figure us out."

Tamara's expression turned somber. "I will. Soon. I don't mean to drag you along, but I have to be sure."

I smiled. "I know. Let's pray." My marriage may have been in limbo, but my spiritual life was solid. I prayed daily for my family's well-being.

I arrived at the office around 9:00 a.m. and busied myself with reviewing the monthly budgeting exercise assignment turned in by the 10 o'clock class. By a quarter to ten, I was thoroughly prepared, and quite proud of my students. The afternoon class was just as productive. By the end of the day, I was floating on a natural high from making a difference in people's lives. I didn't even mind filling in for the evening class teacher, who called off sick. I'd found my purpose. I locked up sometime after five and headed home, totally content.

I'd just turned onto the freeway when I remembered the flowers I'd purchased for Tamara during my lunch break. I'd placed them in the office refrigerator to keep them from wilting in the hot car. I took the next exit and doubled back to the office. No way was I coming home to my baby empty-handed.

I noticed the white van parked in the back lot near the door, but didn't think much of it. Financial Freedom Institute wasn't the only tenant in the complex. I went to punch in the alarm code on the keypad, only to discover the alarm had been deactivated, and the door slightly ajar. Whoever was inside obviously worked for me. I proceeded inside without a second thought.

"Hello," I called out, as I started for the breakroom. Instead of a vocal response, a rumbling sound from the direction of the computer lab greeted me. "Hello. Who's here?" I called again, turning toward the computer lab. More rumbling, then a thud answered back. I ran the rest of the way, thinking someone may be hurt. The door to the computer lab hung wide open. Inside were two men I'd never seen before. Except for the monitors and hard drives tucked in their arms, they looked normal.

"What the…" I didn't finish the question with the obvious answer, before a third man appeared from under a table. It took me a moment to recognize him, it had been so long, and he was at least forty- pounds smaller. Long gone were the designer labels and tailored suits. So were half of his top teeth. He was in desperate need of a shave and a bath. I couldn't decipher if the craters on his face were due to mosquito bites, or dirt.

"Randall, are you robbing me?" I asked the dumb question, but his response was dumber.

"Man, calm down. Your insurance will cover this. If not, you can afford it."

That familiar smirk surfaced, only this time I wanted to knock it off his face. "I'm calling the police."

"Man, I thought your girlfriend said nobody was going to be here," one of the accomplices said, before I unclipped my phone. He set the stolen goods down on the floor. "I'm out of here. I ain't goin' back to jail."

I knew the answer, but I had to ask anyway. "What girlfriend?"

"That chick at the front desk who gave him the key," the second accomplice said, as he walked past me. "Randall, deal with your brother. We out."

It was like watching a bad sitcom, as Randall and his partners in crime argued and cursed one another over how and when to steal my property.

"When your brother drove off, you said we was good to go. I only came because my son needs a computer for school. I could have went to work," the one nearest the door explained.

I shook my head as if to clear it, wondering who would hire him. He looked as ratchet as Randall. The chaos carried on into the parking lot until Randall's boys climbed into the van and drove off, leaving Randall cursing and flipping off the back of the van. The scene was pathetic, and since Randall was my brother, I granted him mercy by not calling the police.

"Man, give me my keys and get out of here," I ordered with my hand out. "Don't ever come back. I don't want to see you, and your girlfriend's last day was today."

He brushed past me, nearly knocking me down and re-entered the building. "I don't care nothing about that broad. I ain't going nowhere until I get my money. Either you pay me in cash or with property. You're the reason I'm living on the street in the first place. If you'd just done what I asked, none of this would be happening."

I hesitated briefly before following him back inside to the computer lab. "I don't have time for this. Put that down!" I ordered in reference to the monitor and hard drive bundled in his arms. "The only thing you're leaving with is your pathetic life." I heard the monitor crashing to the floor just before his fist connected with my jaw, knocking me backward against a table. Drugs hadn't softened his punch; I swear I saw stars.

He grabbed another monitor and started down the hallway. I tackled him from behind, and we tumbled into the conference room. "You think I'm going to let you steal from me?" I asked once I had the advantage by straddling him. "I don't owe you nothing!"

The derogatory names and expletives no longer intimidated me, rather irritated me to the point I slapped him. "Shut up! You sound like a girl. Word on the street is, you are somebody's broad." Making fun of Randall's sexuality proved unbeneficial for me. After spitting in my face, Randall wiggled and wormed until he managed to flip me over onto my back and proceeded to beat me senseless. *I've got to learn how to fight,* I remember thinking between blows. I was dragged, kicked, and then pulled up by the throat against the table, all the while being cursed out. I believed Randall would kill me, but I didn't think to pray. Suddenly, his grip on my throat loosened and he started feeling between my legs. Gasping for air, I kicked and squirmed to get him off me to no avail.

"Whose the...now? I'm going to get my money from your punk...one way or another." He squeezed me then went for my wallet. "Then I'm going to visit that sexy broad of yours and show her what a real man is." I swear his eyes changed colors. "And when that baby gets older, I'm going to play with her just like I played with you." That's when I lost it.

Fight overruled flight as supernatural strength took over. No way was Randall going to ever touch Hailey. I fought from under his grip. The rest is a blurred mess of overturned chairs, slams against walls, blood and broken glass.

Present Day

CHAPTER 21

Right to Remain Silent, but Why?

A S THE SIRENS grew louder, the adrenalin wore off and reality set in. I killed my brother. I killed Randall. I waited for the tears to fall, or regret to set in, but neither happened. My ears rung from Mama's horrific cry after I told her. The ringing could have been from one of Randall's punches. I wasn't sure, but I knew I didn't have much time before I'd be cuffed and toted off to jail. Carlton's reaction was the total opposite. Dead silence filled the line after I broke the news to him.

Pain also set in. I attempted to turn a chair upright so I could sit, but when I bent over a squeezing pain filled my chest cavity. I tried taking a deep breath to alleviate the pain, but the discomfort only worsened. I leaned against the wall, gripping my chest with my left palm. Throbbing and swelling rendered my right hand inoperable. Even my face throbbed, causing me to shut my eyes."

"Put both hands up against the wall."

I attempted to obey the male voice, but the pain in my chest was too intense. "I can't," I moaned. I opened my eyes and saw a female officer kneeling over Randall, who called for a second ambulance in the radio, then began CPR.

A pair of medics rushed in and went directly to Randall. I wanted to lower my head while they worked, but it was too heavy. I watched the medic pronounce Randall dead under the guard of the male officer. Still no tears.

"I'm Officer Wearing," the male officer stated, while steering me away from the body and out into the hallway. "What's your name?"

"Alexander Bennett," I heaved out. "My ID is in my wallet in my back pocket."

"The ambulance will be here shortly," he said, retrieving my wallet. "In the meantime, Alexander Bennett, you have the right to remain silent…"

I didn't need to hear the rest of the Miranda rights; I'd made up my mind to plead guilty and accept my punishment. No need to waste time and money on a lawyer.

"Do you understand these rights?"

I winced from pain. "Yes."

"Would you like a lawyer?"

"No."

"Mr. Bennett, what happened here?" The officer now had a notepad and pen in hand, but the crime scene tape the female officer marked the door to the conference room with distracted me. "Mr. Bennett," he repeated.

"That's my brother in there. We, um, we had a fight," I grunted out. "He tried to rob me." *Thank God,* I thought, when the second set of medics rushed in, and the officer stepped back. More officers also arrived.

After a barrage of medical questions and probing, I was placed on a gurney, and wheeled out to the ambulance, with Officer Wearing following close behind. I couldn't make out the faces, but several people gathered, appearing to catch the scene on their phones. I hoped and prayed Carlton would reach Tamara before she learned her husband now carried the title of murderer on the evening news or social media.

The glaring lights from the police cars and ambulances, along with the streetlights, wreaked havoc on my head. I was no match for the onslaught of sudden nausea and dizziness. Regurgitating on the medics shoes was the last thing I remember before the lights went out.

I pressed through the grogginess induced by the painkillers and tried to listen to the doctor's words. I had no reason to doubt his assessment, and my battered body confirmed it. Three fractured ribs, a broken wrist, multiple lacerations, and a concussion was a small price to pay to protect my family. I'd been at the hospital over twenty-four hours and had undergone a procedure under anesthesia to reset my wrist, X-rays, and a CT scan. My head was bandaged, and it hurt to breathe, but my family was safe. I wasn't allowed any contact with my family due to my police custody status. The only persons allowed into my room were medical and police personnel. I was also denied telephone and television luxuries. Medication had me floating in and out of consciousness and the pain made me want to escape. During those conscious moments, my resolve remained the same: I would plead guilty and go to jail. I would also divorce Tamara, although I wasn't sure if the pain or the medication conceived that thought. What I did know was I didn't want her wasting her life waiting around for me. I'd probably get twenty-five years.

"If your breathing and blood pressure remain normal throughout the day, you'll be released tomorrow," the doctor announced.

"Thank you," I said, thinking I would be released from the hospital's care to that of the judicial system. Officer Wearing's sudden appearance after the doctor left confirmed it.

"I hope you're feeling better, Mr. Bennett. We need to complete your statement." I barely nodded before he pressed forward, with pen and notebook already in hand. "You said your brother, Randall Williams, tried to rob you and a fight ensued. Is that correct?"

"Yes." *Oh my, God! How do I explain this to his daughters, my nieces?* Up until now, I hadn't thought about Randi and Kendall. Randall was a lousy father, but I'm sure his daughters loved him, and would probably hate me for taking him away permanently.

Officer Wearing reeled in my mental rant. "Tell me what happened from the beginning."

My beginning with Randall was so pathetic; I assumed he meant how I killed my brother. "I forgot something in the refrigerator, and came back and found Randall and two of his friends stealing computers. I tried—"

The door swung open and one of the partners from my father's law firm burst into the room. I'd seen him at Mama's house on numerous occasions. He also attended my college graduations. "Don't say another word," he ordered, then turning to Officer Wearing, added, "Attorney Rosenberg. My client will make a statement only after I have had a chance to speak with him, and only in my presence."

Officer Wearing huffed and slammed the notebook shut. "I'll be outside," he said, and left the room.

"I didn't ask for a lawyer; I don't need one. I'm guilty, no need to drag this out."

"Alexander, you didn't need to ask for a lawyer. Your father was Alexander Bennett, Esq, and founding partner. That means you have a group of criminal lawyers at your disposal whether you think you need one or not, which you do. Your mother understands this."

"So my mother sent you here?"

He smirked. "More like ordered me. She and your wife are quite persuasive, not that I needed much persuading. Your father and I were friends, and I respect Glenda to the highest."

"I don't understand."

He pulled the chair close to my bed and sat down. "Your mother stormed into my office this morning and demanded I get down here immediately and represent you. Never mind I was in the middle of a staff meeting. Cute daughter, by the way. Congratulations."

"Why does Mama have my daughter?" I prayed my drama hadn't caused Tamara more trauma.

"She doesn't. Your wife and daughter road shotgun with Glenda, making sure I dropped everything and came straight here, even followed me over. They're waiting for me downstairs in the lobby. So let's get started before they break police protocol and sneak in here." He pulled an iPad from his briefcase. "Tell me what happened and don't leave anything out."

It hurt to smile, but I endured the discomfort. Mama's heart was shattered, yet she fought for me. "How is my mother doing?"

"She's grieving, but she's determined not to lose you too."

I suppressed my emotions and erected a mental block to keep me from thinking about what I was about to lose forever—Tamara, Hailey and Mama—and gave my attorney the details as I remembered them.

Rosenberg explained that until the medical examiner ruled Randall's death a homicide, murder was a working theory. I didn't understand that, I thought it was a slam-dunk case given the circumstances. A police investigation was taking place, as I lay in the hospital to determine if I should be charged with murder or not. Mama, Tamara and Carlton had already been interviewed. I could remain in police custody for seventy-two hours before being charged or booked. The odds were in my favor of being released since the autopsy could take several days to complete. If I were charged, I could post bail and remain free until trial. He then coached me on how to give a statement to the police.

Officer Wearing returned to the room noticeably more cordial. I gave my statement just as my attorney instructed, without any expectations of a different outcome. Officer Wearing wanted me to relive the day from start to finish, which I found strange, but didn't voice. He also drilled me about my relationship with Randall and confirmed I was seeing a therapist. I didn't see how that was important, but apparently, Rosenberg did, since he instructed me to answer.

The interview, more like an interrogation, left me both physically and mentally drained. Rehashing the details forced me to relive the event, only this time I absorbed the pain of taking a life and felt remorse for the freedom I'd given up. My head throbbed and the veins in my neck began pulsating, and my chest burned.

My nurse barged into the room and took control. "This visit is over. My patient is in distress."

"I'm not done," Officer Wearing protested. "Just a few more questions."

"Your questions will have to wait. I have to get his blood pressure under control." She pointed to the door, and to my relief, Officer Wearing left the room.

"You too," she added, pointing at Rosenberg.

"Get some rest," Rosenberg said, standing to his feet. "I'll update Glenda and check in on you later."

"Tell..." I started to send Tamara a message through Rosenberg, then decided against it. Our life together was over. I needed to condition my mind to live on memories. I nodded, then turned and watched my nurse inject medicine into my IV line. The medicine knocked me out cold. I awakened hours later with the dark sky outside my window greeting me.

This became my routine. I'd tolerate the pain until it became unbearable. Then the nurse would shoot up my IV and I'd float off to la-la land. My dreams varied from Disneyland-like fantasy to real-life heartache. I grieved for Randall in my dreams, and when I woke up in the middle of the night. I no longer neither admired nor respected Randall, but he was my brother. I loved him, and didn't desire him dead, especially at my hands. "I should have called the police," I'd wake up mumbling. I found solace in the images of Hailey's face floating through my mind. I'd prayed she'd one day forgive me for missing her life.

CHAPTER 22

Freedom's Cry

I T TOOK THREE days to manage the pain in my chest and to stabilize my blood pressure to the point I could be released from the hospital on non-narcotic pain meds. I washed up at the sink and dressed in the clean clothing Tamara sent by Rosenberg—a difficult task with three broken ribs and a broken wrist. Good thing they were sweats and not the button-up slacks and button-down shirts I usually wore. The lacerations on my head and face had begun to heal. Facial discoloration remained from the many blows I'd endured, but I was alive and able to get through the day without a narcotic painkiller.

Getting dressed sapped my energy. I eased into the chair beside the bed to rest, and to wait for the police to escort me to jail. My eyes just closed when Carlton barged into my room followed by Rosenberg.

Carlton stood over me, staring before speaking. "Hey, man." His smile wasn't full. "How are you feeling?" I couldn't tell if he hated me for killing our brother or not, and was too scared to ask.

"I've been better."

His pulsating palms on my shoulders answered my question. My brother still loved me, but he also loved his full-blooded brother. "We'll get better. Together," he added, after a pause.

Rosenberg cleared his throat. "Alexander, you're all cleared to leave. Let's hurry and get you back to Glenda before she horsewhips me. I promised to have you home before the sun sets."

"And to Tamara," Carlton added. "I don't think she's slept since you've been in here."

I ignored Carlton's statement and focused on my fate. "What time do I have to be in court?"

"You don't. Alexander, you're free to go home and resume your life. The police cleared and released you this morning." Rosenberg beamed.

I eased to my feet with Carlton's assistance. "I'm sure Officer Wearing will be knocking on my door soon with an arrest warrant. At least I'll get to sleep in my own bed tonight. I also need to meet with my estate attorney."

"You didn't hear what I said. Alexander, the police *cleared* you this morning. You're free. No charges will be filed against you," Rosenberg explained.

"*What?* I killed my brother with a blow to the head. How can I just walk free?"

"No, you didn't. According to the medical examiner, Randall died of a heart attack brought on by excessive drug use. The little knot you put on his head was nothing compared to the damage repeated cocaine use did to his heart vessels. It was just a matter of time before his heart gave out. There wasn't any external or internal damage done by you that caused his death."

"What?" Tremors made standing upright impossible. I fell against Carlton for support. "You mean I didn't kill him?"

"No, you didn't. He did more damage to you than you did to him."

I looked to Carlton for confirmation. Maybe some residue of the narcotic remained in my system. "No, you didn't," he confirmed. "Our brother died because of his own devices."

My brother's arms caught me before I collapsed in the chair. I wept like a baby in his arms, despite the discomfort in my chest. "I can go home and stay? I don't have to go to jail?" I asked, once again for clarification.

"You're free," Carlton whispered in my ear.

Almost in slow motion, I eased from Carlton's grip and slid to my knees. Up until now, I shied away from public prayer and praise, considering it as something personal and done in private. Now that God had totally delivered me from the life sentence I deserved, I didn't care who saw or heard me give reverence to God. My body's discomfort was irrelevant compared to the joy in my heart. "Thank you, Lord," I repeated, until a language I couldn't comprehend, nor control flowed from my spirit. I literally felt weight dropping from my shoulders. I knew I was completely healed. Of course, I grieved the loss of my brother, but condemnation no longer ruled me. When I finally recovered, I maneuvered to my feet without assistance, not that I didn't need assistance, but Carlton and Rosenberg were caught up in their own private moment.

The ride home confirmed what my heart already knew—going forward my life would never be the same. Everything looked different and brighter, like me. After being confined to a hospital room for four days, I gained a new appreciation for the outside world. I welcomed the traffic congestion on Interstate 80, and smiled at pedestrians crossing the street against the red light. I rolled down the window, stuck my head out of the window, and inhaled as much of the polluted air my lungs would allow. A few tears escaped when Rosenberg pulled into my driveway. Home never looked so good.

I expected Mama to meet me at the door. I envisioned my mother pacing back and forth in the foyer like she used to do when Randall or Carlton were late coming home from school. I couldn't have anticipated Tamara's reaction in my wildest dream. My feet barely touched the ground before she ran out to me and wrapped her arms around me, squeezing me and nearly knocking me down. I braced myself against the car with my legs and good hand to keep from falling.

"Alex, baby, I've missed you so much! I'm so glad you're home." She rained kisses all over my bruised face between words. That was my angel, always loving me just the way I was. I winced, but didn't ask her to release me. She smelled so good and I missed her warmth.

"I missed you, too," I said through labored breaths, trying to endure the soreness in my chest which would remain for a while.

"Man, get inside and sit down before you injure something else. Then y'all can lip-lock all you want," Carlton ordered, poking fun at my effort to balance myself and sneak a kiss at the same time.

"Oh, baby, I'm sorry." Tamara released me, as if suddenly remembering my injuries. "Did I hurt you?"

I wanted to say yes, in hopes of getting her back into my good arm, but she had other plans.

"Let's go inside. You need to rest and you must be hungry. Hospital food is disgusting." She placed her arm around my waist, edging me forward. "Mama Glenda and I made all your favorites. I picked up some bath salts to help soothe your muscles. After a hot bath, I'll give you a massage once Hailey goes to sleep."

I could hear Carlton and Rosenberg chuckling behind me, as I struggled to keep pace with Tamara by trying to walk "cool" like I wasn't wounded. They could laugh all they want. I was home and my wife had plans for me.

I stepped through the threshold and savored the smells permeating the house. Fried chicken, collard greens, and cake I distinguished right away. My home was cluttered with all of my close relatives, minus Randall. Both hugs and condolences greeted me. Even my in-laws hugged me. I anticipated Tamara's parents would be around to support her, but her sisters' presence was unexpected. So was Ramon's. Neither was I prepared to see my nieces so soon, unsure if they knew the details of their father's death. My effort to avoid them failed once they latched on to me in a group hug. Their grief moved me, and I let their unconditional love outweigh my body's discomfort and hugged them back.

"I'm happy you're back, Uncle Alex," Randi whispered in my ear. "Sorry Daddy beat you up."

"Sorry about your father," I whispered in both their ears. I held them a little longer, but there was one other person I needed to hold, and to be held by. "Where's Grandma?" I asked, gently releasing them.

"I'm right here, baby."

I turned and found Mama standing behind me, next to Rosenberg, with her arms stretched wide and tears streaming down her cheeks. Without hesitation or reservation, I embraced my first love. Mama still smelled like cocoa butter.

"Thank you, Jesus. My baby boy is home," she repeated, while stroking my head and back. Everyone else seemed to stand still.

"I'm sorry about Randall. If I'd known about his heart, I would have—"

The strokes ceased, and she stepped from my embrace. "Don't do that," she ordered, while holding my cheeks. "Randall's spirit may have left here four days ago, but he left us a long time ago. No matter what he believed, I loved him before I birthed him and every day since, but for some reason Randall chose to love only himself. He came by the house the day before he died, bearing flowers. They were wilted, but colorful. He told me he was tired of doing drugs and living in the streets. He wanted to change his life, even asked me to pray for him. I prayed and fed him a good meal. I don't know what happened after he left, but I do know sixty dollars were missing from my purse. My heart has a permanent whole. I will miss him, but the only person to blame for his demise, is Randall.

"But—"

"No buts, baby," she interrupted. "This is not your fault. Listen to me," she ordered, adding pressure to my cheeks. "Mourn your brother, but go on with your life. Live *your* dreams."

"Yes, ma'am," I conceded. Mama's words were on point, and as always Mama displayed more strength than I possessed. I prayed her strength would remain during the difficult times ahead.

"Good." She released my cheeks and kissed my forehead. "Now, let's eat. You look like you've lost some weight."

I was starved, but there was one more person I needed to see. "Where's my daughter?" On cue, Tamara inched between Mama and me with Hailey tucked under her arm. "She woke up just in time for you."

Only four days had passed since I last saw my baby girl, but it felt like a lifetime. She looked bigger than her five weeks. "Hi, princess." I kissed her forehead, but didn't risk holding her with my bad wrist. Bright eyes turned my heart into mush. I didn't take my eyes off her until Mama steered me away.

"You have all night to stare at her. You need to eat and get some rest."

I followed Mama into the dining room. Everyone else followed behind. For the first time, I sat at the head of my table, and *felt* like the head of my home. Grace turned into a mini-praise service once I began thanking God for His deliverance. What should have been an atmosphere of sadness was filled with joy and peace.

For three plates, and through constant chatter, Tamara never left my side. I also took note that Rosenberg never left Mama's side either. Carlton and I looked at one another as if we received the revelation at the same time. Rosenberg's hand was the first man's hand to rest on Mama's shoulder since my father died. Through the years, Rosenberg had remained the most visual from the law firm. I'd always assumed because of his friendship with my father. Now, I wasn't so sure. I'd ask Mama about that later. Right now, all I wanted to do was soak in all the attention from my wife.

Tamara fed me those three plates of food, going as far as to wipe my mouth. The smile never left her face. Her actions exemplified her love for me, yet I found myself staring, trying to read her thoughts. I couldn't. Long after the last bite, Tamara clung to me until Hailey required nursing.

"Everybody, it's time to go." Mama made the announcement after my sisters-in-law and nieces finished storing food and cleaning the kitchen. "Alex needs to rest and spend some quiet time with his wife and baby. Besides, we'll be seeing a lot of each other in the next week or so with Randall's service and such." Her voice trailed off toward the end, reminding everyone the two-fold reason for the gathering. A tear barely escaped before Rosenberg handed Mama his handkerchief.

"We'll get together tomorrow," Carlton said in his departing hug. "I love you, man."

"Love you, too." I replied. In fact, I told everyone present I loved them before they left. My near-jail experience taught me to cherish those dear to me.

I assumed Tamara had that talk with her mother since my mother-in-law left with the rest of the guests.

I set the alarm after the last guest and started the long trek upstairs to my bedroom. I only had to stop once to catch my breath. With every step, I thanked God for being able to struggle up *my steps in my house.* I stopped by Tamara's room first to test my chances of getting that massage she'd promised earlier, but she wasn't in there. I continued on to my room, assuming she was in the nursery getting Hailey ready for bed.

I'm not a wimp, but I cried like one after surveying the master bedroom suite. In my absence, Tamara had done some reorganizing and redecorating. Removed from my bed were the plain black comforter set and pillows, replaced by a multi-colored block-print set with shams and decorative pillows. Tamara's robe lay draped across the bed. The furniture had been rearranged to accommodate Hailey's portable crib. Tamara's breast pump and a novel rested on one nightstand, a floral arrangement on the other. Vanilla and almond scents fragranced the room and soft jazz flowed through the built-in surround sound system. Inside the bathroom, the sink and vanity that had been bare just days before were now cluttered with Tamara's personal items and haircare products. Tamara's shoes lined the shelves of the second walk-in closet and her many outfits, grouped by color, overflowed from hangers. I tripped over her pink fluffy house slippers, not expecting them to be planted at the edge of the bed.

She entered the bedroom with Hailey in her arms at the perfect time. "What happened?" Her voice near panic upon finding me bent over, gripping the bedpost with my good hand and tears running down my bruised face. "Are you in pain? Do you need your meds?" She rushed and placed the sleeping Hailey inside the crib. "Sit down," she ordered. "I'll ran downstairs and bring your meds and some juice up."

I straightened up and grabbed her arm before she whisked from the room. I stared, struggling to find adequate words to express my heart.

"What? Talk to me. You're scaring me."

I released her arm, sat on the bed, and surveyed the room again. Her eyes followed mine until I stroked her robe; then awareness set in. If only I had the strength, I would have done a back flip and a split, when she lowered her lashes and blushed. I settled for the next best thing.

"I hope this is real, because I can't take losing you again," I said, opening my arms to her.

She disagreed, but stepped into my arms anyway. "You didn't lose me, Alex. You broke my heart and forced me to evaluate how deep and real my love really is. You pushed me into living forgiveness and not just preaching about it. Do I trust you? Not completely, but I'm willing to give you a chance because I understand the reasons behind your deception. And I know in my heart, you really love me. After the crying, yelling and screaming you're still my soulmate."

I needed my medication, but I wanted her more. I enclosed my arms around her. "Are you sure you want to take another chance on me?" I voiced the question inches away from her lips.

"Now, more than ever. If nothing else, the past four days have shown me how precious your presence is to me. I nearly went crazy with worry that you'd be locked up away from me. I couldn't sleep, barely ate. Until Rosenberg's visit, I didn't know if you'd been maimed, or disfigured. What I did know, is no matter how bad the damage, I needed you here with me. I'm better with you. It's really somewhat ironic. You caused me to backslide and pick up that cursing demon, then turned me into a prayer warrior, trying to pray off a murder charge."

Her soft giggles mixed with mine.

"You won't be sorry, Mrs. Bennett. I love you." I didn't wait for her to return the sentiment to taste her. I loved her mouth with every ounce of passion in my soul, using my forearms to squeeze her closer. She joined me with total abandonment, stroking my upper body in the process.

"You should probably get that medicine now," I whispered, resting my chin against her forehead. Injured, or not, my body never failed to respond to my wife's touch. Unfortunately, until my ribs healed, and Tamara cleared her six-week checkup, complete satisfaction would have to wait.

"I'll be right back." Her gaze fell to my groin, causing her to blush before leaving the bedroom.

I looked up at the ceiling and grinned. "Thank you, God."

Tonight, I fell asleep between the two most important females in my life—my angel and my daughter. Tamara cuddled underneath my arm. I used Hailey's crib to elevate my impaired wrist. Tomorrow, I will sit down with my mother, brother and nieces to plan Randall's funeral. Afterward, I will meet with Ramon and continue my discovery journey. Then I will stop by the office and meet with staff. In the days and weeks ahead, I will grieve the loss of life, but I won't entertain guilt or condemnation. My life will go on.

In her sleep, Tamara snuggled closer and kissed my cheek. Hailey stirred in her crib. I grinned from ear to ear. My life isn't perfect. I'm not perfect, but I'm free.

Discussion Questions

1. Alexander was his mother's love child, and thus treated differently from his brothers. Have you witnessed this type of favoritism within your family? If so, were you the victim or the recipient?

2. Due to his skin color, Alexander didn't fit in at home or at school. In 2017, do you think too much emphasis is placed on skin color within the African-American community?

3. In families, it's common for the older siblings to watch the younger children while their parents work outside the home. Considering the age difference between Alexander and his brothers, and the things Alexander was exposed to while in their care, should this practice be re-evaluated?

4. Depression, low self-esteem, and manipulation are not topics normally discussed or directed toward men. Usually, women are the victims. Do you believe men suffer from depression and low self-esteem as much as women? Have you witnessed a male being controlled and manipulated by another male?

5. Alexander used sex to medicate his emotional pain. What are some other physical methods, both men and women, use to suppress emotional and mental pain?

6. Considering his lifestyle, why do you think Alexander was attracted to Tamara?

7. Considering Tamara's strong family foundation and spiritual strength, should she have recognized Alexander's deceit early on?

8. Alexander was so engulfed with Randall, he couldn't appreciate the love Carlton had for him until he hit rock bottom. Have you ever been in a relationship where you disregarded genuine love and friendship for the temporary attention of someone else?

9. What did Tamara's reaction to Alexander's deception say about her character? Should she have come back? Do you view her actions as wise or foolish?

10. Was Randall's hatred of Alexander unfounded or misdirected?

11. What secrets/pain was Randall using drugs to suppress or medicate?

12. Share your thoughts on Glenda's response to Randall's death?

13. Which characters would you like to know more about?

More titles by Wanda B. Campbell:

First Sunday in October

Games (e-book only)

Illusions

Right Package, Wrong Baggage

Silver Lining

Unresolved Issues

Doin' Me

Back to Me

www.ingramcontent.com/pod-product-compliance
Lightning Source LLC
Chambersburg PA
CBHW021328250626
47155CB00002B/642